FOUR CORNERS

KATE MCMURRAY

Published by
Dreamspinner Press
5032 Capital Circle SW
Ste 2, PMB# 279
Tallahassee, FL 32305-7886
USA
http://www.dreamspinnerpress.com/

This is a work of fiction. Names, characters, places, and incidents either are the product of the author's imagination or are used fictitiously, and any resemblance to actual persons, living or dead, business establishments, events, or locales is entirely coincidental.

Cover Art by L.C. Chase
http://www.lcchase.com

ISBN: 978-1-61372-696-9

Printed in the United States of America
First Edition
August 2012

eBook edition available
eBook ISBN: 978-1-61372-697-6

This novel would not have been possible without the patience and support of a lot of people, including but not limited to Marsha, Alexis, Livvy, and Sean; the guy at the Apple Store Genius Bar who did me a solid by surreptitiously trying to recover the file for this novel when my hard drive died; everyone in my writers group who read and gave feedback, even after the rainbow unicorns got involved; and all of my friends and family members in Chicago who let me ask stupid questions about the city. Thank you all from the bottom of my heart.

THE wake was bad enough, but then I saw the one person in the world I least wanted to see. The one person I least expected to see. Adam Boughton. The one who left us. The one who got away.

I was at the wake to say good-bye to my old baseball coach. I hadn't actually seen him in years, but he'd been such an important part of my adolescence that I felt I had to come pay my respects. Seeing him in the casket and seeing a bunch of old teammates had brought back a lot of memories. I spent the better part of an hour recounting games I hadn't thought about in fifteen years, listening to others' memories about the coach, and mourning both the man and that part of my childhood that I'd long since left behind. Someone even asked if I still played the game, and I struggled to think of the last time I'd picked up a bat and glove. How could that have been? There'd been a time in my life when I'd pretty much lived for baseball. Coach's wife came up to me and told me she remembered me, she remembered all of us from that particular team, the last to win a state championship under Coach's tutelage. It was a sad way to pass an afternoon.

Then I saw Adam. He stood looking ridiculously handsome in a black suit, his dark hair a little disheveled, his hands shoved in his pockets. He made an interesting contrast to the red frippery of Room B at the Hull Funeral Home. He didn't seem to be looking anywhere in particular, just around at the other wake attendants, but then he turned his head and our eyes met. I froze.

"Oh, Jake," Kyle said behind me. "Jakey. Jake-Jake. Earth to Jacob. Hello?"

It took some effort, but I managed to turn around and face Kyle. Brendan stood next to him, his eyebrows raised.

"You have a seizure?" Brendan asked.

"Adam," I whispered.

Both of my friends looked over my shoulders and saw him. I didn't see their reactions because I was too busy looking at my feet. Brendan patted my shoulder, but Kyle, being Kyle, pushed past me and held out his hand. "Well, if it isn't Adam goddamn Boughton, right here in the flesh."

I heard Kyle making loud conversation but didn't listen to it. I looked at Brendan instead, who gave me a sympathetic smile. "Well, that was a little unexpected," he said.

"Excuse me, I have to go vomit."

I went to the men's room and splashed some water on my face, hoping for a few minutes to gather my wits and make sense of Adam's appearance and the cavalcade of things it made me feel. I looked at my reflection in the mirror, thinking I deserved some credit for not actually vomiting. And then, of course, who should walk in but Adam.

"Jakey," he said.

"What the hell are you doing here?"

"Well." He shoved his hands in his pockets and leaned against the sink. "Don't know if you remember, but Coach Lombard was my baseball coach too."

"You don't have to be sarcastic."

"My mother called and told me he died, and I'm in Chicago on business anyway, so I figured I'd come by and pay my respects. I wasn't sure if you would be here, but I thought you might be. With Ox and Longo in tow, of course. Nothing's changed, I see."

There was a part of me that wanted to have it out with him right there. To explain that Ox and Longo—Brendan and Kyle—had stuck by me when he hadn't, that we'd remained friends through the years. That I was Kyle's daughter's godfather, that I'd been Brendan's best man. That I was the one who had stayed. Adam had left. He'd left us. He'd left *me*.

Adam pulled his hands out of his pockets—hands with long, elegant fingers—and then he reached for his back pocket. He and I both knew that we were not going to have it out, not now, not like this. Not with Coach Lombard's family within earshot, not when there were so many more important things to think about than a friendship that had been lost five years before.

He pulled a card out of his pocket. He grabbed a pen that had been left on the edge of the sink and then scribbled something on the back of the card. He handed it to me. "I'm in Chicago through the rest of the week. I'm staying at a hotel in the Loop. Stop by or give me a call. My cell phone number's on there. We'll talk."

I looked at the card. One side proudly proclaimed his name as "Adam R. Boughton, CEO, Boughton Technologies." On the other side, he'd written the name of a very pricey hotel and room number 1126.

"Adam…."

"Or don't. Worth a shot, right?"

I noticed all of a sudden that the act of him handing me the card had put us within a few inches of each other, and he was right there, his broad shoulders and strong chest looming, his tie a little loose at the neck, a couple of days' worth of dark stubble standing out on his chin. He looked fantastic up close. Then I remembered who I was dealing with here, and I looked up at his eyes. His gaze was intense, focused unblinking on me.

"I like what you've done to your hair." He reached up and flicked a lock that hung near my face.

I couldn't speak. I looked at his mouth. He licked his lips. For a second I thought he would kiss me, but instead he let out a breath. He took a step back.

"Okay, Jakey. See ya around."

"Yeah."

Then he was gone.

A HALF hour later, after most of the crowd had dissipated from the wake, I found Brendan sitting on the granite steps in front of the funeral home, sipping a beer. I sat next to him.

"Where'd you get that?" I asked.

He pointed the neck of the bottle at the package store across the street. "Seemed like an appropriate occasion for drinking. You want one?"

"Sure."

He pulled another longneck out of the paper bag on the step below where he sat. He tossed me his keychain, which had a bottle opener dangling from it. I popped the top off mine and took a long drag before I handed him back his keychain.

"God, nothing like a funeral to remind you of your own mortality," said Brendan. "When we were in high school, I thought Coach was invincible. I mean, he had a body like the Hulk. But cancer got him. Jesus."

"I know. It's pretty freaky. And I feel awful because I hadn't even thought about him much in a couple of years, and now he's just… gone."

Brendan nodded and took a sip of his beer. He shot me a sidelong glance. "So Rosie."

"Yeah, Rosie."

"You talk to him?"

"Briefly."

Brendan nodded. "It's a hell of a thing, him showing up here. Longo just swooped right in there and shook his hand like we're all still best buds. Rosie looked like he didn't know what to do about that."

"Well, he came and found me. Said he's staying at a hotel in the city on business for the rest of the week and that I should stop by so we can talk."

"'Talk'?"

"I know, right? But that's what he said."

Brendan picked up a bottle cap and hurled it toward the street. It landed in the middle of the row of hedges that lined the curb. "You gonna go?"

"No. I don't have anything to say to him."

"Sure you don't."

Kyle appeared before I could protest. He leaned against a column at the foot of the stairs and gestured for Brendan to give him a beer. "What an awful goddamn thing that's happened. Can you even believe it? I just spent ten minutes reliving that play-off game we lost junior year with Hank Hernandez. It felt like that happened yesterday."

"Aw, man, I remember that game," said Brendan.

"Yeah, it was brutal." Kyle turned to me. "So Rosie."

"Yeah, yeah." I hooked my thumb back toward the door of the funeral home. "We're here because Coach died, not because Adam fucking Boughton decided to return to Glenview and grace us all with his presence."

"Touchy," Kyle said, holding up his free hand.

Brendan gazed out at the parking lot. "I should probably go," he said. "I told Maggie I'd be home by six. She's gonna wonder what happened to me."

Kyle imitated the sound of a whip cracking.

"Oh, whatever," Brendan said, standing. "Just 'cause you can't get a girl to stay with you doesn't mean those of us with successful marriages are whipped."

Kyle laughed. He took Brendan's place on the step beside me and threw an arm over my shoulders. "I sometimes think Jakey has the right idea. No guy would ever demand that you be home in time for dinner."

I sipped my beer but didn't respond.

"Of course, in exchange for no nagging, you'd have to suck dick," Kyle said.

"Don't you have a kid to go home to?" I asked him.

"She's at Michelle's, so no. I'm a free agent tonight, man. You wanna leave Ox to his ball and chain and go get wasted at Dickie's? It'll be just like old times."

"Nah, that's all right. I think I'll just go home."

"You want a ride to the train station?" asked Brendan.

"Yeah, that would be great."

Kyle rolled his eyes. "You're no fun anymore, Jakey."

"I'm just tired. Today has been kind of draining, don't you think? But if you want to go out tomorrow, I'm game." I stood up and moved to follow Brendan to his car.

"Okay, tomorrow, then. I'll come to you, we can go somewhere in the city. But no gay bars this time."

I laughed despite myself. The last time we'd gone out, I'd taken Kyle to a gay bar in my neighborhood. Kyle's sexuality was an open question, though he tended to end up in bed with women more often than not. I'd been sort of curious to see what would happen to him in a room full of men. As I'd suspected would happen, he'd eaten it up whenever a guy hit on him.

"Hey," said Kyle, "I can't help it if I'm irresistible to gay guys. Present company excluded, obviously."

"It's because I've known you since we were this tall." I held my hand about three feet above the ground to demonstrate. "It's made me immune to your charms, apparently."

"Yeah, yeah." Kyle stood and dusted off his pants with his hands. "Tomorrow, Jakey. You and I will tear through Chicago, leaving a trail of destruction and broken hearts in our wake. It will be glorious. You can come too, Ox, if your lady is willing to let you out of the cage."

"Ha, ha." Brendan pulled his keys back out of his pockets. "Let's go, Jake. If I remember the schedule correctly, there's a train in about twenty minutes."

I gave Kyle the Standard, the elaborate handshake we'd crafted as kids. These days it was more out of habit than anything else, but it had come to mean a lot of things: "Hello," "Good-bye," "I love you." Kyle surprised me by pulling me into a hug and giving me a mighty pat on the back.

"It was tough, saying bye to him," Kyle said near my ear.

"Yeah." I wasn't sure if he meant Coach Lombard or Adam.

I'D HAD long hair the last time I'd seen Adam. I'd had shaggy hair through most of my teenage years, not for any specific reason other than that my mother hated it. I'd grown it even longer in college, mostly out of laziness, but then I'd dated a guy sophomore year who loved to run his hands through it, so it stayed. One of the last times I'd seen Adam before he skipped town, it had been a few inches past my shoulders, an insane, unruly blond mane. Adam had tugged on a stray curl and told me it looked ridiculous, but I could see the admiration in his eyes.

I'd cut it partly because I'd gotten sick of trying to comb it and partly because Adam liked it so much.

I ran a hand over my short hair as I let myself into my apartment on West Melrose, near Boystown. It felt like a cliché to have moved to the Gayborhood, but the apartment itself—the second floor of a lovely brick house owned by a middle-aged gay couple who were hardly ever home—was gorgeous. I'd fallen in love at first sight with the wood floors and the warm-colored walls and all the elaborate woodwork.

I dropped my keys on the table near the door and tossed my jacket over a kitchen chair before I fell onto the couch and rubbed my face. *Adam*, I thought. *Oh, Adam.*

Nothing needed to happen. I could have just not responded to his invitation and bided my time all week, and then he'd be gone, out of my city, out of my life again.

I took the card out of my pocket and turned it over. There was his handwriting, the same as I remembered it, effortlessly neat letters all in a straight line. Room 1126.

Fretting about it wasn't going to get me anywhere. I wondered if he even really wanted to talk or if he was just being polite.

Five years, it had been. Five years since I'd seen him. So much time and no time at all.

I tossed the card on the coffee table. I walked over to my kitchen and pulled a bottle of Wild Turkey out of the cabinet. I didn't even like Wild Turkey, but it was Kyle's liquor of choice; he must have left a bottle the last time I'd hosted a party. I poured a couple of fingers into a highball glass. Before I could take a sip, my phone buzzed in my pocket.

I thought for a moment that it might be Adam, even though I hadn't given him my number. But no, the display said it was David.

"How are you?" he asked after we exchanged pleasantries.

David was pretty low on the list of people I wanted to talk to right then. Still, I felt like I owed him some honesty. "Well, I've been better. My high school baseball coach died."

"Oh, I'm sorry to hear that. That's terrible. How are you doing?"

"I'm all right. It's sad, but we hadn't spoken in years."

"I'm very sorry for your loss."

"Thanks. I appreciate that." I did not want to have a heart-to-heart conversation. I didn't want David to comfort me. I probably should have, which only made me feel worse.

"I could come over," he said.

Oh, boy. "No, that's all right. I'll be fine."

"I know you will, but…." He sighed. "I know things between us are a little weird right now, but I *am* your friend."

"I'd really rather be alone right now. The wake was today."

"How did it go?"

"All right." I wrestled with how much to tell him. I came down on the side of more. I figured I'd either piss him off enough to make him go away or I'd find out if he was really my friend. "I, uh…. Adam was there."

"Adam." He sounded displeased.

"Yeah, uh, he's in town for business. I'm… I mean, I hadn't seen him, not since he left. I only talked to him for, like, a couple of minutes."

"Are you going to see him while he's in town?"

"He invited me to, but probably not."

There was a long pause. Then, "Why not?"

That was a surprise. I couldn't imagine David being supportive of my meeting up with Adam. And how to even explain? Because Adam had left. Because Adam had looked so good, so tempting. Because the air still crackled between us whenever we got within a foot of each other. Because it was *Adam*. "Oh, well. You know," I said.

David chuckled, but there wasn't much mirth in it. "Jesus Christ, Jake."

I didn't know what to say.

The simple explanation was that David was an ex I'd run into a few weeks before the wake at my local watering hole, and we'd hooked up. The truth was that David had once meant a great deal to me, but now things were confused. Even though we'd slept together again a few times since running into each other, I had told him we were not getting back together, and he seemed okay with that. He was putting a solid effort into rekindling a friendship with me, though. I was still deciding if that was what I wanted.

David coughed and then said, "At least tell me where he's staying so I can punch him in the face. He owes me one for ruining my relationship with you."

"He didn't…. You never even met Adam."

"No, but I feel like I know him from all the time he spent in bed with us."

I didn't want to have this argument. "I'm sorry," I whispered.

"How long have you been in love with him? Since, like, the tenth grade, right? Come on, I know this better than anyone. It's Adam. It's always been Adam. And he's in town now and he said something to you, so you're *not* going to see him?"

"It's too late. After what he did, how can I even—"

"Maybe it *is* too late." There was a whistling sound through the receiver, and I could picture David flaring his nostrils the way he did when he was angry or upset. "Maybe not, though."

"I have to go."

"Suit yourself. See you around." He hung up.

I tossed the phone on the kitchen counter. Then I downed the glass of Wild Turkey in one long gulp.

I DON'T know if this happens to other guys, but everything became clear to me in one magic moment when I was fifteen years old and sitting in a booth at Mama's Pizza.

We'd come in after a baseball game and argued for several long minutes about what, exactly, should go on the pizza. Kyle and I would eat anything, but Adam was going through a phase where he wouldn't eat vegetables and Brendan had always been fussy about what he ate. We settled on meatball, and Adam got up to go to the counter. When he came back, he shot me a toothy grin full of conspiracy—he knew meatball was my favorite pizza topping, and his face seemed to say, *Hey, we just won!*—before sliding back into the booth next to Kyle, across from me.

Kyle and Brendan were having an involved conversation about the batters for the team we'd just beaten—Brendan thought they were bound for the regional play-offs, and Kyle said, "Fat chance!" in response—so I figured I'd start my own conversation with Adam. I was about to mention that my dad had gotten me new cleats for my birthday when I noticed that he was still grinning.

His dark brown hair was plastered to his head but curled out near his ears, the perfect example of terrible hat hair. He ran a hand through it but didn't really fix the problem. He didn't seem to notice; he just kept on smiling. I couldn't look away. He had a dusting of freckles over his nose—something we had only recently lost interest in teasing him about mercilessly—and there was a cut on his lip from when he'd slid into third base at practice the other day. His hazel eyes looked at me with an intensity I'd never seen before. Everything around us seemed to fade: Kyle and Brendan's voices sounded like radio static, the bustle of the restaurant receded into the background. Adam kept on smiling.

Kyle elbowed Adam in the ribs and said, "Good job not busting your face open when you slid home in the sixth inning, Rosie."

"Gee, thanks."

Adam turned to Kyle, and the moment was broken, which was probably just as well, because I was about to have a nervous breakdown. Intellectually, I knew this was merely confirmation of something I'd already suspected, but emotionally, it was like being caught in a nightmare. Because Adam had smiled at me and I'd popped wood. Because I'd already been wrestling with the fact that my wet dreams had all involved big, sweaty men. Because I'd known in the back of my mind for a long time that I was gay, but there'd never really been concrete evidence of it until this moment. Because I had a big, fat, honest-to-god, full-blown crush on Adam Boughton, a boy I saw every day, who lived in the house kitty-corner to mine, whom I'd known since we were infants, who had hazel eyes and freckles and wide shoulders and was everything I wanted.

I was mortified.

Ted, the guy who worked the counter on weekdays, called out, "Hey, boys, your pizza's done."

I froze. My instinct was to bolt from the table, but I didn't want to advertise my present state of arousal to the whole restaurant. Kyle, Brendan, and Adam argued over who should go up, so I took a moment to think about baseball and talk down my erection.

"I got it!" I shouted when I succeeded and bolted up out of the booth.

I fetched the pie and returned to the table. None of my companions seemed aware that this Tuesday was at all different from any other Tuesday, and they grabbed slices and started eating and talking and laughing. I took a slice, and then I sat there staring at it, because my whole life had just taken a left turn.

Adam reached across the table and poked my arm. "Aren't you gonna eat, Jakey?"

"Oh. Yeah, of course." I took a huge bite of my slice, bigger than was really advisable. The cheese burned my tongue, so it took some effort to chew it.

Adam laughed and pulled a piece of meatball off my slice. I watched him pop it in his mouth. I couldn't take my eyes off those lips.

"What the hell is wrong with you?" Kyle asked me.

I blinked a few times. "What? Nothing."

"Okay, weirdo. So as I was saying…."

I HAVE this memory from when I was maybe nineteen of sitting on the floor of Adam's parents' basement, reading a book or a magazine while Adam shouted a lot at the video game he was playing. We'd do that a lot, hang out in the same room without actually interacting with each other. It was winter break and we were both home from college, so by some unspoken mutual agreement, we were spending all of our free time together.

Adam's avatar met a grisly death in the game. He grunted and tossed the controller on the couch cushion next to him. I glanced up at him but then went back to what I was reading.

"So did Longo tell you?" Adam said. "He thinks he's bisexual now."

"What?"

I looked up at Adam again. His eyebrows were raised, and a smile played out on his lips.

"Are you fucking serious?" I asked.

"I know, isn't that crazy? He says he's really curious about what it would be like with a guy. I guess some gay guy came on to him, and now he's thinking he might go through with it."

I wasn't really comfortable having this conversation with Adam, so I shook my head and turned back to my reading.

After a long pause, he said, "You ever think about what it would be like?"

He sounded so serious he surprised me. I wasn't able to look at him, though. I worried my face would give me away. Of course, I didn't have to wonder what it would be like to be with a guy; by then, I knew. I shrugged.

"Oh, I forgot, poor little Jakey is still a virgin. You're so pure, I bet you don't even jerk off."

I felt my face flush hot enough to set my hair on fire. I didn't dare turn around; Adam couldn't know how much time I spent not only jerking off, but jerking off while thinking of him. I said, "I'm not a virgin."

"Oh ho!" Adam laughed. He reached over and tugged on a long strand of my hair. "When did this happen? Why didn't you tell me?"

I squared my shoulders. "Last year, and it's none of your goddamn business."

"Who's the girl? Do I know her?"

"No. It wasn't—" I almost said, *It wasn't a girl*, but thought better of it. "It wasn't a big deal."

"Sure it is. You had sex. You're a man now."

"That's bullshit. It's just sex." A memory of that first time flashed in my head. The guy's name was Brad. I wouldn't have said he looked like Adam, but he did have the same dark-hair-and-freckles thing going on. Our relationship consisted mostly of long make-out sessions in each other's dorm rooms until one day he'd flashed a condom at me and I thought, well, what the hell?

It's not that I treated sex lightly. For starters, shortly after the Pizza Incident, I'd had to sit through a documentary about AIDS in my health class, and the teacher had put extra emphasis on the way the disease ravaged the gay community. In my head, I equated intercourse with disease. But after a few weeks of making out with Brad, I was horny and becoming less afraid by the day. Plus, I was curious. Brendan had recently met Maggie and called me the day after they'd slept together for the first time to regale me with the tale in way too much detail, but it got me thinking that I'd very much like to have sex with someone, risk be damned.

So by the time Brad got to me, I was ready and willing, and though I'd had these ideas about sex being about love or emotion, the moment Brad took his pants off and I saw his erection tenting his underwear, I decided that sex was about sex. I liked Brad well enough and he was hot and he wanted me, and that was all that was needed to balance that equation.

Back in Adam's basement, I found myself regretting Brad and the guy who'd come after and the guy who lived on my floor in the dorms that year that I sometimes fooled around with if no one else was in the communal showers. The thing was, I *liked* sex. A lot. So when opportunities arose, I took them. But really, I wanted to be having sex with Adam.

Adam hummed to himself and picked up his game controller again.

An interesting thought occurred to me. "Are *you* a virgin?"

"No," he said in a way that I somehow knew meant yes. I opted not to pursue it.

THE four of us went to four different colleges, flinging us far and wide across the Midwest, but when we were all in town, we'd go out together fairly often. Sometimes we'd go out for pizza, claiming our old booth at Mama's as if no time had passed. Senior year, after we'd all turned twenty-one, we started going to bars. It was at a bar that I wound up coming out to my oldest friends, in fact. We were at Dickie's Pub, which was a blandly decorated sports bar with a limited beer selection, but it was cheap, and Kyle liked it because the girls who worked at one of the women's clothing stores at the nearby strip mall would come in after work. On this night, Kyle and I were both spectacularly drunk, daring each other into doing shots of whiskey so cheap it might as well have been battery acid. Adam was playing designated driver and Brendan had never been a heavy drinker, so it was just the two of us doing the shots.

Kyle threw an arm around me and pointed to a blonde woman standing on the other side of the bar. "I would like to fuck her," he said.

He got murmurs of approval from Adam and Brendan, though Brendan was quiet about it—he was engaged to Maggie by then.

Kyle turned to me. "What about you, Jake-Jake?"

I laughed. "I don't want to fuck her."

Kyle nodded. "All right. Blondes are not your thing. You see anyone here you *would* like to fuck?"

And because I was drunk and I wasn't thinking, I pointed to a guy in a leather jacket with neatly trimmed stubble. "Leather daddy at two o'clock." It was the sort of thing I would have said to my friends at school, but in my stupor, I'd forgotten that none of these guys—my boyhood friends, my brothers—knew I was gay. It was only when all three of them stared at me, mouths agape, that I figured it out. It struck me as hilarious for some reason, so I laughed. "Oh, whoops!"

Kyle guffawed. "Why, little Jacob Isaacson."

Brendan's eyebrows came together as he frowned, which made him look like my father. Or maybe that was the confused disapproval in his eyes. He said, "Ew, really, Jakey?"

I threw my arms in the air. "Oh, hey, by the way, I'm gay!" Nothing in my whole life had ever been funnier, and I doubled over, laughing so hard I had trouble breathing.

Kyle whacked me on the back when I started coughing. "Whoa, there, sport." He lifted my chin and looked into my eyes. "So is this true, Jakey? Are you gay?"

"I'm here and I'm queer," I said. It was still funny until I noticed how serious everyone's faces were, Adam's in particular. "Uh. You guys don't hate me, do you?"

Kyle was the first to answer. "No. Why would we hate you?"

"I always kind of suspected," said Brendan.

And that was that, I figured. Kyle and I went back to doing shots like nothing had happened. At 2:00 a.m., we all piled into Adam's car, which was how I came to be sitting in the passenger seat as he pulled into his own driveway, figuring he'd just shoo me across the street. Except when he put the car in park, he stayed in his seat.

"Adam?"

"You." He sounded angry. He opened his mouth as if he was going to speak again, but no further words were forthcoming.

"Right. Well, good night." I moved to get out of the car.

He reached over and put a hand on my thigh. That hand felt like it was made of lava, so hot did it feel on my skin. "Jake. Wait."

"What?"

"You are…. So does this mean you've fucked guys?"

"Yes, indeedy." I was still riding that drunk. The alcohol was making my head spin, and also made everything funny, most especially the so-very-serious expression on Adam's face. I giggled. "I even let a few fuck me."

Adam's face seemed to cloud over. He turned away. "Oh, Jakey."

"Whatever." I felt my stomach sink. "I don't want any of your homophobic bullshit. See, this is exactly why I didn't want to tell you. You're an ass, Adam. Thank you and good night." I moved to get out of the car again, this time because I felt like I was crammed into a space about the size of a shoebox with Adam, whom I'd spent the last eight or so years loving and lusting after, and I could feel the panic cutting into my buzz.

"No, I didn't mean…. Like, I get it, but—no, don't get out of the car, just let me say this one thing…."

I didn't wait for him to explain himself, because suddenly I was mad. I got out of the car and slammed the door. Then I ran across the intersection to my own house.

AT SOME point when we were in middle school, we figured out that "Mad Adam" was a palindrome. It was a particularly apropos nickname because Adam was angry a great deal of the time when we were teenagers. He had a short fuse, but rarely was his anger directed at us. Mostly he was angry with his teachers or parents. He had four older brothers, all of whom picked on him relentlessly. The Boughton family had six kids in all, of which Adam was the fifth and best behaved, so he didn't get much attention from his parents. Before they put the TV in the basement, Adam and I spent many an afternoon lounging on the couch in the Boughtons' living room. I can't tell you how many times Mrs. Boughton breezed into the room, looked at us, and said, "Adam, honey, Jake is here. Why so surly? You like Jake, don't you?"

That's sort of how his nickname came about. When we were sophomores, Stephen King's *Rose Madder* was published. Kyle and I spotted it in a bookstore while killing time at the mall one afternoon. Kyle started making puns with the title. "Who makes Rose madder? Who is madder than Rose? I bet Mad Adam is madder than Rose." We went to the movies with Adam that night, and the whole time, Kyle kept working on those puns, calling Adam things like "Rose Mad Adam" or "Adam's Mad at Rose" until finally he shortened it to just calling Adam Rose. It drove Adam bananas to be so christened with a girl's name. That only fueled Kyle's fire. Kyle started calling him "Rosie" not much longer after that. Soon we all did.

Adam's anger was never directed at me as far as I could remember. Or it wasn't until the months after I came out. After that he seemed angry with me all the time. He didn't do anything specific, but he was often standoffish and short with me. One night a few months after the big reveal, we were all at Dickie's having what I thought was a great time. I was relating a story about something that had happened at work. At the time, I was working at a bookstore while I was putting together applications for grad school. I told some stupid customer story.

Adam said, "You know, you wouldn't have to deal with shithead customers if you just got a better job."

It was the most he'd said to me in weeks. I was so shocked, it took me a minute to gather my wits enough to respond. "It's temporary," I said.

Adam sat on a stool and seethed. Annoyed, I meandered over to the jukebox and dropped a couple of quarters in it. While I was flipping through the song selection, a tall guy with blond hair walked up to me. “Hello, there.” He smiled broadly.

“Hello, handsome,” I said, charmed by the way he grinned at me. “Wanna help me pick out a song?”

I’d written Adam off as a potential love interest by then, so I didn’t have any compunction about flirting with guys in front of him. I let the tall blond drink of water help me pick out a couple of songs, and then slipped him my number before returning to my friends.

Adam was now furious. “What the hell? Do you fuck every guy that hits on you?”

“What? Whoa. I just gave that guy my number. Who said anything about fucking?”

Adam grabbed his jacket. “I’m out of here.” Then he stomped out of the place.

“What got up his butt?” Kyle asked. Brendan just shook his head.

AFTER Coach's funeral, I tried to put aside Adam's business card and his reappearance in my life. I was actually only able to do that for an hour here or there; I could get things done, but then I'd walk into the living room and see his damn card on the coffee table and be reminded all over again.

My way of coping was to go to the gay bar at the end of my block Sunday night. I'd considered calling David, but that was a thornbush I figured I should stay away from. I supposed that right there was the advantage to living in Boystown. The bar was pretty quiet, all things considered, but there were enough guys there that I had my choice of potential hookups. There was a redheaded guy dancing in a crowd that caught my eye. I wondered if I was drawn to him because he looked so different from Adam, which only made me realize that I was a damned mess.

"You all right there, Jake?" asked Ken the bartender.

"Fine," I said. "Scotch neat."

He poured me a glass. "The redhead's name is Trey."

"That's nice."

"He comes in here a couple of times a month. Last I knew, he was single."

"Good to know."

Ken nudged the glass toward me, so I took a healthy sip. I enjoyed the burn as it went down my throat. I polished off the glass, and Ken poured another.

"Go dance with him, Jake."

I took Ken's advice and got up from the bar. I insinuated myself into the crowd of men. My mind went blank for a good long moment. I put my hands on Trey's waist, and we danced together. Trey leaned in and whispered, "You're adorable!" in my ear.

I laughed. "I live nearby."

Trey quirked his mouth up in a half smile. He leaned over and kissed my cheek. "I don't put out on the first date, darling," he said, "but I'm already putting our second date in my calendar."

All I did with Trey was make out with him a little in the corner of the bar, which was unfortunate, because it wasn't enough to make me forget but was enough to make me feel guilty. I went back home that night and saw Adam's stupid business card sitting on the coffee table. I sat on the couch and picked it up.

I don't know what came over me, but soon I was dialing the number. He answered on the third ring.

I barely spoke before he whispered, "Jake."

"You want to talk? Talk."

I *KNEW* he was gay. I don't know how. Call it intuition or gaydar or what have you, but when we were in our early twenties, I looked at Adam and I just *knew*.

All four of us wound up back in the Chicago suburbs after college for some reason or another. Kyle had gotten a job pushing paper at a pharmaceutical company in North Chicago and had moved into a tiny hovel of an apartment nearby. Brendan and Maggie had gotten a place together in Glenview, near our high school. I'd had no particular purpose upon graduating from college with a degree in biology, so I moved back in with my parents until I figured it out. And Adam had wound up back living in his parents' basement.

Somewhere in there, I met David. I had just turned twenty-four and had been accepted to the chemical and biological engineering program at Northwestern. David was a post-doc at Northwestern who liked to spend his idle time in the coffee shops near campus. I'd seen him around, and he always looked spectacular: blond, fit, strong, neatly put together. Finally, three days after orientation, I ran into him again and asked him out. He gave me an award-winning smile and accepted.

I hardly saw my friends at all that semester until the Thanksgiving break. That Friday, I met up with Brendan, Kyle, and Adam at Dickie's.

"How's school?" Kyle asked me when I arrived.

"Tough. Good, but very hard. Sorry I haven't been around much."

"We get it," said Brendan. "You're working to save the world. Or something."

"Something," Kyle said, laughing.

We each leaned on the bar, drinking. Kyle faced the seating area, and I followed his gaze as he watched a couple of pretty brunettes talking to each other on the other side of the room. Brendan was mostly watching the game on the TV over the bar. And Adam, somewhat to my surprise, seemed really interested in the guys playing pool at the table over by the jukebox.

Kyle said, "I'm glad you're doing something useful with your life. Speaking of which, how's the boyfriend?"

Adam's eyebrows flew up. I hadn't wanted to say anything until David and I were a more firmly established couple, and I especially hadn't wanted to tell Adam because that would put the nail in the coffin of any hope I had for something with him. But Kyle had called one night when I was spending the night at David's, and David had answered my phone. It took Kyle about fifteen seconds to work out why another man might be around, and I hadn't been able to lie.

"He's good," I said, unable to keep the smile away. For all I didn't want to talk about him, I was pretty darn smitten with David. To Brendan more than Adam, I gave David's vitals: name, age (twenty-seven), and how we'd met.

"That's very cute," Brendan said.

"Or something," said Adam with an eye roll.

"Look, he's not even really my boyfriend," I said, probably a little too defensively. "We just go on dates sometimes."

"Well, and you're sleeping with him," Kyle said. "When you combine that with the fact that you go on dates sometimes, it sounds to me like he's your boyfriend."

Adam blanched. I very badly wanted to change the subject, although part of me hoped Adam was jealous. But Kyle poked at me, so I said, "Well, sure. And I like him a lot. It's just not, like, an official thing."

Kyle laughed. "See, that's the beauty of dating a guy. No girl nagging you about commitment."

"How many guys have you dated?" asked Adam.

"Well, none, now that you mention it. It's a damn shame I like tits and pussy so much. If only I were gay, sex would be so much easier."

I laughed. "Right. Because being gay is a cakewalk."

"I just meant that men are easy. Don't get your panties in a bunch." Kyle elbowed me in the ribs. "What about you, Rosie? How's that lady friend of yours working out?"

It was news to me that Adam was dating anyone. "How do you know so much about everyone's love lives?" I asked. The question was partially motivated by not wanting to hear Adam talk about this girl. And really, a woman? Did *Adam* know he was gay?

"I'm a nosy bastard," Kyle said. "So, Rosie. I want details, too. I would have asked Jakey for specifics, but I figured that would gross out Ox."

"Hello? I'm right here," said Brendan. He turned to me. "I'm not grossed out by the gay thing."

"It's fine," I said.

"Rosie," said Kyle.

Adam grunted. "She dumped me."

There were sympathetic groans all around. "What happened?" asked Kyle.

Adam raised an eyebrow at him. "You *are* a nosy bastard." He took a long sip from his beer. "We were barely dating, first of all, so it's not a big deal. And second of all, she, well…. It just wasn't working out."

Kyle dropped it, and Brendan changed the subject to the baseball game on the TV. Adam's comments on the game were mostly restricted to single syllables. While they talked, I hung back. Adam looked up as he talked, and his gaze met mine. I felt a little like he was seeking me out. And I saw everything there, everything he was going through, everything he needed me to know. I considered the men he'd been watching play pool—all of them attractive, a couple of them wearing very tight T-shirts—and I knew why his latest relationship had failed.

I excused myself to go to the men's room. Adam came in as I was washing my hands.

"Don't tell them, okay? I'm not ready for Ox and Longo to know. Especially Longo. I'd never hear the end of it."

"Tell them what?" I couldn't face him. I busied myself at the sink.

"About me. You know."

I wasn't sure how long I should drag out this game. I felt angry and a little bit ashamed. Why was it okay for me to be gay but not okay for Adam? Why did he feel like he should hide it? If he was ashamed of himself, was he also ashamed of me? And why should I be the only one subjected to the scrutiny of our friends? Not that it even mattered; Brendan and Kyle didn't give a shit about who I slept with. But the way Adam was acting didn't make sense.

"Tell me," I said. "Say it out loud."

"You know what I'm saying," Adam said, walking to the sink and getting into my personal space in a way that made me uncomfortable. That was just plain weird—Adam and I had been sharing tents and beds and things since we were kids, and there had never been any awkwardness—but I started to panic a little as he crowded me into the sink.

"Back off, Rosie," I said through my teeth.

He winced and took a step back. "Okay. Sorry. But I know you know what I'm talking about."

"I do, but I want you to say it."

"I can't. I…."

"Say it to me. Say the words. Get it all out on the table."

He stalled, his mouth agape.

"Fine. Why did that girl dump you?"

He put a hand over his mouth and pinched his lower lip before dropping it. "It didn't work out."

"And why didn't it work out?"

He shook his head. "Because I couldn't…. Because I wasn't…. I mean, I liked her, but I'm… not attracted to her."

"Uh-huh. And why do you think that is?"

"Are you really fucking that guy you're seeing? David?"

I balked. "None of your business. Stop changing the subject."

"Are you?"

"Yes, I'm fucking him. Now you can fuck off. I'm not playing this game anymore. Two little words, Rosie. 'I'm gay.' See how easy that is?"

"But that's not…."

I pushed past him and left the men's room without waiting for a response. I met Kyle's raised eyebrows with a grunt. "I gotta go," I told him before rushing out of the bar.

BACK in the present, Adam laughed. It sounded breathy and familiar, even filtered through the phone speaker. "What should I talk about?"

"I don't know. I have nothing to say to you, I know that for sure. You're the one who wanted to talk."

He laughed again, but it sounded more nervous this time. "I don't even know where to start. I am glad you called, though, I—"

I sighed. I dropped his card back on my coffee table and sat back on the couch. "Let's start with the basics. Why are you in town?"

"Tech expo." That, at least, I believed. I knew that one of the bigger expositions of the year was going on in Chicago that week. It was the sort of big event that got a ton of press coverage regarding the new gadgets everyone would be buying in the coming years. The words "Boughton Technologies" seemed to jump off the front of his card.

"All right. And why do you want to talk to me?"

"Well, that's a little harder to answer." He was quiet for a moment, so I waited. Finally, he said, "You want to go out this week? I'm free Wednesday night."

"Oh, no you don't. You can't just waltz back into my life and expect to pick things up where we left off."

"Why not?"

I leaned forward and rubbed my forehead. It was good he couldn't see me, because I'm sure there was no way I could have kept the emotions off my face. "It's too late. You left us, Adam. You left five years ago with nary a word at all, just took off, and I'm expected to swoon because you happened to show back up again?"

"Then why did you call?"

"I don't know. I'm a little drunk."

"I see."

There was a long silence. Eventually he said, "Well. So how are you? You still seeing that David guy?"

"No." Although that wasn't strictly true, was it?

"Oh, I'm sorry to hear that."

"We still see each other sometimes, though. And I'm kind of seeing this other guy." I wasn't sure that a half hour of making out with Trey really qualified as "seeing" him, but we did have a date scheduled for the following weekend. Although, let's face it, Adam and I both knew "seeing" meant "fucking," and that was certainly an exaggeration where Trey was concerned.

"Oh." It was such a neutral sound that I couldn't read his voice. Was he jealous? Did he care?

"You?" I asked. "I mean, since we're making small talk, are you seeing anyone?"

"No, I…. That is, I was seeing someone, but we, ah, called it quits. That was a couple of months ago, I guess. But it wasn't really a big deal. I mean, we just didn't…. It just didn't work out."

I couldn't fight my own curiosity. "Male or female?"

"What?"

"The person you were seeing. He or she?"

He coughed. "Well, 'he', if you must know."

That was something, I supposed. I wanted to quiz him about it, but even through the drunk haze, I understood that it wasn't my business and that, if they'd broken up recently, Adam probably didn't want to talk about it. So I said, "Good."

"Good that I dated a man or good that we broke up?"

"I don't know. Maybe both."

He laughed. There was a pause, and then he said, "Can I see you?"

"For what?"

"Just to hang out while I'm in town. I want to see you. We can talk or… not."

"Adam—"

"Think about it. Come by the hotel tomorrow night. I should be wrapping up at the expo around six, so any time after that."

I really wanted to see him, and also I really didn't. "I'll think about it."

"Good. Please come."

"Maybe." Then I hung up, because I knew I shouldn't go, but if he said "please" with that yearning in his voice again, I wouldn't be able to refuse.

BEFORE Adam left Chicago, he'd been working for a major telecomm company that had been pioneering video chatting. Adam hadn't written the code on their most popular program, but he'd modified it to make it more user friendly, and his changes had propelled it to being the best-selling program of its kind. He was fond of saying in interviews, "I wanted to make this program something everyone's grandma could use." By all accounts, he'd been very handsomely rewarded for the breakthrough. He had then used the money to start his own company that took what he'd developed to the next level, and his program had become a runaway hit.

Of course I'd kept tabs on him. Sometimes I wondered if I'd find the answer for why he'd run out on us in between the lines of the interviews he did. I never found what I was looking for, though; mostly the articles told me things I already knew. Adam Boughton was incredibly smart, charming, and handsome. Some articles went so far as to call him a genius. He was well-regarded in the industry, and he, or at least his company, was becoming a household name in certain circles. And he was so young that everyone said he undoubtedly had a great career ahead of him.

He'd always liked fixing things. There had been one afternoon when we were in our early twenties—when we were both living in our respective parents' basements, after I came out but before David—when I came home and saw him in his driveway, gazing at a banged-up motorcycle.

"What the hell is that thing?" I asked.

He grinned ear to ear. "*This* is a Ducati. Best motorcycles in the world. Costs more than your yearly salary, normally. I bought this one for a song from a guy in Waukegan."

"It's in terrible shape."

"Nah, that's mostly on the outside." He ran his hand over the front suspension. "What you're looking at is a 1973 750 SuperSport. It looks like shit because the owner left it in his yard to rust for fifteen years. I think he also had some kind of accident, which is why the casings are all scratched. But I intend to restore it."

"Does it even work?"

"Sure. The engine is sound. I drove it around the high school parking lot a little yesterday to be sure. The exterior is banged up, but inside, she purrs like a kitten." I couldn't think of a time I'd heard so much reverence in Adam's voice. He walked a lap around it, then stood next to me, still admiring his purchase. "You want to go for a ride?"

"Absolutely not."

He laughed. "Okay. Well, so, I've got a connection to a parts dealer through my dad." Adam's father was a mechanic, which I suspected was half the problem here. "I've already talked to him. He's willing to sell me what I need at the wholesale price, and then I just need to paint it. I was thinking about red."

I wrinkled up my nose. "Ugh, that's such a cliché."

He frowned. "What's your favorite color?"

"I dunno. Green?"

"Green it is. But not, like, bright kelly green. Army green. Manly green."

I continued to stare at the thing. All I could picture at first was Adam perishing in a fiery crash. But then I started to imagine Adam decked out like a biker in tight leather pants and a slick leather jacket, the motorcycle humming between his thighs….

I coughed and took a step backward.

"You all right there?" he asked.

Jesus, I thought. *Adam in head-to-toe leather.* I felt the flush rise up my neck to my face. Because that was an image to keep me warm on cold, lonely nights.

Then I realized Adam was staring at me, and I snapped out of it. "This is a terrible idea," I said.

"I have my motorcycle license. I've been riding with my brothers for a couple of years. It'll be really great. And I promise you, Jakey, I'm gonna get you on the back of that thing one of these days, and you will love it."

"Over my dead body."

He laughed. "Don't be such a stick in the mud."

I sighed. "I can just hear my mother." I cleared my throat and affected my mother's terrible Brooklyn accent. "Ach, Jacob *bubele*. You'll crack your skull open!"

Adam snickered. "That's pretty good. But I promise, when I get this thing fixed up, I'll buy you a helmet. I'm good on a bike. You'll be perfectly safe."

I wasn't quite convinced, but it was hard not to get caught up in Adam's enthusiasm. "Then you'll crack your head open," I said, but I had a hard time hiding a smile.

He smiled back and rocked on his heels. "C'mon, don't you think motorcycles are sexy? I'd look totally hot on a motorcycle."

He was killing me. "You won't look so hot if you're dead."

"You're no fun at all." He petted the handlebars and then looked up at me with an eyebrow cocked. He was totally sexy in that moment, and there was the image of him on the bike with the leather dancing through my mind again. I had to shift my legs a little, terrified he'd realize the effect he had on me.

He walked around the bike, and then stood next to me. We gazed at it together for a moment. Then he elbowed me in the ribs. "Think about it, Jakey. The hum of the motor, the wind in your hair as you zoom down the highway, the bike vibrating beneath you. Does none of that appeal?"

"I don't know."

He threw an arm around me. "It'll be great, I promise."

IT MIGHT have been romantic if room 1126 was a swanky penthouse suite, but it was just a normal room on one of the middle floors of the hotel. Still, even the corridor leading to Adam's room was much nicer than the interior of any hotel I'd ever been in before.

I stood there staring at the numbers on the door for a good five minutes before I raised my hand to knock, and even then I almost turned and ran back to the elevator about six times. I'd been like that all day, one moment swearing I had nothing to say to Adam and no reason to go see him but then the next feeling oddly compelled to at least hear him out. Under everything, all my hurt and anger, I still missed him. I still wanted him. I'd gone to a bar after work and tried to decide if I should go see him or not, and the alcohol had mostly served to weaken my resolve enough for me to do what I pretty much wanted to do anyway, which was go to his hotel.

I knocked, and he answered. His whole face lit up. "Jake!"

"Hi, Adam."

He stepped away from the door and ushered me inside. "I didn't think you'd come."

"I didn't either."

He smirked, and there was so much of the boy I remembered in that look. But we were basically strangers now, I reminded myself.

"Well, now that you're here, do you want some coffee or something? Or we could break into the minibar."

I shook my head. "Look, I just came because you said you wanted to talk things through, and I had a lot of whiskey before I got on the El and came over here, and somehow that persuaded me that seeing you in person was a good idea, but now that I'm here, I kind of think it isn't, so just say what you have to say, and then I'm going home." The words tumbled out of my mouth rapidly.

"Breathe, Jakey."

"Just… what is it you want from me?"

He looked away from me and then started to pace. "Well, I thought that we could be friends again, for starters."

"Are you fucking kidding me?"

That just hung in the air for a while, the echo pinging around the room. Or maybe that was just my imagination. Everything went still. Then Adam rubbed his head and resumed pacing. "I'm quite serious, actually. I know I made some mistakes—"

"Mistakes? You call disappearing for five years a mistake?"

"And I know you're still mad at me. Maybe it will take some time to repair the damage, but come on, Jakey, we've known each other since we were infants. How can you just throw all that away?"

"Maybe you should have thought of that before *you* threw it away." I reached for the door, thinking I should bail before I got more upset. It had been a mistake coming to see him. I could see that now. I didn't know what I'd expected of him. It seemed clear now that nothing had changed. "It's too late, Adam. I'm not little Jakey Isaacson anymore. I've grown up. Shit's different now. You can't expect me to just drop everything for you like in the old days."

"Tell me why it's too late. I know you still have feelings for me. Otherwise you wouldn't have come here at all."

Was that what this was about? "Maybe I just wanted some closure."

"Maybe you want me."

"Fuck you, Rosie."

His skin went pale at the nickname. I'd stopped calling him by it when he'd asked me to, all those years before. Now I wanted him to feel everything it represented, both to me and to him.

Still, he looked so thrown off by it that I couldn't stop myself from apologizing. "I'm sorry. But it's too late for us."

"Why?"

"Because you left us!" My anger grew like a cancer through my body. "Because one day you just took off and didn't tell anyone where you were. Because five years went by when things happened to us, happened to me, that you weren't around for. Because you're not a part of my life anymore. Because you *chose* to leave."

That was about when I broke. My knees got wobbly, and the anger started to dissipate, like it had just been waiting for me to say these things. Adam stared at me, but I didn't understand the look on his face. His eyes were wide, his lips were pressed together, and I found it all completely inscrutable. So I sat on the edge of the bed and told him one last truth.

"Because I spent five years wondering what was so horrific about kissing me that it made you run away."

WE WERE in our midtwenties before I stopped calling him Rosie.

The night began the way so many had in those days, with him talking me onto the back of the Ducati. It had terrified me the first few times we went riding, but I found it thrilling too. I'd put up a little bit of a fight, but then the allure of sitting behind him, our bodies inches apart, became too much. Often I'd have to press close behind him, and I'd hold on to his waist as we rode, partly because I was terrified I'd go flying off the back and partly because I just liked touching him.

This particular night, we rode out to a small park near O'Hare. Adam's fascination with all machinery was a key element of this particular trip, mostly because he liked lying on the grass and watching the planes come in. He'd name the make and model of each plane that flew over us and try to teach me some physics, but I didn't really care. Mostly I just liked lying on the grass next to Adam and listening to him talk.

He was in the middle of explaining the fuel capacity of the DC-10 that had just landed when my mind started to wander. I liked his enthusiasm, because this was after I'd started dating David and Adam had gotten surly. He was in rare form that night, though, jabbering away with me as his appreciative, albeit captive, audience. It was nice, was what I kept thinking, to have Adam back, for things to be like they'd been when we were kids, before David, before I'd come out and fucked everything up between us.

Adam lifted his arm and glanced at his watch. "We should probably head back," he said. "I'm twenty-four years old, and my mother still thinks I need a curfew."

"I told my mother I was going riding with you. She told me to wear a helmet, and then she told me to tell you not to drive too fast."

He laughed. "You like it when I drive fast."

"Which is why I didn't tell you not to."

We both stood and looked at each other. There was a strange moment in which it felt like the words we'd just exchanged had been laced with double entendre, even though we'd both spoken the literal truth. Our parents had nothing to worry about as far as we were concerned back then. I did always wear a helmet when I rode with Adam on the motorcycle; it wasn't a euphemism for safe sex. Though I think we both understood for one fleeting second that it could have been.

He cleared his throat and walked back over to the Ducati. "How's David?"

"All right."

"Does he get mad when you go out with me?" His back was to me, but he turned his head slightly when he asked this, and he looked at me out of the corner of his eye.

"No," I said, omitting the part where he didn't get mad because I didn't tell him. David was teaching a class that night.

"Oh."

"I mean, why would he get mad? You and I are just friends."

"Of course we are."

Adam tossed me my helmet. I caught it and turned it over in my hands.

"You don't really want to know about David, do you?" I asked.

He shrugged and threw his leg over the motorcycle. "He's your boyfriend, right? I care about that."

"Why do you care?"

He turned away from me. "Same reason I care about Maggie."

I didn't believe him but made the decision not to ask too many questions. I didn't want to throw off the balance we'd struck. I started to walk toward the Ducati, getting ready to hop on and head back.

He said, "I'll tell you the same thing I told Ox. I care, but I don't want to know anything about your sex life. Especially not *your* sex life. Gross."

"Shut up, Rosie."

I moved to get on the back of the motorcycle and realized he'd gone completely still. I waited a moment to see if he would breathe, but he instead tightened his grip on the handlebars until his knuckles went white.

"What?" I asked.

"Don't call me that."

"Call you what?" I honestly didn't know what he was talking about.

"You know. That name. The one you guys call me."

It took a moment for recognition to dawn. I hadn't done it consciously. "Rosie" had just popped out of my mouth, same as it had for ten years. "I'm sorry. I wasn't thinking."

"Well, think next time, all right. It's a *girl's* name. Bad enough that Ox and Longo call me that, but *you*, Jakey? You of all people should know why I don't like it. So please. I can't make Longo stop, but you, at least, can stop calling me that. Okay?"

"Okay," I said. I got on the back of the bike and put my hands on his waist, but it was awkward now, his body still stiff. "Okay, *Adam*."

"Thank you. You all set?"

"Yeah."

He revved the motor, and we zoomed out of the park. I stopped calling him Rosie.

IN HIS hotel room, he stared at me, eyes wide in confused surprise. "What?" he said. He stood before me, a few yards from the bed, looking down at me where I sat on what was, frankly, an incredibly ugly green bedspread. I felt intimidated.

But I kept talking. “You kissed me.” I mimed this by pressing my palms together. “And then you ran away.” I dropped my hands to my sides. “Clearly kissing me was a horrific experience.”

He stared at me for a long moment. “What? No. No, of course it wasn’t. Oh my God, is that what you think?” He squatted on the floor at my feet. “No, it was far from horrific. That was probably the most incredible kiss of my life.”

That didn’t compute. “Then why did you leave?”

“I panicked.”

He shifted a little until he was kneeling. He seemed so big. He was broad and corporeal and present in a way he hadn’t been in so long; this was the real Adam, not the wispy cloud of my memory.

With me sitting above him on the bed, I felt like he’d given me the upper hand. Still, I waited for an explanation.

Eventually, he said, “I don’t even know why I did it to begin with. I guess I was curious. But it confirmed some things for me. And then there was this huge fight with my mother, so there were a lot of things going on. I had a job offer in California, and I was freaking out, seriously everything was going to hell, so I took the job and decided to try to start over. That’s what happened. There was nothing awful about kissing you. Quite the contrary, actually.”

I was having a hard time processing what he was telling me. I’d gone for so long clinging to my own interpretation of what had happened that I couldn’t make sense of his. “What did it confirm for you? That kissing your best friend was a mistake?”

“No, I—” He closed his mouth and shook his head. “I wasn’t ready, I guess. I still had a lot of things to figure out.”

“Did you figure those things out while you were gone?”

He bit his lip and looked up at me. “Yeah.”

“What did you come up with?”

He put his hands on my knees. “I think you know.”

“I need the words, Adam.”

He closed his eyes. "I'm gay."

I didn't want his words to make my heart soar. I didn't want my skin to tingle where his palms rested. I didn't want to get aroused by the way he smelled. I didn't want the proximity of our bodies to make me shiver. All of those things happened anyway.

I took a deep breath. I watched a bead of sweat fall from the line of his hair, down toward his nose. Everything seemed to be moving in slow motion.

"So… what?" I asked quietly. "I proved you were gay?"

"Well, I'd thought I was for a while, obviously, but—"

Suddenly I was angry. "You came across the street to the first convenient fag to test out your theory that you might be one too? You kiss me and prove it and then run off to fuck your way through California?"

He jerked backward. "No! No, that's not what happened at all. Don't you get it? I had feelings for you and I acted on them, and then I freaked out."

"Do you have any idea what you did to me? What really happened? You came to me and you kissed me, and I thought, *Oh dear Lord, finally! Adam came to me and he wants me and everything is perfect!* I'd had a crush on you for so long. Did you know that?"

"No, I didn't."

"You know what I did after you left my house that day? I broke up with David. I took the train into the city and I ended things, and it was awful. We argued and cried and had a completely terrible time of it. I really hurt him, and that wasn't really what I wanted, either. I did care about him a great deal. I thought I was making the right decision, though, that you had come to kiss me because you wanted to be with me and that we'd have this great life together. But then I went to your house the next morning and you were gone. Your mother wouldn't tell me where you'd run off to, just that you were gone and never wanted to see me again. Then she slammed the door in my face!"

He looked appropriately chastened. "My job transferred me."

"That's bullshit," I said.

"Did you really break up with David for me?"

"Well, what was I supposed to do? I thought you wanted me. I'd wanted you to want me for so long, and you finally seemed to, and I wanted to act on it but I couldn't cheat on David. He deserved better than to be treated that way." He deserved better than me, I thought. David was a good man who deserved more than the guy who would always be half in love with someone else.

He backed away slightly. "I did want you, but I wasn't ready yet. It kills me that I hurt you in that way. That was never what I intended, and I know I acted selfishly, but I wasn't ready emotionally to get into a relationship with another man, I just wasn't ready. That.... Kissing you was the first time I'd ever done *anything* with a guy, and I panicked as soon as I did it."

"You wanted me?" I was trying to hold on to my anger, but the closer he got to me, the more he confessed, the faster it seeped away.

"Of course I did!" He leaned forward a little until his palms pressed into my thighs. He smelled fantastic. It was making things short-circuit in my brain. I had to work to focus on what he was saying. "God, Jake, don't you get it? I kissed you because I wanted to, and it was even better than I ever would have expected. But then things went to hell with my family. It's not really worth it to relive it, but...."

"What happened with your family?"

He squirmed a little. This was not something he wanted to talk about. But I needed to understand. When he didn't speak, I leaned forward.

"My mother... she...." He frowned. "She saw us. Kissing."

"What?"

"It's not like she threw me out of the house or anything. But she knew about this offer I had in California, and she was pushing me to take it. She thought you were a bad influence. The minute she found out you're gay, she told me I should stop seeing you. I couldn't do that, obviously I couldn't, but then, I don't know. I thought if I kept my distance, it would be all right, but everything was building up between us, and it was just, ugh. I had to kiss you. I *had* to. And I know none of this makes any sense, but—"

He was so close to me that he was affecting my ability to think, like an electronic device causing radio interference. I knew he was telling me something important, but I grabbed on to the one part that jumped out. "You wanted to kiss me."

"Yes, that's what I'm telling you. I'd been wanting to for months. And now that you're here, I really want to do it again."

"Is *that* why you asked me here?"

"I did want to talk." He leaned in a little further.

His lips were *right there* and looked so perfect and kissable. "About kissing?"

"Well."

I kissed him. Something in my brain exploded. Our lips just fit together, like we were made to kiss each other. He sank into me almost immediately, his mouth opening and his body going slack, leaning against my legs. I put my hands on the sides of his face and became suddenly aware of everything: of how smooth his freshly shaven cheeks were, how warm his skin was, how sharp his minty aftershave smelled. He tasted sweet and metallic.

He moved his hands up my thighs while we kissed. They skimmed over my hips and rested on my waist. I opened my legs to pull him closer. I *needed* him close to me like I needed to breathe. He pressed against me and moved his lips to my chin, where he began to kiss and nibble at my jaw.

There was a moment when this situation stopped being about the five missing years and became about missing Adam. I'd missed him when he was gone, but more than that, I'd missed the opportunity to hold him in my arms. I'd missed the chance to prove to him that I'd loved him, that I'd be a good partner for him, that he and I were good together. Then the situation changed as my brain got a little cloudier, as my libido took over, and it became about having this incredibly hot man in my arms, having his body pressed against mine, his lips on my skin, his teeth nipping at my jaw. It became about the heady smells and the harmony of our moans and hair and skin and sweat.

I put my hands on his face and brought his lips back to mine, and our kisses were full of hunger and yearning. His body bent toward mine. I had to have him closer, needed his skin against mine, so I undid the buttons on his shirt. I got him out of that and the T-shirt he had on under it, and then I leaned back a little to get a good look.

He was gorgeous. It was difficult to reconcile this body with the scrawny teenager I'd known. He'd started filling out in his early twenties, but this was something else entirely; he had a gym-sculpted body and dark hair that fanned out over his chest. I ran my hands over his nipples and curled my fingers, touching the hair, loving the texture.

I kissed and touched him and tried to remember what this body used to look like, the times I'd seen him naked. We'd changed clothes in front of each other dozens of times and taken post-game showers all through high school, but I'd spent so much of that time willing away erections that I'd never really let myself look at any of the other boys, let alone Adam, so often the object of my desire.

I decided it didn't matter and concentrated on the man before me. I scooted back on the bed and pulled him close to me. He pulled off my T-shirt and ran his hands over me, making my skin tingle and come alive under his touch.

"Jakey," he whispered, pushing me back on the bed. "Jake. Jesus, Jake. You're so beautiful."

The awe and yearning in his voice undid me. I clutched at his skin, tried to pull him closer, but he held me off. Instead, he stood up. I lay on the bed watching him. He undid his pants and pushed them to the floor, and then he toed off his socks. The fabric of his briefs strained over his hard and impressive-seeming cock. I sucked in a breath.

He leaned over me and pulled off my pants, and then he was suddenly on top of me, our bodies pressed together, his hairy chest rubbing against mine. I reveled in the alternately smooth and rough textures of his body, sliding my hands over any bit of skin I could reach, pressing my hips against his. His erection rubbed against mine, making my blood rush and pleasure course through me like waves. I must have cried out, because he shushed me and then kissed me again.

This was good, but I needed more. I plunged my hands into his briefs and grabbed his ass. It was smooth and tight and perfect, and I was impressed all over again by how strong and muscular his body was, so different from what I remembered. Not that I'd ever been with him like this—and my mind reeled with the knowledge that this wasn't just some guy I was about to have sex with, but *Adam*—but my memory of him was of a much thinner guy, a troubled man, an awkward teenager.

My capacity for rational thought soon flew out the window, though, because Adam got a hand between us and started stroking my cock through my underwear. I decided I'd had enough of this clothing business, and I angled my hands to peel off his briefs. There was a fleeting moment of squirming when he seemed to become all knees and elbows, but then we were back, pressed together on the mattress, him on top, both of us naked, me happy enough to surrender to whatever he wanted to give me.

Everything became a blur of touching and feeling and stroking and exploring. I moved my fingers anywhere they would go, over his nipples, his hip, his thighs, his ass. I parted my legs a little to pull him closer, and truth be told, I wanted him inside me, but I also wanted him in a frantic way that wouldn't allow for stopping to properly prepare for that. Instead I wiggled my hips until our cocks lined up, and then we were *there*, thrusting against each other, grasping, gasping, moaning.

Adam let out a sputter of curses and moans, and he breathed out my name a few times. "Shit, I'm gonna come soon," he muttered—words I'd never before heard him utter, words that made my pulse pick up the pace. His words surprised me until I felt the head of his cock rubbing against my own shaft, and tingles became something tangible. My very skin seemed to sing as we lunged toward the cliff. Then he let out a groan, and I felt his cock pulse before I felt the stickiness on my belly. I wanted to see his face, so I pushed him up a little, and our eyes met, and he was so completely fucking gone, and then I was overwhelmed. His body vibrated against mine, pulling at me, drawing my very soul to the surface.

He wrapped his hand around my cock and stroked firmly but not too hard. "Come for me, Jake. I want to see you fly apart."

I arched my back and thrust my hips, and then I was coming, and it was like a flashbulb went off in my face. I couldn't see anything, but

I sure as hell felt Adam's body against mine, and he continued to tug at me as I rode the orgasm. When I felt it waning, I grabbed his hair and yanked him close to me. I kissed him, thrusting my tongue into his mouth, wanting to thank him aggressively for the great orgasm and for being Adam.

He held me for a while as we lay in the middle of the bed, getting our breath back. He didn't speak, which gave my mind the opportunity to wander. Had we ever had a frank conversation about sex? I was sure we'd told dirty jokes or stories about other people or talked about it in the abstract, but the actual fact of Adam's sexuality had always been off limits. And yet, he'd just come against me. We'd just engaged in a sex act together. I was wrapped up in his naked body. What we'd just done had been hot and messy and sexy as hell. None of it made any sense.

"I have a proposition," he said, breaking into my rambling thoughts.

"Okay."

"Seeing as how we're all sticky, how's about we take a quick shower and then order room service. Have you had dinner?"

"No."

"Great. I hear the restaurant downstairs makes a good steak. How does that sound?"

My stomach rumbled in response. We both laughed. "It sounds great, Adam."

He lifted up a little and smiled down at me. "Come on, let's get cleaned up."

He pushed up and then seemed to hop off the bed. He held out a hand for me. I took it.

WHEN we were high school juniors, the baseball team made it to the state championships, which meant we were good enough that scouts were starting to look at all of us.

I had no particular desire to play baseball after high school. I enjoyed the game, and I was a decent player, but I viewed it as a hobby. Kyle told me once that he felt the same way. Brendan went through a phase in which he was convinced he'd grow up to play in the majors, but I suspected that, deep down, he really wanted to stay in the suburbs and work for his father. Adam, however, took the scouts seriously, not so much because he thought he had a future as a professional ballplayer but because getting a baseball scholarship meant he could go to college. After putting four kids through college—and Adam's brother Danny was then a junior—it was starting to look like the Boughtons wouldn't have any money left to pay for Adam's education.

So Adam took baseball very seriously, and that involved as much extra practice as he could fit in his schedule. We were at the batting cages one night for this reason, and we were working on our swings. Or Adam was; I got sick of the machine throwing balls past me pretty quickly, so mostly I was hanging on the backstop fence behind Adam, picking apart what he was doing.

"Your left elbow is too high," I said.

"Bullshit." He moved his elbow. "Up like this? That's how Ken Griffey, Jr., hits. He got that insane homer against the Sox last week, did you see it?"

"No."

The machine vomited a ball at Adam, which he hit. It would have been a grounder right down the middle. He grunted and adjusted his stance a little. The next one whooshed by him and hit the fence about a foot to my left. He adjusted again, and this time he lowered his left elbow. The ball hit his bat with a *clok* and sailed up and away before getting caught in the net.

Adam did a little victory dance, imitating the roar of the crowd before adding in his best sportscaster voice, "Boughton gets a hit, and that ball is going, it's going, it's *gone*! Boughton hits a grand slam!"

"I told you so. See what happens when you put your damn elbow down?"

"Oh, shut up."

He assumed the position again. His batting stance actually looked pretty good. He swung at the next three balls and connected with two of those. "Unfortunately, the machine doesn't throw a curve ball," he said once he had it down. He devastated the next pitch, sending it far and away into the net.

"I think you got it now. The stance thing, I mean. It looks good."

He turned back to me. Our eyes met briefly. At the time, I thought I imagined the electricity that crackled between us. He turned off the machine. "It can't just be good," he said. "It has to be perfect. There are gonna be college scouts at the game Tuesday."

"You think?"

"Yeah, Coach told me it's all but a sure thing. At least the guy from Urbana."

"You want to go to Urbana?"

"I'll go wherever they take me."

"Dad thinks I should apply to Michigan or Iowa State. Somewhere with a good science program."

"You should."

"There's a decent program at Illinois."

He picked up a bat and contemplated it. "What are you saying?"

"Us going to the same school, genius. We could, I don't know, room together or whatever."

An incredibly awkward moment followed, in which both Adam and all of the air around us froze. Eventually he coughed and said, "Eh, I don't know about that. I heard that when friends room together, they end up hating each other."

"I don't think that would happen to us."

He set the bat down against the fence. "I'd rather not test that." He picked up a ball and walked around the fence. "Let's practice throwing and catching."

"Aw, Adam. I'm tired. Let's go to Mama's and get extra cheese."

"You're a whiny bitch." He cracked up and tossed the ball at me. I caught it easily. I rolled my eyes and picked up my glove.

He said, "As members of the infield, we have to get this down. In order to be effective, we have to operate as one, be able to communicate wordlessly—"

"Talk a lot of nonsense." I threw the ball at him.

He caught it in his glove. "You suck."

I caught the ball he lobbed at me. "You love me." I stuck out my tongue.

He gave me the strangest look, his head cocked to one side and his eyebrows raised. "Yeah, well. Throw me the ball again." He held up his glove.

He did end up getting that scholarship to the University of Illinois. I don't know how he managed to play ball and finish a computer science degree with honors, but he did it. In the end, I picked Michigan over Iowa, figuring there would be more gay kids there, or at least fewer Iowa farm boys who would make fun of me. Being apart from Adam was awful, and I missed him a great deal, although we did email and talk on the phone frequently, and I think being apart gave me some perspective. Or it gave me room to explore my sexuality without having to tell him what was going on. Being apart gave me freedom I probably wouldn't have had otherwise. I certainly couldn't sit around waiting for him before starting my life.

THE night after I slept with Adam, I met Kyle in a bar near his office. We were close enough to Millennium Park that there were tourists moving in packs along the sidewalk outside. I watched them through the bar's front window and tried to figure out if I should tell Kyle about what had happened with Adam.

We were just shooting the shit when, behind us, a woman's voice said, "Kyle Longo!"

Kyle and I both turned at the same time. There was a busty blonde walking toward us.

"Wow," she said. "I haven't seen you in a while! How've you been?"

She put a hand on the bar and leaned in close to him, bowing forward a little in a way that gave him the best view of her ample cleavage. Kyle's gaze lingered there as he said, "Well, hey… you."

They flirted for a minute, after which time she tucked a piece of paper with her phone number into his shirt pocket. "We should do it again sometime," she said in a low, husky voice. She patted his chest before turning and sauntering back from whence she came.

When she was gone, Kyle grinned at me.

"You know," I said, "I'm starting to think that the only reason you think you're bisexual is that you've run out of new women to fuck."

Kyle frowned. "You don't think I'm bisexual? Because I have slept with a few men. Not as many as you, probably, but—"

I rolled my eyes. "Come on, Longo. I appreciate your sense of sexual adventure, but at the end of the night, wouldn't you rather go home with a woman?"

"Sure. Who wouldn't?"

"I wouldn't."

He raised his eyebrows. "No? Not even a little?"

I sipped my beer. “I suppose my life would be easier if I did. I would have spared my poor mother some grief. But no, at the end of the night? Give me someone with chest hair and a penis.”

He laughed. “Fair enough.”

“Besides, aren’t you the one who’s always joking about how much better it would be to be in a relationship with a man?”

“Well, I imagine it would be a lot like this—” He waved his finger at the space between us a few times. “—but with sex.”

“There’s a *little* more to it than that.”

“How so?”

I couldn’t figure out if he was joking, but it seemed not. I also couldn’t think of how to explain. “I don’t know. There just is. There are lots of differences between a friendship and a romantic relationship. There’s companionship, sure, but there’s also romance and emotion and, like, those things, you know. Don’t you have female friends you don’t sleep with?”

He narrowed his eyes at me. “This is not a concept I’m familiar with. Women I don’t sleep with?”

I groaned. “And suddenly it becomes clear why none of your relationships have lasted.”

He smiled and slapped me on the back.

By the second round, we were watching the baseball game that was playing on the TV over the bar. Kyle was disproportionately amused by the White Sox’s pitcher, who did this weird shimmy before hurling the ball at the batter.

“What I don’t like about this guy,” he said, angling his glass toward the TV, “is that he’s got the goods, but he chooses to pitch defensively. Like, he’s capable of throwing a ninety-five-mile-per-hour fastball that’ll whizz right by this guy, right? Or a curve or a change-up or whatever. But instead, he throws these slow pitches into the right corner. Which, sure, will throw off a batter, but it’s a cheap shot, you know?”

My focus wasn't really on the game. I was a die-hard Cubs fan, which made me ambivalent about the White Sox, but Kyle's dad had worked for the White Sox organization for years, so he'd had his team loyalty imprinted on him at birth. We watched the game, Kyle rambled, and I zoned out. My thinking meandered toward Adam more often than not. I wondered what he was doing that night. I wondered if I'd made a mistake the night before. I wondered if this meant anything in the greater scheme of things.

I blurted out, "I slept with Adam."

Kyle stopped, his beer halfway to his open mouth, and then he slowly put the glass back on the table. "You what now?"

"Adam invited me to his hotel, and I knew it was a dumb thing to do, but I was curious. I went to see him last night, and we had sex."

"Uh-huh." Kyle's face was inscrutable. He pursed his lips and looked down at the bar, but I couldn't tell if he was displeased or confused or angry or what. "Why would you do that? And why are you telling me?"

"It's all I've been able to think about for the last twenty-four hours."

Kyle shook his head. "He'd better have a huge cock. Otherwise I can't think of a good reason for you to have done that."

"Well, he—"

Kyle held up his hand. "No, don't tell me. I don't want to know."

"Anyway, it was probably a mistake. We didn't really resolve anything. He still… well, you know what he did."

Kyle nodded. "I guess you know now for sure that he's gay."

I shrugged. "I knew that anyway. I just…. I mean, I don't know what good this did. He's only in town for the rest of the week. I'm still pretty mad at him, too. On Friday, he'll go back to wherever it is he lives now, and then what? Will he come back? Can we even be friends again? Will he just disappear and then come back every five years like Brigadoon?"

He laughed. "That's maybe the gayest thing you've ever said."

"Fuck you."

"Look, Jake-Jake, I don't know what to tell you. It's *Adam*. That's fucking weird."

"Even weirder for me."

"I can't even picture Rosie in a sexual context. I mean, I saw him at the funeral, he's looking good these days, don't get me wrong. But I just keep remembering the kid he was in high school, with the freckles and the bad hair, and I see him getting mad about something stupid like he always did, and there's nothing sexy about that. Like, one time we were at the arcade and he started yelling at me because I beat his pinball score."

"He yelled?"

"Yeah. You can't be surprised. You knew him too. In this case, it was mostly defensive. Like, 'I would have gotten a better score if that snotty kid hadn't walked by and made a noise that distracted me for half a second,' or whatever." He dropped his voice and did a reasonably good impression of Adam.

"What did you do?"

"I punched him."

I laughed. "Of course you did."

Kyle smiled. "Hey, I may be wiry, but I've got a mean right hook. Then we started to wrestle and got ourselves kicked out of the arcade. Then Adam *really* let me have it in the parking lot while we waited for my mom to come pick us up. He shouted until he turned red, and we started whaling on each other, but my mom pulled up before we did any real damage. He used to annoy me so much. Nothing was ever his fault." Kyle shook his head. "I mean, he was like a brother to me. I knew that, if I needed it, he'd direct all that anger at any of my enemies, that he totally had my back. Just… you know."

I nodded. I did know. That was the thing about Adam. Even after I came out, when he seemed mad at me all the time, when I was so angry and frustrated with him, I knew he'd lay down his life for me if he had to. That was the thing about us: things weren't going to be idyllic all the time, but I knew I could count on my three best friends when push came to shove. Except Adam's leaving had shaken all that up. I couldn't count on him the way I used to.

"But that was all in the past," Kyle said, echoing my thoughts. "He took off for all that time without telling any of us where he went. He's not… I mean, what kind of friendship is that?"

"I know. I know all of that." I knew that better than I suspected Kyle did. Hell, my heart was still hurting from what happened. And yet I hadn't been able to stay away. "But he's just… Adam."

Kyle took a long sip of his beer and seemed to regard me carefully. "How long have you felt that way about him? Since before he left, I assume."

"Yeah."

"I think I suspected, but you never said."

"How could I have?"

"That certainly would have changed things in our little family, wouldn't it?"

"What? If Adam and I had hooked up?" As soon as the words were out of my mouth, a million images from the previous night zoomed through my head. It was mostly flashes of body parts, skin, sensation, Adam's low moan reverberating around my skull. My whole face heated up. "Before last night, I mean."

Kyle cracked up and slugged me on the arm. "If you had gone out with each other, yeah, that's what I meant. It would have changed the whole dynamic. Like, if I made out with Ox or something, that would make things different." He crinkled his nose. "Uh, I want you to know, for the record, I'm not making out with Ox."

"Please don't."

"I'm just trying to make a point. I have a hard time imagining what that would have been like. You and Rosie, I mean, not me making out with Ox, because dear God, why would anyone want to make out with Ox? I mean, I love that guy, but no thank you."

"Maggie seems to enjoy it."

"She can have him." Kyle shuddered. "Well, I guess we would have adjusted. And talked about sex less. I do *not* want details, by the way."

We sipped beer and watched the TV for a minute. "Seriously, though," I said at length. "Do you think I made a mistake?"

"Time will tell, I guess. Do you want to see him again?"

"I don't know." I moved to take another sip and noticed my glass was empty. I signaled to the bartender. "I mean, I *want* to. But I'm still mad about what happened when he left. Because it's not just that he left, it's that he jerked me around, and I fucked everything up with David, and everything is all tied to that one stupid thing he did." I groaned. "It's all a mess."

"But you like him." Kyle didn't wait for me to respond; he merely nodded. "He's in town for the rest of the week, right? Make the most of it. Fuck his brains out, and then take it from there."

"I thought you didn't want to talk about me and Adam having sex."

He grinned. "I don't. I'm just trying to give you the best advice. That makes me a good friend."

"Whatever you say."

FOR as long as I live, the memory of that first kiss with Adam will forever be etched in my brain.

I was raking leaves in my parents' front yard. It must have been late spring, just after the cherry tree in the front yard had shed all its blossoms. The Ducati zoomed by my house, went to the end of the next block, and then turned around. I kept busy raking while Adam parked at his house and hopped off it. My stomach did a little flip in anticipation of talking to him, but I concentrated on the task at hand.

He, of course, jogged across the intersection and walked across the area I'd already raked, dragging desecrated cherry blossoms with his boots.

"Hey, Jakey," he said.

"Hey, Adam. How was Disneyland?"

"Happiest place on Earth." He grinned.

What I didn't know at the time was that the family trip to California had doubled as a sort of fact-finding mission for Adam's career. That the company he'd been working for in Chicago had offered a promotion if he was willing to transfer to the Silicon Valley headquarters. That he'd looked at apartments in San Jose before he and his family had flown to LA and taken a few of his nieces and nephews to Disneyland. That at the same moment he stood in my front yard with bits of cherry blossom stuck to his boots, he still hadn't made up his mind about whether he'd take the promotion.

"Hope you said hi to Mickey for me," I said.

"I did. Got my picture taken with Donald Duck just to make you jealous." He laughed. "How were things in Glenview while I was gone?"

"Oh, you know. Same as always."

He took a step closer to me. I kept raking. He said, "Yeah, I bet it was a real riot."

"Eh. Longo got plastered at Dickie's the other night, and Ox and I had to carry him home. He puked in Ox's car. Ox may never forgive him."

"So it was a Tuesday."

We both laughed. I became aware suddenly that Adam was staring at me with a strange intensity. "You okay?" I asked.

"Fine."

A rare awkward moment passed between us. I sifted through my memory for conversation topics, and I remembered that he'd mentioned the potential promotion before he'd left, albeit without telling me it required a transfer. "Oh, hey, did you ever find out about that promotion?"

He raised his eyebrows. "Oh. No, it's not a done deal yet."

"I'm sure it'll come through. Your company would be stupid not to promote you."

"Yeah. Thanks."

He seemed distracted. He kept glancing at me and then at my hands and then at the house. I found it unnerving, so I kept raking. Although "raking" by then meant I was scraping the rake over the same thinning patch of grass.

"Jake, stop for a minute."

Startled, I looked up. He was standing there biting his lip, a sure tell that he was nervous about something. I took a step back and leaned my rake against the front porch. I stepped forward, closing the space between us.

"What is it?" I asked.

That was when he kissed me. He put his hands on either side of my face and drew me in until our lips touched. I was too surprised to react at first. He opened his mouth and prodded at mine with his tongue, so I let him in. I parted my lips and pressed my tongue forward, tasting him, letting him taste me. Our lips slid together as we explored each other's mouths, and somewhere in the back of my mind, fireworks were going off. There's a certain simple pleasure in a really good kiss, and my adrenaline kicked up as I enjoyed this one, but more than that, I couldn't shake the fact that this was Adam kissing me, and that touching him like this, simply kissing him, was at once a totally new experience and yet somewhat familiar. I knew his scent, I knew the texture of him, I knew his shape and the gentle press of his hands. I put my hands on his waist and I kissed him back with my whole heart and it was better than anything I ever could have hoped for. I catalogued the experience in my mind, hoping to remember every moment of it later. His lips were soft and tasted like bubblegum. His stubble scratched at my face.

But then, just as soon as we'd really gotten started, he backed away again. He took a step away from me and wiped at his mouth with the back of his hand. His eyes darted up and down the street. No one was outside.

"Jesus, Jake, I—"

"Adam, wait, I—"

"I have to go. Um. You know. Thing with my parents." He hooked his thumb back toward his house. "I, um. We'll talk about this later?"

"Sure, Adam."

He nodded once, then ran back across the intersection to his house. I wouldn't see him again until Coach Lombard's funeral.

WHEN I opened the front door of my building, Adam stood on my stoop. "Boystown, Jakey? Really? Isn't that kind of a gay cliché?"

"What the hell are you doing here? How did you get my address?"

"You're still on Mom's Christmas card list."

I looked around him and saw the Ducati was parked in my driveway. "Your dad told me you sold that."

"I did," said Adam. "To my brother Danny. Take a ride with me."

"You're kidding."

"Serious as a cancer diagnosis. I even brought you a helmet."

I took a long look at him. He was wearing tight jeans that looked expensive in that distressed-just-so way and a white T-shirt under a well-worn black leather jacket. He looked like sex on legs, frankly. I thought of all the times in my early twenties that I'd pressed against Adam while riding on the back of that motorcycle, and I felt my skin flush. It was nearing twilight, luckily, so I was pretty sure Adam wouldn't be able to see me blushing.

"Did you really ride that thing here through the city?"

He guffawed. "What are you, my mother? It's perfectly safe. You trust me, don't you?"

"That's kind of a loaded question."

He rolled his eyes and grabbed my hand. Since I was apparently not being given a choice, I pulled the door closed as he pulled me toward the bike. I checked my back pocket for my wallet and was disappointed to find it there, and I could feel my keys in my front pocket, thus taking away my excuse to run back inside. When we got to the Ducati, he let go of my hand and unstrapped his spare helmet from the back.

"Put this on," he said.

As I strapped the helmet to my head, he took his off the handlebars.

"Isn't riding in the city kind of dangerous?" I wasn't even that afraid—I did trust Adam, and it wasn't like we'd never ridden over city streets before—but I needed to stall him more. Things were not exactly hunky-dory between us, good sex notwithstanding.

He swung his leg over the bike and motioned for me to get on. "It's fine. But if it'll make you feel better, I'll stick to the back roads."

"I just would prefer not to meet my end by plowing into a city bus."

"So noted." He turned his key, and the Ducati roared to life.

Resigned to my fate, I climbed on behind him. I put my hands on his waist, taking the time to note the buttery quality of the leather on his jacket. Something smelled sharp and spicy. I imagined it was Adam, who had always smelled good to me.

He revved the motor and pulled out of my driveway. We drove to the end of my block, and then he took a right onto Halsted. I closed my eyes, letting the wind and the city zoom past me. I scooted a little closer to him, finding some comfort in the solid presence of his body, in the competent way he leaned into turns. We must have turned a few times, because when I opened my eyes again, we were zipping along some residential street I didn't recognize. I pressed my hands into his stomach, my chest touching his back, and I was a little surprised by how firm his body was, how clammy the skin felt under his T-shirt. I flashed on a sexual fantasy I'd had ever since that bike had first appeared in his driveway, of us fucking like animals on top of it, and I jerked a little, suddenly concerned that Adam would find a way to read my mind.

"You okay?" he shouted.

"Yeah. Where the hell are we going?"

"Almost there."

It was hard not to get aroused with the bike vibrating between my legs and my body pressed against Adam's, the smell of leather and spice flooding my nose, the wind whipping around us. I hadn't realized how much I'd missed our rides together, how much pleasure I got from riding behind Adam on that damn motorcycle, how sexy he was as he deftly maneuvered the bike through the streets.

Eventually we pulled up to a park that I had never been to before. Adam slowed down and coasted along the narrow road that led us past an open lawn and into a shady area. He parked the bike on the grass and told me to take a look around. There was a small grassy area that I soon realized was on a ledge that overlooked the river. It was a quiet spot. The occasional distant honk of a car horn was a reminder we were still in—or at least near—the city, but you wouldn't have known otherwise.

He pulled a blanket out of one of his saddlebags and tossed it at me. I laid it down on the grass and sat down with my legs splayed, enjoying the cool evening air. He sat next to me and handed me a paper bag.

"I got sandwiches at the banh mi place near my hotel. I assumed you still don't eat pork, so I got you chicken. Hope that's okay."

"Yeah, that's good." I pulled two wax-paper-wrapped sandwiches from the bag. He took one of them, and we unwrapped them. That sharp, spicy scent I'd smelled on Adam had clearly been coming from the sandwiches. My stomach grumbled; I hadn't even realized I was hungry until that moment. So I dug in. The sandwich was very spicy and made my mouth tingle and my eyes water a little.

"Too spicy?"

"No, it's good." My voice sounded like I was choking.

He laughed. "You always were a wuss about spicy food."

He polished off the rest of his sandwich and then got up. He came back with a couple of cans of diet soda. I took a healthy gulp from one. That didn't really help; the carbonation made it seem like there was an air bubble stuck in my throat. I started coughing. Adam knelt behind me and whacked me on the back a couple of times.

When I got my breathing back under control, I said, "It's very strange hanging out with you again."

He settled back next to me and opened his soda. "How so?"

"I haven't seen you in five years, which makes you practically a stranger. And yet you know all these things about me."

He shot me a sidelong glance. "Well, I'm not really a stranger. I'm the same guy I was before I left."

I looked at him closely, looked for the boy I'd known. He was so much bigger now, stronger, alluringly masculine. There was a shadow of dark stubble on his jaw, and his freckles had faded a little. I knew now that he had a faint scar on his back and hair on his chest. But the differences weren't just physical. He didn't seem so angry now. Something in his demeanor had changed. His voice sounded the same, but his tone with me was different. It was hard to really put a finger on what had changed, but it certainly was surreal looking at this man who was at once familiar and foreign.

"I don't really think that's true," I told him.

He shrugged and sipped from his soda.

"For one thing, I don't think I'm the same," I said. "Lots of things have happened to me in the time you've been gone. I finished my masters, I got a job at a really great company, I broke up with David, I dated other men, I got my first apartment. My thirtieth birthday just came and went. I'm sure things happened to you while you were in California or wherever it is you live now."

"New York. I moved from Silicon Valley to Silicon Alley." He rolled his eyes. "When I was first starting to plan Boughton Technologies, I got in touch with a guy I went to college with who had some experience with tech startups. He's an MBA type, I mean, really good with money and numbers, and I wanted his help running the new company. But he lived in New York and was unwilling to move, so I set up shop in Manhattan. I like it better than San Jose, which is where I was living before. New York feels a little more like home."

"And yet is still far from home."

He smiled. "You got me."

I managed to force the rest of the sandwich into my mouth and washed it down with the rest of my soda.

"What are you doing these days?" he asked. "With your job, I mean."

"I work for a company that manufactures and develops technology for hospitals. My department mostly develops systems that help screen for various diseases."

"Oh, that sounds really interesting."

"Yeah. It is, actually. I only do a little bit of lab work, but I get to work with computer models. I'm putting my degree to good use, I think. And I like the company. I like the people I work with."

"That's good."

Adam took my trash and got up again, taking the remnants of dinner over to a trash can near the road. I glanced back at him, taking a moment to admire his ass as I tried to ascertain if it really was as quiet as I thought out here. I didn't think anyone had come by in the short time we'd been sitting in the park.

He came back and fiddled with something on the bike. He pulled a second blanket out of one of his saddlebags and tossed it on the ground next to where I sat.

"I bet this was a hot cruising spot back in the day," I said. "All secluded like this."

He stopped what he was doing and then turned to me with a raised eyebrow.

"Just saying." And it was a hell of a thing, putting all this in context. I wondered if that was why Adam had chosen this spot, if he already knew it was the sort of shrub-enclosed area where one could go if one were looking for sex. The night took on a seedy quality, suddenly. I wished I could have gotten to the bottom of what Adam's intentions really were. What did he want with me? Would he stick around long enough to get it? Still thinking about why he was living so far from Chicago, I said, "I suppose it's not worth it to ask why you left home to begin with."

He sighed and stopped what he was doing. He walked to the blanket but didn't sit again. "I told you the other night."

"I guess you did." I crossed my arms over my chest, not feeling especially satisfied with that answer.

"It's not that I don't like Chicago. This is a great city."

"But you didn't leave because of the place. Even I know that." I could imagine him leaving because of the memories, though. I'd found it difficult to live with those memories at times. I'd ride into the city in a car and see the toll booths we blew through as kids who were short on cash. I'd see every shop we saved money for, or us waiting for the El to take us to Wrigley, or just Adam's smile when we stood on Michigan Avenue and let our awe of the city overtake us. I'd go by the new Comiskey—or, fine, U.S. Cellular Field, although I often forgot to call it that—and remember Kyle's dad getting us in to see a game, even though the old stadium wasn't even there anymore. Chicago was full of memories, and I found that, as the one left behind, sometimes I wanted to take those memories and hold them close, and sometimes I wanted to push them away.

Adam started to pace. "My mother saw us kissing. I told you that, right? I had all of this stuff swirling through me, all this pent-up energy and… desire, I guess… and I had no idea what to do with it, but I just thought, I don't know. I thought, *Jake is my best friend and he's gay, and if anyone would know how to handle what I'm going through, it would be him.* When I crossed the street that day, I wasn't even really planning to kiss you, but once we were both standing there, you were all I wanted. You, Jake, it was always you. And I couldn't help myself, I couldn't keep myself from acting, even right there in public. And you know what? My worst nightmare came true. My mother saw us kissing. She was in the kitchen, standing right in the window that faces the street. I didn't even know she was home. When I went back to the house, she let me have it. She called me every name in the book, told me I was going to hell. It was awful."

My heart went out to him. My own coming out had been fairly easy. My parents were initially a little disappointed, but they were supportive. I never doubted for a moment that they loved me.

"Mom was convinced that if I left town, I'd get over it. That I was confused because you *thought* you were gay and we were close friends. I was already freaking out about kissing you, because I'd never kissed a man before, and kissing you was so amazing. I will never regret doing that, never on my life, but I started to believe what my mother was throwing at me, that I had done something shameful, that there was something wrong with me. I just panicked. I took the job, and I left."

"You should have said something. I wish you had come to me and said good-bye."

"I'm sorry about that. I was a coward."

"You left us." This conversation wasn't really about all of us anymore, and we both knew that. This was about me and Adam. "You left *me*. You kissed me and then you disappeared, and I just don't know…. I mean, what was I supposed to think? That sucks, what happened with your mother, and I feel for you, I do. But I waited, Adam, I waited so goddamn long for you to just call or to come back and give me an explanation, and there was just nothing. I missed you so fucking much and I waited for you to come back and you didn't. Now, all of a sudden, you're here and you keep acting like you expect everything to just pick up as if nothing happened, as if five whole years haven't gone by, but shit doesn't work that way. There's still so much going on here that I don't understand, and I can't just accept that things are back the way they used to be, that you won't leave at the end of the week never to be heard from again. How can I trust that you won't bolt again if things get intense between us?"

I could see him getting angry; his pacing was suddenly heavier, his steps more exaggerated. He shoved his hands in his jacket pockets and then pulled them out again. "How can I prove that—"

"You can't! You can't just pretend nothing happened!"

"That wasn't what I was going to say."

"I don't think I can forgive you."

He let out a guttural moan, throwing his arms in the air and crying out in anguish. "Don't you get it, Jake? I came back for you!"

"What?"

Adam tugged on a lock of his hair. "I mean, not consciously. I swear, I only went to Coach's wake because my mom called and told me about it and I felt like I should pay my respects to the man. He was… he was there for me in a lot of ways my family wasn't. I mean, you know that. You were there."

"I was there." I watched him pace, wondering where all this was going. My heartbeat kicked up to the next gear.

"And I kind of figured you would be there at the wake. All of you. You, Ox, Longo. The three fucking musketeers."

"We were once four corners."

"I know that! God, of course I know that. Four corners of the fucking diamond. First, second, third, and Ox the catcher sitting at home." He sighed and rubbed a hand over his face. "Anyway, I figured you'd be there, so I prepared myself to see you again, but me giving you my card, that was a totally spontaneous decision. I mean, when I went to the wake, I knew I would see you, but I just figured we'd see each other and I'd say hi and that would be the end of it. But as soon as I actually did see you, and I mean *you*, Jake, not Ox and Longo… not that I don't… I mean, shit. *Shit.* I'm totally fucking this up."

How long had I been waiting for Adam to really see me? "You're doing fine. Keep going."

"Not that I didn't also want to see Ox and Longo, but they don't…. They're not you and me."

Well. I couldn't really do or say anything beyond watch him pace.

"So, anyway, I saw you at the wake, and… you know all that. And the reason I've been so…" He rolled his hand through the air while he thought of the word. "… aggressive, I guess, is that I realized as soon as you started talking to me again that really, I came to that wake for *you*."

"Adam."

"Look, I know I have a lot to make up for, and I know it was wrong to just run out on you like I did, but I was so confused and freaked out, and then I was in California, and then three months went by, and then six, and it felt like it was too late. Now years have gone by, and that seems impossible, but God, I really don't want it to be too late. I want a chance with you."

I looked up at him. He stopped pacing, and our eyes met. I didn't know what was happening exactly, but it felt like the air between us was electrically charged. He knelt on the blanket and reached for me, his hand stroking the side of my face softly. Then we were kissing. My mouth was still a little numb from all the hot sauce, but his soft lips were pressing against mine and his hand caressed my shoulder, and I certainly felt that.

I thrust my hands into his hair. I opened my mouth, and his tongue found mine. I was overcome by the need to get my hands on him. In the back of my mind, I knew I shouldn't have forgiven him so quickly, but everything he said made me think he was telling the truth, that he had come back for me, that it was okay to let this happen. The years I'd spent missing him caught up with me, overcame rational sense, and this felt like *finally*. Finally he was in my arms, he was home, he was with me.

One of his hands slid under my shirt. His palm was hot against me. The need to touch his skin became acute. I pushed his jacket off his shoulders, and he moved his arms to let me remove it without breaking the kiss. We were *so* going to get arrested, I thought, but I didn't much care, because his hands were back on me, sliding against my chest, pinching my nipples, waking up my body.

I wondered if anyone smelled as good as Adam, if any other person on earth would feel as good under my fingers, would look as good, would taste as good. I didn't think so.

He tugged off my T-shirt and pushed me down onto the blanket. I loved his big body hovering over me, and I let him between my legs. He pressed his growing erection against mine, and I arched and cried out. I pulled off his shirt and ran my fingers through all that hair on his chest.

"You are so sexy," I said. "So fucking hot. When did that happen?"

He sighed and kissed my neck, my jaw, my ear. He bit into my earlobe. "I grew up," he said, as if his inherent sexiness were nothing.

"Jesus, Adam."

He chuckled and then kissed me again. His hands made their way between our bodies and fiddled with the fly on my jeans. I shoved my hands into the back of his pants and felt the soft skin of his ass. He wiggled away from me a little and then started kissing me from my neck, down the center of my chest, over my belly button, to the opening of my jeans. My heart rate kicked up as I realized what he was about to do.

He hooked his fingers into the waistbands of my pants and briefs and pulled them both down to my knees. I was hard and trembling, goose bumps breaking out where my skin kissed the sky. He pressed his nose to the place where my thigh met my hip and inhaled, his breath tickling me. I squirmed a little, and he pressed in more firmly, sniffing and licking. I was practically twitching, wanting him to draw out the tension, to keep me guessing as to what he'd do, but also wanting so very badly for him to do *something*, to bring me some relief.

Then he took me in his mouth.

I nearly screamed. I did bite my lip to keep in the moan, but I didn't much care if anyone heard us, because it felt *so good* to be in his mouth, to feel the texture of his tongue rubbing against my cock, to feel all that slippery heat envelop me. I looked down and thought that Adam's lips on my cock were maybe the most beautiful thing I'd ever seen as he went down on me with expertise and enthusiasm.

He took me into his throat, and pleasure zipped through me like lightning. Then he took his hands away and undid his own jeans, letting his cock fall out. He stroked himself while he sucked on me. He groaned, and the vibration from it sent shivers through my body.

Then he pulled off me and kissed his way back up my chest. His hard cock pushed against mine, and I shifted my hips to try to get more friction, more of him, more anything, my body yearning for release.

He kissed the side of my face and whispered, "I want to be inside you. Let me inside you."

I groaned. "I want that too." Dear Lord, did I want that. "But what about—"

He kissed me. Then he said, "I got it covered."

He backed away slightly. He slid off his pants, but before he tossed them aside, he reached into a pocket. He pulled out a couple of condoms and a tiny bottle of lube.

"You're prepared," I said.

"Just call me a Boy Scout."

"I don't think they let the Boy Scouts do things like this."

He grabbed the other blanket and lifted it until it pretty well covered us. He put the lube and condoms near my head and then started kissing me again.

I pushed at him, and he rolled onto his back. I wanted to touch him everywhere, so I reached over and stroked his cock. He was hard and hot, his skin wonderfully soft, and I rubbed my thumb over the tip of his cock, which pulled a moan out of him. I kissed his face, loving the rough texture of his stubble against my lips, and I moved my hand a little further south, rubbing my palm over his balls. He squirmed and moaned again. I kneaded his skin, thoroughly enjoying the noises he was making as I pleasured him. He put his hands on my waist and pulled me closer, kissing me deeply. My cock was trapped against his thigh, and I shifted my hips, rubbing against him, the friction sending waves of delight through me. His legs fell open, so I took the opportunity to press into the skin on the underside of his balls, and then I slid a finger over his opening.

He went completely still.

"No," he whispered.

I took my hand away and saw that he'd lost his erection. "Are you okay?" I asked.

"Yeah, I… I just don't bottom. Ever. I don't even like to be touched there."

"I'm sorry."

"It's okay. Come here."

He pulled me back into his arms and then took my hand and placed it on his flaccid cock. I rubbed it, and he started to get hard again almost immediately.

I was confused about what had happened, but he started kissing me again. I turned toward him, and our legs locked together, our cocks rubbed together, and my mind went blank, lost to the texture of his body and my growing desire to have him fuck me.

He rolled me onto my back. "Let me prepare you," he whispered.

I opened my legs for him and let him touch me wherever he wanted to. His fingers slid over my cock, my balls, and to my entrance, just dancing over it at first, touching me lightly, teasing me. I thrust my hips at him, hoping to show him I wanted him to press inside. I wanted him inside me badly. My body yearned for him. He kissed me, and I closed my eyes, concentrating on his lips pressing firmly against mine, his fingers trailing over my body, his muscles shifting and moving as he positioned himself. His cock was fully hard again and poking against my hip, and I was happy for it, glad my little mistake had been forgiven.

Something cool slid over my balls and was pressed against my hole, and I realized he'd gotten lube on his fingers and was starting to probe his way into my body. He touched me carefully at first, but it wasn't enough. I needed so much more. I broke the kiss and moaned, "More, Adam."

He shoved his whole finger inside me. It hurt a little at first, but then he slid his finger in and out a few times and my body easily accommodated him. He curled his finger against my prostate, and I saw stars. I dug my nails into his skin and moaned.

"That's it," he whispered.

"More."

He nibbled at my shoulder and added a second finger and then more lube, and then he gently stretched me. I opened my eyes and took him in, the look of concentration on his face, the freckles on his shoulders, the lovely line of his nose. I wanted to devour him. I wanted him to devour me. I pictured us going up in flames together, and I wanted that too.

"Now, Adam. I need you now."

He withdrew his fingers, and I grunted involuntarily at the emptiness. He moved over me and pressed the head of his cock against me. I pulled my legs further apart and shifted my hips to give him a better angle. He pressed in slowly. It felt like he pressed against every nerve ending, and my body was practically screaming as he entered me. I arched closer to him and put my hands on his lower back to urge him further. Pain seared me, but every cell in my body was crying out for him.

When he was fully seated inside me, he grunted and then pulled on the blanket above us to cover us better. He kissed me, shoving his tongue into my mouth, sliding it over my teeth, pulling me ever closer. I felt filled up, excited, on edge.

"Move," I said.

He did, sliding in and out of me, creating electricity where our bodies met. My dick rubbed against his belly as he pushed in and out of me. We kissed, and he pulled me close, and I was surrounded by him, wrapped up in his warm body, and he still smelled like leather and hot sauce, and I knew I'd never be able to think about those things again without remembering how intense this moment was. He lifted his head and looked down at me. Our eyes met, and I felt like I knew a secret.

We began to move against each other, slowly crescendoing, speeding up, driving forward. I felt myself getting closer to toppling over the edge.

"I love being inside you," he whispered. "You're so tight. Feels so good."

His murmuring was doing strange things to me, stirring something in my chest. He picked up the pace, pushing into me, pressing against the sweet spot inside me, everything accelerating and rising up. Then he wrapped his hand around my cock and tugged. "Now, Jake, now," he said close to my ear.

Then I was coming, my body seeming to fly apart, jumping off the blanket, colliding with Adam. I shot ribbons across our chests as he continued to stroke me.

His pace became frantic, and he started to hum, pumping in and out of me, moving his legs, grabbing the bottom blanket in his fists. He shuddered and groaned, and then collapsed forward, pulling me into his arms as he came, muttering love words and nonsense.

We lay together between the blankets for a long time, not speaking, just holding each other. The ease with which this all happened surprised me. I had a brief moment where I thought, *Good Lord, this is Adam!* A moment later, holding him felt like the most wonderful thing in the world.

He sighed and rolled off me. We lay side by side, looking up at the sky through the trees, which is when I noticed that it had gotten dark.

"I could lie here all night," said Adam, "but we should probably get back."

"I need a minute," I said.

He laughed and sat up. "You have a lovely well-fucked expression on your face."

I put my hands behind my head and smiled up at him. He bent down and gave me a quick kiss before he stood and started to find our clothes. He tossed mine to me as he found them, but a few things had gone astray. He used his phone as a flashlight to find the lost items.

I pulled the top blanket up to my chest and sat up, watching him move around. He pulled on his pants before tossing the condom and wrapper in the trash can near the road.

Something occurred to me as I watched him. "Did something bad happen?"

"Huh?"

"The not-bottoming thing. I was just curious if you'd had a bad encounter or something."

"Oh. No, not really. It's just not something I…."

He looked down at the ground and picked up a shirt, which he then tossed to me.

"Come on, Adam. Talk to me."

He sighed. "This guy I dated in California. He used to…. He was not a good person. Used to call me names. I guess it reminded me…." He shook his head and looked at his hands. "You have to understand, my whole life, my brothers picked on me. Every bit of homophobic bullshit you can imagine. Bad enough that I was the youngest for a long time, but I was also the little sissy-boy, the girl Mom always wanted until she had Janine, a pussy, a pansy-ass, all of it. Sometimes I believed it, because I sure as hell felt like something wasn't quite right with me, that there was something in me that made me different from my brothers. And then I got into this situation with this guy, and just…. It's not something I do, all right?"

I wasn't quite understanding what he was telling me. "So, you didn't want to prove them right? That you were a sissy?"

"I'm not a sissy."

"I'm aware. I'm just trying to understand. What I hear you saying is that your brothers picked on you and you had some bad relationship that left you feeling like you were… not masculine in some way?"

"Well, not exactly, but—"

It clicked. "You think that taking it up the ass makes you less of a man."

He hesitated just a moment too long. "That's not what I said."

I threw the blanket off me. "You think what I just did for you makes me less of a man?" I stood up, completely naked, exposed before him. "Do I look like anything but a man to you?"

His gaze raked over my body and settled on my penis. "Of course you're a man. I wouldn't be attracted to you if you weren't."

"Exactly. Because you're *gay*."

He winced.

"That doesn't make you less of a man, either. So who's dealing out the homophobic bullshit now?"

I found my underwear and jeans and pulled them on. He just stood there staring at me. So much passed through my mind. It had puzzled me for years that, when we were in our early twenties, it was okay for me to be gay but not for him. I wondered how his own self-loathing affected what he thought about me. I'd worried for a long time that any judgments he held about himself applied to gay people generally or me specifically, that he couldn't muster up the pride to just say out loud that he was gay, that he condemned me for coming out. I guessed I had my answer.

I felt suddenly cold.

"Jake, come on. That wasn't what I—"

"Fuck you."

He huffed out a breath but stood aside as I stomped over the ground, making sure I had all my things. I folded up the blankets and threw them at him. He put them and his last few things away in his saddlebags.

"Jake, stop. Don't be.... Don't act like this. It took me a long time to get where I am now. I'm not... ashamed. I'm out now. It's not like it used to be."

"But you've still got a ways to go."

He did a brief walk over the ground, and then he walked back to the Ducati. He got on and motioned for me to get on behind him. I felt like the magic was gone, and I wasn't quite ready to touch him or be near him again. I paused.

"I don't think less of you," he said.

"Just take me home."

THE kiss was a poison.

High on excitement from finally kissing Adam, seeing the kiss as a sign that Adam wanted me after all, that he'd finally come to his senses, I spent most of that afternoon in a daze. At some point, I remembered that I had a boyfriend who wasn't Adam. So I hopped on a train and went into Chicago. I went to David's apartment intending to break up with him. I told him the truth, or what I understood to be the truth at the time.

"Adam kissed me."

"He *what*?"

I had to look down because I couldn't look at his face. I took a deep breath. "He kissed me, and I don't know if it means anything, but I think it does, and I want to see if it goes anywhere. So I can't be with you anymore."

I looked up. David stood there, his jaw loose, his eyes wide. "He's not… after all this time, you don't think maybe he's manipulating you? That this is his way of getting you to do what he wants? He's never shown you any interest before. He's too tangled up in his own bullshit to really care about you the way you deserve."

"That's not true! You don't know Adam."

"You're right, I don't! Because you would never let me meet him! You keep me away from your friends like you're ashamed of me!"

"I'm not ashamed of you."

"No, maybe not." He ran a hand through his hair. "Better not to bring me around, though, lest Adam think this thing between us is actually serious. Maybe that right there is a reason for us to break up. I love you, Jake. That's why I've stuck around as long as I have. But to you, I'm just the guy you fuck while you wait for Adam to come around. I deserve better than that."

"I love you too. You think this conversation is easy for me?"

The discussion turned into a shouting match, an opportunity to air all of our resentments and hurt feelings, and I took the train back home later feeling completely devastated.

The next morning, I went to Adam's house and rang the doorbell. His mother answered the door. She looked at me sternly and said, "Adam's not here."

"Oh. When is he coming back?"

"He's not."

"Okay. Well, uh, tell him that I stopped by."

"No, Jake. Adam's gone. He's not coming back."

"Gone? Where did he go?"

She slammed the door in my face.

That was really bizarre to me. Adam's mother had never been the warmest woman, but I'd never known her to be so rude, and I had always thought she'd liked me. I wondered if she knew what Adam had done, if she knew he was gay and she blamed me for turning him. I figured I'd wait for things to blow over and then everything would be fine and Adam and I could have our happily ever after.

Except that Adam really was gone. His mother wouldn't tell me anything about his whereabouts, no matter how many times I asked and got that damn door slammed in my face. Adam didn't respond to phone calls or emails or anything. He was just gone without a word. And I'd just fucked up my relationship with David, the one person who *did* care about me romantically.

Once it became clear that Adam was gone, I wondered whether it was worth it to tell anyone what had happened. I decided to tell Kyle and Brendan first. We were having drinks at Dickie's, and they were speculating as to what had prompted Adam's hasty departure. They weren't quite angry, not yet anyway, and Kyle seemed to enjoy cooking up ever more elaborate explanations. He was embellishing a tale about Adam secretly being a spy when I blurted out, "He kissed me."

They both stared at me. Kyle said, "That bastard." He probed me for more information, but I didn't have anything beyond the simple fact that Adam had come to my house, kissed the hell out of me, and then vanished off the face of the earth. Kyle seemed to find that frustrating. Brendan stayed silent through this whole exchange, occasionally shooting me confused looks. I wondered for a while if he blamed me for sending Adam away, although he never said anything.

After the dust settled, I called David one night and apologized, told him I was an asshole for dumping him and letting Adam manipulate me. I told him Adam was gone for good. I told David I loved him. He didn't take me back. Instead he listened to my apology, and then he told me to fuck off and hung up on me. Which was probably what I deserved.

I did love David, or I thought I did. I cared about him a great deal, and I felt comfortable and safe with him. I genuinely did not want to cause him any pain. But at the same time, David had never made my heart race the way Adam did. I loved David, but he wasn't Adam.

I kept waiting for the other shoe to drop. I waited for Adam to come back. I dated a few other guys. I had some good NSA sex, and that scratched an itch but left me feeling unfulfilled. Then, mere weeks before Adam came back into my life, I ran into David at that damn bar down the street, and we got to talking, and I took him home.

But that kiss would always hang over my head, spreading through the fabric of my rekindling relationship with David. Because I couldn't look at David without thinking of Adam. But with Adam's departure five years in the past, I was certain I would never see him again. When I ran into David, I thought it was worth it to give it a go again, even though I wasn't sure what it was I wanted from him. When we hooked up, though, he said that he still cared about me and thought of me often, but we agreed we should keep our relationship casual. He probably knew what was going on in my head better than I did.

I really did care for David, and I didn't want to lose him from my life. But now I knew that when I'd dumped him, David had gone on with his life. I'd gone back to waiting for Adam.

WHEN we pulled into my driveway, I immediately hopped off the Ducati and beelined for the door to my house. I felt about three inches tall and completely mortified on top of that. I wanted to replay the evening to figure out how it had gone wrong. Adam was the one who'd brought up the possibility of anal sex, he'd been really into it, I knew I hadn't imagined that, but did he really think so little of me that he would ask me to do something he was too ashamed to do himself? But I couldn't even think straight with Adam on my heels.

I fumbled with the keys to my front door. Adam kept saying, "Jake, wait, come on, talk to me, don't do this, Jake, wait, wait, Jake," and variations on same. I tried opening the outside door with the inside key, which gave Adam enough time to run up the front stoop. I successfully got the door open and slipped inside, and then I moved to shut the door in his face, but he put his hand out and held the door open. And he, being both bigger and stronger than I was, succeeded in keeping it open.

"Stop acting like a five-year-old and talk to me," he said.

"You got your rocks off, okay? Leave me alone now."

He looked around frantically.

I pushed on the door. "Oh, whatever, Adam. This house is owned by a middle-aged gay couple who do not give a shit if you are fucking a dude, and they're not even home anyway. Most of my neighbors are gay. You have nothing to be embarrassed about. We're in fucking Boystown." I stuck my head out the door and shouted, "I like to fuck men!" as loud as I could, which earned me a "Woohoo!" from a guy going by on a bicycle. I raised an eyebrow at Adam.

"Will you quiet down?"

"We're done here." I tried to slam the door again.

But he, of course, pushed on the door. "Will you stop for a minute and let me apologize?"

I gave up trying to shut the door. "Fine."

He took a deep breath and let his arms drop. "Look, I'm sorry. What I said… it didn't come out the way I meant it."

"How did you mean it?" I asked. "Because what you said made me feel completely shitty."

"I know, I just… I have some hang-ups, I will freely admit that, but they're mine, and this is not about you. You asked me a question and I answered it honestly, and my answer was not a judgment on you or what we did, it just… is." His brow furrowed as he looked at me, a challenge in his hazel eyes.

And it was hard to deny the central logic there. I had asked, and he had answered.

"Anyway," he continued, "I don't regret what we did."

Truth be told, I didn't either, although I was regretting everything that had come after. I didn't know what to say.

"Can I come in?" he asked.

I stepped away from the door.

SOMETIME shortly after nine o'clock, we both decided we were hungry again. I took Adam to the gay bar at the end of my block because I knew it would be open and still serving food. I also kind of wanted to test him.

Indeed, he paused at the door. "This is a gay bar," he said.

"Good work, Sherlock. All the bars on this block are gay bars. But guess what. *You're* gay."

He scoffed and pushed his way through the door.

I spotted an empty table, so I installed Adam there and then went to the bar to order. Ken the bartender was working, and he shot me a grin when I sidled up to him.

"That's a hot guy you've got there."

I glanced back at Adam, who was intently checking something on his phone. I turned back to Ken and smiled. "I know. Can we get a couple of hamburgers?"

"No problem."

I ordered a couple of beers too, which Ken said he'd have someone bring over momentarily. I turned and walked back toward the table, but before I got there, I heard a familiar voice call my name.

David. Of all people.

He was suddenly standing in front of me. He put a hand on my shoulder and stroked gently. "Honey bear, how are you?"

My stomach flopped. "Honey bear" was a nickname he hadn't called me since well before I'd dumped him, and I guessed by the way he was swaying that he was totally blitzed. This was the dance we'd been doing for the last couple of weeks; usually he called me and invited me out to the bar, and I'd meet him for a drink, and we'd inevitably end up in my bed.

Even though we weren't technically back together, or anything like a couple, I felt a little guilty, because tonight I had Adam. This was the definition of bad timing. I glanced toward the table again to check on him. Adam was gone.

"Shit," I said.

"Fancy meeting you here," said David. "You were just the man I came here looking for. I'm glad you turned up, because I tried calling your phone, but…." He shrugged.

"Listen, I'm here with someone, and I don't think he'd appreciate—"

Then a meaty arm was slung over my shoulder. "Is this guy bothering you?" Adam asked.

Oh, good Lord. I was about three seconds away from vomiting all over both of their shoes.

"Well, hello," said David. "Aren't you a tall drink of water?"

I wriggled out from under Adam's arm and stepped away. "Okay, well, I'm about to blow both of your minds."

They both looked at me.

"Adam, meet David. David, meet Adam."

I almost ducked. The tension all around us was palpable suddenly. Adam and David stared at each other, taking each other in. It reminded me of introducing cats to each other; both of them had practically assumed the arched-back, hair-on-end stance. I wondered which of them would try to kill the other first.

Alas, David was the first to back down. "I see how it is. I guess I'll just take my drunk ass home. I'll call you later, Jake. Or… not."

He went back to whichever corner of the bar he had come from, so I herded Adam back to our table. I saw David leave the bar as I was sitting back down. Then Ken walked over with our beers. I took a deep breath in an attempt to get my queasy stomach back under control.

"So that was David," said Adam.

"In the flesh."

"You know, it's funny. You dated him for a really long time. A few years, right? And this is the first time I've met him."

And there came the nausea again. I could not even begin to think of how to explain.

Adam shrugged. "He's Jewish?"

"Yeah, but that's neither here nor there."

He looked at the table. "I just wondered if that was something that was important to you."

I took a deep breath. "Well, I had to endure a lot of lectures about finding a nice Jewish girl when I was growing up, but once it became clear that I would not be marrying a woman who would be responsible for bearing Jewish babies, my mother pretty much gave up on that."

"But you liked that David was Jewish."

"Well, we had similar upbringings, so it gave us some common ground. But hell, Adam, you and I pretty much grew up in the same house. No one has more common ground than we do."

He looked up at me and had a goofy half-smile on his face. "I suppose that's true."

It occurred to me that Adam was trying to suss out his eligibility to be my boyfriend—if I did care about having a Jewish boyfriend, that would rule out Adam, given that the Boughtons were so very Catholic—and I had no idea what to do with that. I didn't want to ask him about it; this still seemed like too fragile a thing.

A guy in an apron plopped down little baskets with fries and hamburgers on the table. Adam went about making a lake of ketchup in his.

"Are you sad about breaking up with David?" he asked while fiddling with the bun on his burger.

I closed my eyes. "I, uh. Well, yeah, sometimes. He's a good man." I didn't want to tell Adam that we'd been hooking up. It wasn't relevant. I was pretty sure I wouldn't be hearing from him again. "I mean, the breakup sucked. But, uh, we still run into each other sometimes. And now I think things worked out the way they were supposed to."

Adam made one of his fries wade through Lake Ketchup. "But he was, like, your first love, right?"

How could I even answer a question like that? "He was my first long-term relationship." Not wanting to drag out that conversation, I said, "What about you? You mentioned seeing a guy. You date much?"

He popped a ketchup-drenched fry in his mouth. "A few guys. Nothing serious."

I didn't like how evasive his answer was and tried to think of how to phrase a question that would net me more information.

Before I could speak, he tapped the table in front of his food. "I don't know what it is we have here, but I'd like to see you again before I leave. I've got a flight back to New York Friday night. I have to give a big presentation at the expo tomorrow, but maybe we could have lunch Friday?"

I wanted to ask, *And then what happens?* It wasn't like we could have an easy relationship, not with him still struggling with whatever shit he was struggling with, not with our history, not with him living in New York and me in Chicago. Instead I said, "Yeah, okay."

We ate silently for a while. He looked around, and every now and then, his gaze snagged on a cute guy. A few of them checked him out right back. I felt a little smug, given that I was sitting with maybe the hottest guy in the joint.

"It's a trust thing," he said.

"What is?"

He looked down and lowered his voice. "The not-bottoming thing. It's also about trust. I've never trusted any guy enough to… you know."

It took me a moment to adjust to the topic, to understand what he was telling me. "Okay. I can understand that."

"I just don't want you to think less of me, either. But, you know, I… it's hard for me to trust people, I guess, and this is one of those things."

"I get it," I said.

And that was the end of that. We went back to eating as if he hadn't just said something really important.

He polished off his burger and said, "I hardly ever go to gay bars."

"Really? Then how do you…?" I almost asked how he found dudes to have sex with but realized quickly that I didn't want to know the answer. The mental image of Adam with any other guy made me feel ill.

"They serve the same beer in straight bars," Adam said. "The only real difference is the house music on the speakers and the guys over there dancing with each other."

I glanced toward the little dance pit in time to see two men starting to make out with each other. I nodded. "I go to straight bars too, usually with Longo, but this is my regular place, you know? I know the guys who work here, they know my regular order, it's a good thing all around. And I guess I feel comfortable here. I mean, that's part of why I moved to the neighborhood to begin with. It felt really safe. I felt like I belonged, like I was a part of a bigger community."

He nodded. "It's a little strange, being here with you. It's one of those parts of your life I missed out on when I left, I guess."

I reached across the table and took his hand. He stared at it for a long moment. I said, "One of the advantages of being here is that there can be a little PDA and no one will judge us. We don't have to worry about the breeders at the next table getting all offended that two men are on a date together."

"Is this a date?"

"I don't know. I guess kind of?"

He smiled again. "I like the idea of being on a date with you. I thought about asking you out about a million times. Before I left, I mean. But that would have changed everything, I guess. I was so worried about losing you."

It occurred to me that the stakes were lower now. He couldn't fuck up the group dynamic more than he already had. And if it all went horribly wrong, well, he had a ticket home in a couple of days. On the other hand, that seemed to make the odds of all this blowing up in my face much higher.

But for the moment, it was nice, just sitting there holding hands.

THE moment was short-lived.

On the walk back to my apartment, I opened my big mouth and said, "You said you were out before. How out are you?"

"What do you mean?"

"I mean, who knows? Your family, your friends, your coworkers?"

"My immediate family knows. I was the most afraid of telling my brothers, but these days, they're all preoccupied with their own families, so I don't get too hard of a time. Doug swears he always knew. And my dad and my sister have been completely cool about everything. My mom, well…." He tilted his head and grimaced. "She's coming around, I guess."

"I'm sorry if it's been hard."

He shrugged. "I think it helped that they had some forewarning. Mom knew about the time I kissed you, and I let two and a half years go by before I came out for real, so by then, she'd had a little bit of time to get used to the idea. So while my parents were not happy, they didn't disown me or anything. They're adjusting. I, uh, most of my friends in New York know. I don't really keep it a secret anymore. But at work, well."

"I don't think there's anyone who has met me who doesn't know I'm gay."

"Even at your office?"

"Yeah. Put it this way: a few years ago, a boyfriend gave me a Men of Old Hollywood calendar. Marlon Brando, Cary Grant, and so forth. So, thinking that my office was a good place for a calendar, I put it up there. I didn't even think twice about it. But I'm sure people noticed. Like, what straight guy puts up a calendar of sexy men in his office? Once I caught wind of the fact that there were rumors, I just sort of started slipping information in there. Like, my coworkers would be telling stories about their spouses, so I would mention my boyfriend. Or I'd just say something like, "Oh, So and So and I went to see that movie last weekend," or whatever. And then I found that once I was out? I didn't have to try to curb my behavior. I stopped worrying about whether my clothes or my mannerisms made me look gay, because everyone at work already knew I was. It was kind of liberating, actually." That was true. I ran into homophobia every now and then, but I was working for a biotech company where everyone mostly kept their heads down and got their shit done.

He was silent for a moment. "I view it more as need-to-know. And most people don't."

"So you're closeted at work."

"Not really. I just don't advertise. I think most of my senior staff probably knows, but I do a lot of work with clients and customers. You know what happens when people find out you're gay? They think about sex. I meet a new client or customer, and if they know I'm gay, they're thinking about who I have sex with and not the work that I can do for them. I want my customers to know me for my work, not who I fuck."

"Yeah, but—"

"It's not about me. It's not me who thinks that way, it's everyone else." The volume of his voice rose, and he was starting to get really worked up. "You're not an engineer or a tech whiz or a businessman anymore, you're a *gay* engineer or businessman or whatever, which implies that you're different in some way. But my being gay has nothing to do with my ability to get my job done. I'm fucking good at my job."

"I'm sure you are, but—"

"It's all well and good that you've got calendars with hot men and rainbows in your office or whatever, but I need for people to think of my work first. My personal life has no bearing on my job. It's not relevant. My sexuality is not part of who I am, it's not my fucking *identity*, it's just what I do on the weekends, okay?"

I held up my hands. "How can you say that? After everything you went through with your family? It's just a thing you do? Really?"

He kicked a rock down the sidewalk. "Maybe that's a bad way to phrase it. It's just not…. I don't want my sexuality to define me. I want to walk into a room and say, 'Hi, I'm Adam, I run a company that will do amazing things for you.' Not 'Hi, I'm gay.'" He tacked a lisp onto the end of that diatribe and then lifted his hand and bent his wrist.

"That's…. I'm kind of offended."

He shook his head. "I'm sorry. But you have to understand how it is. I mean, come on, it's not like you live in a bubble. I'm happy for you, Jake, that you're out and proud and everybody loves you. But things don't work that way in my world."

"That sucks for you, then."

"It's just the way things are. I'd change it if I could, but I have to work within a certain reality." He grunted. "Clearly someone found out, because last week I got an email from a reporter who wants to do an article on the most prominent gay businessmen in the country. She asked me for an interview."

"Are you gonna do it?"

My house came into view. Adam said, "Probably not. Too much of the wrong kind of publicity, I think. And that kind of public media? I'd give my poor grandmother a heart attack."

I felt really flustered by this whole conversation. His little speech had me feeling inferior again, like I wasn't as good as he was because I didn't have some fancy-pants business-oriented job. Because I also felt that my sexuality *did* define me, that being gay was a big part of who I was, and I didn't like Adam telling me something was wrong with that. I couldn't help but think that it was complacency like Adam's that kept setting the gay rights movement back. Although, that was a can of worms I didn't really want to get near. I took a few deep breaths, trying to calm down. I didn't really want to fight with him, but I found his attitude frustrating.

"You're mad," he said.

"It's not…. Well, yeah, a little. I guess we just see things differently."

We stood at my front stoop for a minute. He looked at me. "I should get going. I have to give a presentation tomorrow. But I do want to see you again before I fly back to New York."

I wondered if it was worth it. After all that, I was feeling hurt and confused and wondering if life would be easier if I let Adam go away and forgot about this whole interlude.

But I nodded.

He kissed my cheek and squeezed my hand before he walked back to the Ducati. He put on his helmet, then gave me a wave, hopped on the bike, and took off.

IT SOUNDS like a cliché now, but I always knew there was something different about me. It took me until I was a teenager to really figure out what that was, but I'd look at other boys and feel like something was off. I suppose I lucked out; I had baseball to help me blend in. I figured playing second base on a Little League team that won more than it lost probably saved me from getting picked on too much.

When we were ten, Adam came with me to my parents' synagogue. He actually was a Boy Scout, and at the time he was working on some kind of comparative religion merit badge that required him to learn about a faith other than his own. How convenient, then, for the Catholic kid to have a Jewish best friend. My parents thought it would be fun for him to come with us to services on Purim.

My family was sort of nominally Jewish as far as religion went. I thought of us more as cultural Jews. We took our heritage seriously, but we mostly only showed up at synagogue for bar mitzvahs and the High Holy Days, and we only really kept kosher during Passover.

But I'd liked Purim as a kid. The synagogue made a big party of it. I didn't really understand the real meaning of the holiday until I was older, but I did know it was an excuse to put on ridiculous costumes.

I was having trouble coming up with what I'd wear that year, so I took Adam to the community room at the synagogue, where a bunch of congregation members had put out boxes of costume bits. Adam and I pawed through the boxes, thinking we'd do some costume together, maybe pretend to be twins for the day. He pulled a fake beard out of one of the boxes that looked like it belonged in a production of *Fiddler on the Roof*, so I started singing "Tradition" and stomping around in a circle. Adam cracked up and kept rummaging.

A bright pink feather boa caught my eye, and without even thinking about it, I picked it up and tossed it around my neck. I'm not sure what compelled me to even pick it up. I really liked the color of it, I guess. I went back to digging for other gems, until I noticed Adam was staring at me.

"What?" I asked.

"What's with the pink feathers?"

"Dunno." I tossed one end around my neck and struck a pose with my hands on my hips. "Don't you like it?"

Adam's face contorted as he tried to suppress a laugh. He shook his head. "You look like a girl, man."

Feeling a little spiteful, I dug through one of the boxes until I hit pay dirt. There was a dress that looked like it had once been part of a flapper costume: short and rectangular with silver fringe everywhere. It was a little beaten up, but it sure was sparkly. I pulled it on over my head, right over the modest white-shirt-and-brown-dress-pants combo my mother had put me in that morning. I readjusted the feather boa so that it draped neatly over the dress.

Adam started getting mad then. "Don't be such a cornball. We're supposed to be finding real costumes."

"Who says I'm not?"

I knew I was being ridiculous, but I loved to poke him. He started huffing and shaking his head, but then he found a box full of superhero costumes.

"Fine," I said, raising my voice an octave. "You can be Superman. I'll be Lois Lane."

"You can't be a girl."

"I could so be a girl. Don't you think I'd be a pretty girl?" I preened.

And of course, my mother walked in right then. She stared at me for a moment, like she didn't recognize me. I froze, feeling like I'd been caught doing something I shouldn't have been doing.

But then she laughed. "Well, that's certainly a way to go. You look like a little blond Ethel Merman."

So, as is required, I broke into a bombastic rendition of "Rose's Turn" and changed the lyric to "Everything's coming up Ja-a-a-ake!" (If I hadn't followed Adam onto the baseball team, I probably would have been a theater geek in high school.) Adam turned red and hid his face behind an equally red cape.

My mother told me later that this was the moment she figured out I was gay.

Adam started shaking, and I worried that he was about to walk over and punch me. Then he dropped the cape, and I realized he was laughing. He laughed so hard, in fact, that his whole body shook but no sound came out. He sat on the floor and rubbed his face.

"You're crazy," he informed me when he was able to speak again.

I pulled the flapper dress back off. Part of me felt like I should have apologized for pushing it too far, but Adam didn't seem particularly offended. He was still wiping tears out of his eyes, actually. Instead I said, "If you don't want me to be a girl, I'll do something else. We can go back to our brothers idea."

My mother laughed. "You boys could not look less alike." She ruffled my hair. "I love the idea of you dressing up as brothers."

Adam stood up. "No, it's okay. I'll be the hero, you can be the damsel in distress." He smirked, then produced a long blond wig and tossed it to me.

So I pulled it on my head and batted my eyelashes at him. "Oh, Adam. You're so strong and brave."

He tied the red cape around his neck, then assumed the classic superhero stance: chest puffed out, fists on his hips.

My mother, bless her, found all of this hysterically funny.

When all the laughter died down, I pulled off the wig. Adam walked over to me and threw an arm around my shoulders, and we stood there grinning like idiots, which was about when my mom pulled a camera out of her pocket. And thus, to this day, there's a photo sitting on the mantle at my parents' house of me in the pink feather boa and Adam in the red superhero cape, standing in the community room at the synagogue with our arms around each other. The photo was sort of an afterthought until Adam left and I started to wonder if he'd loved me because of who I was or in spite of it. I worried that photo was somehow related to the reason he'd come to hate me.

TRUE to his word, Adam took me to lunch Friday at a steakhouse near his hotel. He'd been enthusiastic on the phone about seeing me again, but I was preparing myself for this to be good-bye.

Once we were seated, Adam grinned at me from across the table. He looked so young then, much more like the kid I remembered than this adult I knew now, and I thought of a dozen meals out we'd had at pizza places and fast-food joints, wrestling over french fries, with me living for every time he touched me. I wondered if there had always been something like that going on for him too.

A very cute waiter came over and took our drink orders. Adam said, "Hey, man, you guys got the White Sox game on?"

"Yeah, I think it's on the TV over the bar."

"Mind finding out the score for me?"

"Sure thing."

The waiter left, walking toward the bar. He had a really cute butt too. When I moved back to look at the menu, I noticed that Adam's grin had turned into a smirk.

"You were checking him out," he said.

"So sue me. You were checking out guys at the bar the other night."

"That's true. I realize that you are male and have a pulse, as am I, so it's only natural. I'm just giving you a hard time. He's cute if you like freckles."

"Um, hello?" I pointed to Adam.

He laughed. "Well, nice to know you have a type."

The waiter came back a minute or two later. "Sox are up three runs, bottom of the fourth."

"Excellent," said Adam. "I'll go with the prime rib, then. Might as well celebrate."

It dawned on me that Adam was trying to do some kind of macho hetero bonding thing with the waiter in an effort to deflect attention from the fact that this was a date. This bothered me, maybe more than it should have. Either that, or he was very awkwardly flirting with the waiter, but I didn't see the point in that, especially not with me sitting right there, penis and pulse notwithstanding.

I ordered some chicken contraption that was the only thing on the menu I didn't think would clog an artery, and while I was deciding which kind of potatoes I wanted, a blonde woman in a very tight pink dress waltzed in. I thought she looked a little trashy, frankly, but she sure had our waiter's attention.

Adam said, "Nice."

The waiter turned to him, a little bit of awe on his face, and said, "I know, right?"

So, hetero bonding. The waiter left to put in our food. I was about to comment on Adam's attempts to be bros with the waiter when his phone rang. He looked at it and said, "It's my assistant, I better take it. Hang on." Then he answered the phone, "Hey, Jim. Oh, it went pretty well. Yeah, I have all the specs on that, but they're packed away. I'm getting on a flight back in a couple of hours. Can I call you back from the airport? I'm at a business lunch. Yeah, sure. Take care."

After he got off the phone, I started to really get mad. "A business lunch?"

Adam slid his phone back into his pocket. "What?"

“First you do some kind of weird ‘hey we’re all straight dudes here’ thing with the waiter. Then I’m a business lunch?”

“What, you want me to tell my assistant that I’m having lunch with the guy I fucked two days ago?”

My face started to burn red hot. “No, but you could have said you were out with a friend.”

“Why does it matter? Jim doesn’t need to know who I’m having lunch with. It has zero relevance to his job, or mine for that matter.”

“I don’t want to be your little secret,” I said through my teeth.

“Who said you are?”

“I’m not asking to put up a sign declaring that we’re on a date, but a little acknowledgement from you that I’m not just your buddy would be nice.”

His eyebrows went up. He hooked his thumb back toward the bar. “That guy could be a homophobic asshole who’d spit in our food if he knew we were on a date.”

“You don’t know that. But again, you don’t have to *tell* the guy we’re on a date, but it would be nice if you didn’t go so far out of your way to pretend like we’re not.”

He sighed. “Look, I admire that you’re all rainbows and sparkles now, but that’s not who I am, okay?”

“I’m not asking you to be anything other than who you are. But who you *are* is a gay man, and I don’t see how we’re ever going to make any progress if you keep hiding that. Don’t you want to be able to have the freedom to just be who you are, without getting your food spit on?”

“I don’t have a lot of interest in gay activism or gay culture. My sexuality is incidental to who I am.”

I finally got what he’d been trying to tell me since Wednesday night. I was capital-G Gay: I was out to everyone, I lived in Boystown, I had rainbow tags on my luggage. He was lowercase-G gay: he was attracted to and had sex with men, but that was where it ended as far as he was concerned. I was more flabbergasted than angry then, surprised I hadn't put that together sooner, and also feeling a little hurt.

"Don't knock it," I said weakly.

He played with his napkin. "Well, whatever. Just don't ask me to get on a float in your Pride parade anytime soon, okay? I don't need it."

"What if I do?"

"What?"

"What if I need the Pride parade and the sparkles and rainbows? What if I need to be out and proud? Can you still be with me?"

"I don't see what that has to do with—"

"Say I decided to wear something outrageous or otherwise draw attention to myself. Would you be embarrassed to be seen with me?"

"No, but why would you do that?"

I groaned. "Maybe we're just fundamentally incompatible."

I wanted him to assuage my doubts, but instead he propped his chin up on his hand and looked out the window.

Before I could really say anything, the waiter came back with our lunches and an update on the Sox game. Adam yukked it up with him while I sat there and stewed, my appetite gone.

When the waiter left us alone again, Adam scowled at me. I scowled right back. With his big body and square face, he looked very much like the adult he was, and I could see how he'd be an intimidating figure in a boardroom—or anywhere, really. Some of that slipped away as I stared at his face, because he was also still Adam. It was difficult for me to separate out the parts of him I knew.

The scowl faded, and he sighed. "When did all this happen?"

I wasn't entirely sure what he was referring to, but I said, "You were gone for five years, Adam. You can't have expected everything to stay static."

"I didn't. But it's not just that. It's weird to spend time with you because on the one hand, you're the same guy I've known since forever, but on the other hand, you're not at all."

I nodded. I knew all about that feeling.

He ate a forkful of potato. "But all this started to change long before that. When we left for college, everything changed. And not just because we didn't see each other every day. I mean, you were… you were out in college, weren't you?"

"Yeah." No sense in denying it.

"But you didn't tell us until, what, senior year. Didn't you trust us?"

"It wasn't about trust."

"I was your best friend. And you were keeping things from me."

"Well, if you recall, when I *did* tell you, you freaked right the fuck out, which is exactly what I expected would happen. So you'll excuse me if I wasn't in a rush to share with you that I'm gay. Besides, I thought being gay wasn't a big deal."

He squirmed in his chair. "That's not what I said."

"What you said was that it's incidental to who you are. An incidental part of you that, hello, you also kept from me. Much longer than I kept it from you."

He frowned at his plate. "Look, it took me a long time to be okay with this. And I acted like an asshole, I won't deny that either. It's not that being gay isn't a big deal, although it isn't, it's more that I don't want it to be my be-all end-all. If, say, someday I should get into a long-term relationship or marry a man or what have you, that doesn't change a single thing about who I am or how I do my job. That's all." He took a deep breath. "But my point is that you had this whole life that I wasn't a part of."

I sat back in the booth. *I was your best friend* kept ringing through my head. "How could I have told you?"

He sighed and began to eat his steak.

"I was afraid to tell you," I said. "I thought it would change everything. Surely you, of all the fucking people in this world, can understand that."

He nodded, though the tension in his shoulders indicated to me that he was still hurt. But I couldn't figure out why he was hurt. Was he mad I hadn't told him sooner? That we'd missed out on all of those years we could have been bonding over it? Had he even wanted to be a part of my gay life back then, when we were nineteen and he was making fun of Kyle's alleged bisexuality, when we were twenty and he was still trying to date women? Or even when we were twenty-five and he needed to kiss me while we stood on the lawn in front of my parents' house?

None of this made any sense.

"No point in dwelling on this now," he said. "The past is the past and we can't change it. But we could, well, not start over, exactly, but try to do this right going forward. Maybe we weren't meant to have a happily-ever-after romantic relationship, but I do want you as a friend again. Maybe I fucked it up too much and you won't ever forgive me, but I do want to try."

"Even with you in New York?"

"They have these funny things called phones. And as it happens, I know a guy who runs a company that specializes in voice-over IP and video chatting. He could probably hook us up." He winked and then shoved a forkful of steak in his mouth. After he chewed, he added, "And we can visit each other. It's not like I live on the moon."

I realized that I wanted him as a friend again too, despite everything. I nodded, but he kept looking at me, as if he was expecting me to say something. I tried for a joke. "We can still have sex, though, right?"

He laughed. "Sure."

IT DIDN'T really hit me that I'd spent a week with Adam until after he left.

I'd have these flashes of memory, of us in his hotel room, or on the grass in that park, or making out on my sofa, or even just laughing over hamburgers at the bar. I'd think on the moment fondly, and then it would hit me like a slap to the back of my head: I'd done all those things with *Adam*. At times, I thought I'd imagined the whole week, but the strange ache I felt when I thought of him was certainly real.

A week went by, and I assumed he'd go back to hiding. I knew where he was now, at least, and I had his phone number, so I figured I had the power to get in touch with him instead of waiting around helplessly, but part of me wasn't ready. I wanted to hold on to the good memories, and I knew that contacting him would mean confronting the bad stuff too. Because I felt like he was holding out on me still. Because I hadn't gotten everything off my chest yet. Because a part of me was still angry and hurt.

So I carried on with my life. A week after Adam left, I went on a brunch date with Trey, the redhead from the bar. I had a great time on the date, and Trey was everything I could have wanted in a guy: hot, brainy, and charming, plus he had a wicked sense of humor. And yet he had one fatal flaw: he wasn't Adam. I didn't ask him back to my place after the date, but then again, he didn't ask me to his, either.

I walked back home from brunch and noticed it was unseasonably cold. An icy wind whooshed by me. I was wearing only a hoodie sweatshirt as a jacket, and I pulled it a little tighter against my body as the wind picked up. I wanted to reflect on my date with Trey but instead found my mind wandering toward Adam. I wondered if I'd ever be over Adam or if a part of me would always just be waiting for him.

Of course, the wind seemed to whisper.

I sighed and stuffed my hands in my pockets.

That afternoon the cleaning bug overtook me. I tended not to be as diligent at chores as I should have been, but when the mood struck, I indulged in some binge cleaning. I was, in fact, in the middle of giving my shower a good scrub when my phone rang. I pulled it out of my pocket and looked at the caller ID. It was Adam.

"Hello?"

"Jakey!"

I put the rags I'd been using and the bottle of cleanser aside. "Hi," I said, walking into my living room, not really sure what to say to him.

"I probably should have called sooner, but I got caught up in work this week. What are you up to?"

"Right now? I was cleaning my bathroom."

"Sexy." He laughed. "So what are you wearing?"

I balked at the phone. Had he really just asked me…? Did he mean it that way?

"Uh, old sweats," I said.

"Wow, you suck at this game. Even if that's true, you're supposed to lie and tell me something enticing. For example, I am currently sitting in my apartment wearing only my underwear, which is a pair of gray boxer briefs. That is the God's honest truth."

I couldn't stop the mental image of Adam splayed over an armchair, an erection tenting those gray boxer briefs. I was instantly hard thinking about it. "Did you really call me for this reason?"

"Well, I'm in New York and you're in Chicago, so it's not like I can sex you up in person."

It hit me suddenly how different this relationship we were forging was from anything we'd had before. "I'm not having phone sex with you."

"Aw, come on, Jake. It'll be really hot. I've been thinking about you all week, and this is the first moment I've had to do anything about it."

I liked that he'd been thinking about me, because I'd certainly been thinking about him, but I found the prospect of phone sex potentially mortifying. "I'm bad at dirty talk. I always get too embarrassed."

"Just follow my lead. What are you doing now?"

"Sitting on my couch."

He laughed. "Well, I'm sitting on a chair in my living room, thinking about you. I'm thinking about what you looked like that night in the park, lying on the blanket, all open and ready for me."

A million images flooded my mind. I felt the flush come to my face as I imagined what I must have looked like lying naked on that blanket, and then I remembered Adam, naked with me, how his skin had looked in the moonlight, his hard cock pointing skyward….

I sucked in a breath and reached into my sweatpants to adjust myself, because this was getting silly.

"Yeah, that's right," Adam said. He was a little breathless. I figured he was lost in the same memory. "I'm remembering how your skin felt under my hands, and your hot body, and your hard cock. It felt so good to touch you, to be inside you."

I couldn't help it. I moaned.

"Yeah, that's it," said Adam. "You were so tight. You make these sexy little sounds when I'm fucking you, like little mewls, it's so fucking hot." He swallowed and made a little gasping sound. "Touch yourself, Jake."

I did. I slid my hand back into my pants and wrapped it around my cock, and it felt like relief. Not wanting to get off too quickly, I just traced my hard-on lightly, and then I ran a finger over the head, feeling the moisture there. I hissed involuntarily at the touch. Good Lord, he had me worked up.

"I'm touching myself too," he said.

Part of me thought that sounded a tiny bit ridiculous, but it was also ridiculously hot. I pictured him writhing on a chair in his living room, his hand rubbing his big, hard cock, and the image had me so charged up I moaned again.

"I'm pretending my fist is your body," Adam said, his voice changing registers, now low and throaty as he spoke. "You loved having me inside you, didn't you? Loved it when I fucked you."

"Yeah," I said, stroking myself more aggressively. "Yeah, I loved it."

"I want to do it again. Please tell me you'll let me."

"I will. I want it too."

He started panting into the phone. "So good, Jake."

"I know. I'm getting close."

He groaned. "Yeah, that's what I want to hear. Keep stroking yourself. Pretend your hand is my hand, or that your hand is my mouth. God, I want to suck you again. So fucking hot. I want you to come in my mouth."

Arousal screamed through my body. I picked up the pace of my stroking, bucking my hips, the friction and heat flowing through me. I was right on the edge when I heard Adam mutter, "Jesus Christ," before letting out a long groan. I knew he was coming, and imagining what that must have looked like was enough to propel me right over the cliff, and soon I was shooting all over my hand.

I lay on the couch, spent and out of breath. I heard him breathing through the phone, indicating he was in a similar state. Eventually he said, "You want to voice those objections about phone sex again?"

"Good Lord."

He laughed. "You're a piece of work, Jake Isaacson."

WE FELL into a routine. We talked on the phone a couple times a week. Sometimes we'd have phone sex, but sometimes we'd just talk. We'd tell what had happened during the five missing years. We talked about our respective jobs a lot. I told him about the work I was doing, how what I was really interested in was getting promoted into the department that was working on rapid HIV testing. How I loved that I was doing something that could really help people. He gave me the basics about his own company, the projects he was working on, the contracts he hoped to get, the ways he wanted to expand. He told me stories about things he'd seen and done since moving to New York. I'd tell him about living in Boystown and the people I'd met in the neighborhood. Sometimes we'd talk about dating. He'd ask about David or about any of the guys I'd gone out with since David and I had broken up, and I quizzed him right back, since his dating life as a gay man was something still completely foreign to me. He was a little cagey on details but generally left me with the impression that he went on a lot of first dates and very few second dates. He did tell me that he'd spent a few months of the previous year seeing the same guy, but to hear him tell it, the relationship lacked emotional intimacy. "I liked him, but I don't know," he said. "It just didn't work out."

We just talked and talked some nights, and I remembered why I'd valued our friendship. He was easy to talk to. He listened to me. He had interesting things to say. I had missed the hell out of him.

Then again, it was easy enough to keep him at arm's length. I enjoyed our phone calls, but I didn't see much coming from them.

The barrier of time seemed to be melting away as we filled in the blanks of the last five years, but space was becoming more of a problem. When I complained that it sucked not being able to see him, he offered to send me a tablet computer with his company's video chat software installed so that we *could* see each other when we talked on the phone, and I turned him down, first because I didn't want to accept a big gift from him like that—it just didn't seem right or appropriate—and second because it just wasn't the same. I wanted to hold him and touch him and see his pretty hazel eyes; seeing a blurry picture of him on a computer screen was not going to cut it.

So I'd sort of resigned myself to this being our relationship. We were getting to know each other again, sure, and that was certainly a good thing, but it didn't do much to alleviate the longing I felt for him, and I thought maybe our days like this were numbered. I enjoyed talking to him for all those hours, but I felt an ache all the time. I didn't think what we had was sustainable.

But then, after a few weeks of this, he said, "I want to see you. I can't really get away, but if you wanted to come to New York, I'd pay for your flight."

I wanted to see him too, yet at the same time, I wasn't sure I did. I was concerned that the little bubble we'd been living in where everything was nice and safe and distant would burst, that all the hurt feelings would come back if I saw him in person again.

But I said, "Sure, I'll come. But I can pay for my own flight."

THOUGH our high school baseball team made it to the state championship both my junior and senior year, there was one game that stood out in my mind whenever I thought of my would-be career as a first baseman.

We were down four runs in the bottom of the eighth. It looked bad. As the home team, it was our turn at bat. I dutifully trotted up to the plate and took a few practice swings, already pretty confident that I would suck out loud. My batting average was about .300 that season, which is good for a pro, but considering how amazing the team was that season—Adam, for example, was hitting above .400 pretty consistently—it wasn't that great. We were pretty far in the hole, but we really should have been slaughtering this team, and that had killed everyone's morale. Plus it was drizzling.

I glanced back at the dugout, where Adam was squinting at me. Brendan sat next to him, giving me the "you better not fuck this up" face. I looked back at the field. The pitcher took his sweet time, tossing around a chalk bag. Kyle stood at second base, staring toward third; I assumed he was calculating if he'd be able to steal the base or not. One of our teammates was at first.

When I looked back at the dugout again, Adam gave me a thumbs-up.

For whatever reason, that did actually comfort me. Adam had faith in me, I thought, so why didn't I have faith in myself?

Baseball is about half skill and half psychology. There are a lot of high school players for whom one mistake can mess up the rest of a game, or the rest of a season. One of our pitchers had quit in a huff a few weeks before, in fact, because he'd pitched one lousy game and just never recovered after that. On paper, I had the basics down: I could run pretty fast, I had quick reflexes, and I could hit a ball if I concentrated. But I was always psyching myself out. I was a decent player, but the guys on my team were great. Adam and Brendan in particular were spectacular players for high school kids. I always felt like I was the weakest link.

But for whatever reason, that stupid thumbs-up from Adam was all that I needed to know I could do this.

I missed the first pitch, but I connected with the second, sending a grounder toward the empty space between first and second that none of the opposing players could get their gloves around. That was good enough for me; I got a base hit, so the bases were loaded when Adam came up to bat.

He had an arrogant swagger that made him look like he was a major league hitter who had deigned to come hit for some scrawny high school team on his day off. He did a bit of trickery, spinning the bat in his hands, kicking it with his cleats; he basically did a whole dance routine up to the plate and assumed his stance. When he got it right, he was unstoppable, but he only got the stance we practiced at the cages right about half the time. I don't know if it was nerves or arrogance or what, but sometimes he'd raise his elbow too high, or he'd swing at the ball a second too late. But when Adam was good, he was amazing.

The pitcher looked around the field and seemed to notice for the first time that the bases behind him were stocked. He bit his lip and turned back. He shook his head at the catcher a few times. When he got the call he wanted, he nodded and then lobbed a pitch at Adam.

Adam was good that day. The *thunk* of his bat hitting the ball reverberated around the field, could probably be heard from the parking lot. That ball soared over everyone's heads, clear out of the field and into the line of trees that separated our baseball diamond from the football field. Adam had already taken off running when the announcer called it as a home run, and then Kyle, our other teammate, me, and then Adam tapped our cleats against home plate and fell into a mob of cheers and hugs and back pats. Just like that, the game was tied. It was one of the most amazing things I'd ever seen.

And it wasn't even over. Brendan went up to bat next. The opposing pitcher was shaking in his socks by then. He threw three pitches in a row toward Brendan that were so wild I thought for a moment the umpire might pull him out of the game. He wound up walking Brendan. Then he walked the next two batters. And then he had another bases-loaded situation.

The last at bat of the inning involved our batter hitting a ground ball right at second base. The second baseman got the second out of the inning, but not before Brendan plowed through home plate to pull us into the lead.

Thus we started the ninth inning up by a run. I stood at first base full of conviction now, like we'd rescued this game from the jaws of defeat.

Adam grinned at me from second. Kyle saluted from third. Brendan sat behind home plate, his face hidden behind a hockey-style catcher's mask. We all looked at each other, and we all knew that we had to get through this inning without letting the other team score a single run. Then the game was in the bag.

The first batter came up. He pulled two strikes before hitting a grounder toward Adam, who easily tossed it to me. First out.

The second batter hit a pop up that went directly into the air and then right down into Brendan's glove. Second out.

The third batter bunted, and the ball hit the dirt before ricocheting toward Kyle. He lobbed it at me, but the ump declared the runner safe.

The fourth batter sent a ball flying right over Adam's head. The center fielder got it and threw it at Adam, but again, we weren't fast enough to stop the runners from advancing. Actually, by rights, that should have been a double, but the opposing players chickened out. There were now runners at first and second.

Our pitcher stalled, which gave Kyle, Adam, and me time to look at each other and suss out a possible strategy. There was a limit to what we could do without shouting across the field. Kyle tried hand signals, but I couldn't figure out what he was trying to say. But then Brendan called a time out and ran up to the mound. The four of us plus the pitcher and the shortstop stood there and stared at each other. Brendan said to the pitcher, “Remember, this kid totally flipped when you threw that curveball in the sixth.”

“So, curveball?” asked the pitcher.

“No,” said Kyle, a lightbulb going off over his head. “Here’s what we’re going to do.”

From my point of view at first base, I couldn’t tell what pitches the pitcher threw, so I didn’t know if he was following the plan. All I knew was that the batter totally whiffed over the first pitch. But he connected with the second. It veered toward third base, where Kyle caught it before the runner got there. Kyle didn’t even need to, but he threw the ball to second anyway, and we got our fourth out of the inning. And that game was done. Our whole team ran toward the mound.

“What happened?” I asked Kyle.

“Tommy threw the curveball first. Then he threw a fastball. But the batter thought he was getting a curveball again, and he was angry, so he swung at it. Which is what I expected to happen. He overcompensated a little, which was what sent the ball to third. It’s all very scientific.”

“Ah.” I wasn’t convinced the outcome of the last inning had been anything other than dumb luck, but I didn’t question it, either.

“Who cares?” said Adam. “We just won that fucking game!”

Then I got sucked into the cheers. Sometimes a victory could be boiled down to one teammate making a significant play—an unlikely catch, a home run at the right moment—but that game felt like a real group effort. I don’t think I’d ever felt prouder to be part of a team. Nor do I think I’d ever been so happy to have these guys as friends.

I DIDN’T feel nervous until the plane touched down, at which point I was struck by hangover-after-a-bender-level nausea. It only got worse as I made my way through the airport. I spotted Adam at the baggage carousel, but I wasn't sure how to act. Would we have one of those movie reunions when we ran in slow motion at each other and collided in a spectacular embrace? That was what I pictured, but then he looked toward me, made eye contact, and continued to stand where he was.

When I got to him, he smiled. He said hello and asked if I'd checked any luggage. When I said no, he gestured toward the door and said we'd get a cab. That was it. No hug. Not even a handshake. Didn't someone you'd fucked at least merit a handshake?

The cab was full of awkward silence as we rode to Adam's Upper West Side apartment. I spent the whole ride wondering if it was okay to touch him.

When we got to his place, I thought, *Finally! With no one around to see us, he'll drop the aloof act.* But he didn't. He carried my bag to his room, where I followed him, and he placed it in a corner.

Then he said, "If you want to clean up or whatever, there's the bathroom. We're going out in a little bit to meet some friends of mine for drinks. I have to make a phone call."

His indifference made my arms feel empty. I'd been longing to see him again, to touch him, for weeks, and what I got was Adam's voice in another room, speaking to someone in a clipped, businesslike tone.

I pulled a clean shirt out of my bag and used the bathroom to freshen up before walking out into the living room. He was still on the phone, so I took a moment to look around. It was a nice place. Adam's taste in furniture was very midcentury modern, and he seemed to favor dark upholstery with light wood. The place was also immaculate; I wondered if he'd cleaned for me or if it always looked like this. He'd been fastidious as a kid, but this was showroom shiny.

He hung up the phone and smiled at me. "So, the bar is just down the block. You're gonna like these guys, I promise."

I wondered if he didn't want to be alone with me. If he were coming to see me, I would have cleared my calendar for at least two days so we could get to all the sexing. Instead it was like there was a wall between us. Rather than making sweet love to me, he was taking me to meet his friends. I decided that was something, but it wasn't what I wanted just then.

Soon enough, we were walking up Amsterdam and then into a fairly nondescript Irish pub. Adam led me to a table right in the middle, around which sat a woman with square-rimmed glasses and dark hair, a tiny Asian woman, and a guy with blond hair. The Asian woman and the blond were clearly a couple; they leaned into each other, and the blond threw his arm around the woman when Adam and I approached.

"Hey, guys," Adam said. "This is Jake."

He introduced me to everyone in turn. The girl in glasses was named Mara, the blond guy was Tim, and the Asian girl was Lana. Adam installed me at the table, then immediately took off to buy us drinks.

"Uh, hi," I said, feeling abandoned but trying to make the most of it. "So how do you all know Adam?"

Mara grinned. "I used to live in the apartment next door to him, but I left the building for the greener, cheaper pastures of Brooklyn. We got to be friends before I moved out, though. Our relationship was built on mutual hatred for the family who lives upstairs. They have a teenager that loves to dribble his basketball at odd times. So if you're staying with Adam, fair warning."

"Ah, thanks. And you guys?" I turned to Tim and Lana.

"Adam and I went to college together."

"Really? I don't remember him mentioning a Tim." Realizing that these guys might not know my relationship with Adam, I added, "I knew him back then."

"We know," said Mara. "You're the infamous Jake."

Before I could ask what she meant, Adam came back and plopped a gin and tonic in front of me. We spent the next half hour or so drinking and making small talk with Adam's friends. I found myself getting increasingly annoyed as I got increasingly drunk. I was sure that these were perfectly nice people, but Adam was forcing me to be social with them when we could have been out on a date or, even better, having wild monkey sex at his apartment. He also hadn't briefed me at all on what it was okay or not to say. Nothing in the conversation gave me any hints about whether or not Adam was even out to these people, let alone what I could say about him and what we were to each other. Mostly I steered clear of controversy.

Adam excused himself to go to the men's room at one point, and Tim and Lana were making eyes at each other, so I turned to Mara. "So I'm 'the infamous Jake'."

Mara laughed. "I didn't really mean anything by that. Just that we've been hearing about you for weeks. Longer than that, actually, I think. You're the boy who grew up across the street from him?"

"Yeah."

"Interesting." She smiled. "Well, this is something of an auspicious occasion. Adam has never brought a boyfriend to meet us before."

The word "boyfriend" startled me, but I nodded. I supposed that was something, that Adam had been honest about the nature of our relationship. "Oh," I said.

Mara laughed. "You're surprised, aren't you? That he told us, I mean."

I shrugged. "I don't really know what's going on with me and Adam, so I certainly don't know what he's telling people about me."

"All good things." She took a sip of her drink. "Adam is the most closeted out gay man I have ever met. If it makes you feel better, he doesn't date much. He doesn't even like to go to gay bars. I've offered to take him and act as his wingwoman, and he always turns me down. The last guy he went out with was this guy *I* set him up with, and as far as I know, that was just a sex thing. It was short-lived, at any rate. Um, sorry if you didn't want to hear that."

I laughed. "It's okay. I'm not exactly a blushing virgin, either. We haven't seen each other in a while. It's kind of interesting to find out what his life is like now." To put it mildly. I wanted to grill her, in fact, but I didn't think that would be appropriate.

"I feel somewhat obligated as his friend to tell you that Adam's a good guy, even though he acts like a jackass sometimes."

"Yeah, I know."

Adam came back, and I saw that he'd detoured to the bar for another round. The night wore on, conversation got sillier, and Adam got drunker. The funny part was that drunk Adam got a little handsy. He finally touched me, and not in a shy way, either. At first it was just little brushes against my hand or my thigh, but eventually he placed his palm against my knee or my lower back, and then he put a hand on my shoulder, and then at one point he surprised the hell out of me by kissing my cheek.

While I processed that, Tim asked, apropos of nothing in particular, "Is it just me, or do all the gay men in New York have beards now? Is that a thing? Present company excluded, obviously."

"What are you talking about?" Adam asked, laughing.

"Maybe this trend hasn't hit Chicago yet," Tim said, eyeing me, "but take that guy over by the bar. The redhead."

We all looked. There was indeed a guy at the bar with red hair and a beard, and he was very obviously flirting with the male bartender. Our collective movement must have caught his eye, because he turned to look at us. He made eye contact with me and winked. Adam curled a hand around my waist and gave a tiny tug. His message was clear: *Back off, Beard-o. This one's mine.*

"Maybe you should grow a beard," Mara said to Adam.

Adam shook his head. "Right. So I can look just like that douche."

"I don't know," I said. "It could work. It would go pretty well with that whole muscle bear thing you have going on. It would be very butch. Like a lumberjack."

Adam rolled his eyes. "Yeah, I'm sure the beard would go well with all the fucking freckles."

Mara tilted her head. "Muscle bear?"

Mara had seemed hip to gay lingo, so I didn't feel the need to explain it. Instead I waved my palm over my chest to demonstrate that Adam had the goods. Mara raised an eyebrow at me. Adam blushed.

"I could grow a beard," I said, rubbing my chin.

"You're too blond to pull that off," said Adam.

"Not true. My dad has a spectacular beard. His hair is only a little darker than mine."

Adam held his hand about six inches below his chin, miming the length of my father's beard. He exaggerated, but only by a little. If my dad weren't otherwise well-groomed, he might be mistaken for a dirty-blond yeti.

"Historically, my people are a hirsute group," I told Mara.

And so the evening went. Mara had a dry, acerbic wit that I found kind of endearing. Tim kept trying to bond with me by bringing up the gay thing, often by making mildly homophobic jokes. Lana mostly talked to Tim and ignored us. I started getting a little angry because Adam apparently needed the alcohol to behave in a way that indicated we were more than strangers.

Then I yawned.

Adam leaned close. He whispered in my ear, "Tired?"

I glanced around the table. "Yeah. Traveling is always draining."

"Mmm." He stuck out his tongue, and it tickled my earlobe.

I giggled. "I mean I *could* go to bed, I suppose."

"Yeah?"

"Jeez, get a room, guys," Mara said.

Adam kissed my cheek and went off to pay his tab. I sighed and turned to Mara. "He's really never brought a boyfriend to meet you?"

"Nope."

"So clearly asking you to decode his behavior won't get me very far."

"What do you mean?"

"Eh, it's probably nothing. He's just been all kinds of awkward since I landed in New York. We're still working out the kinks of our new relationship, I guess."

"I wouldn't read too much into it. I mean, if you're asking if I think he likes you, then yes, he really does. I've never seen him like this with anybody else. I almost wondered if he was making you up, you know? Wouldn't it be awfully convenient for Adam to have a boyfriend in Chicago? We wondered if he just invented someone to get us to stop asking if he was dating anyone."

I pinched my thigh. "I seem to exist."

Adam came back. "You ready to go?" he asked.

"Sure." I hopped up.

We said our good-byes, and then I followed him back out onto the street. I considered asking what the point of this whole interlude was, but then I thought about what Mara had said. It occurred to me that perhaps Adam wanted to show me off. Or prove I was real.

I reached for his hand as we walked, but he moved away from me, just out of reach. We didn't really talk on the way back to his apartment, aside from him pointing out a few of the highlights of his neighborhood. A lot of his commentary was mundane—he pointed to the Korean grocery that he often went to for basics, the Laundromat where he had his laundry done, and so on—but in my slightly intoxicated state, I didn't mind because I liked the rumble of his voice.

When we got back to his place, I didn't know what to expect. It had seemed like he'd wanted to have sex when we were back at the bar, but he locked up and then walked toward his room, saying only, "I'm pretty tired," in a way that implied my night would not involve any nudity.

I stood in the living room for a long moment before I followed him into the bedroom. "Did I do something?" I asked. "Did you not want me to come to New York?"

"What are you talking about? Of course I wanted you to come."

"Because except for toward the end there in the bar? You've been kind of ignoring me since I got here. And I don't really get it. I thought we were really on to something. Was I wrong? Am I delusional?"

"Jake, come on." He walked over to me and touched my shoulder. "That's not what this is about. I just…. This is really weird, okay? I don't know how to act around you yet. Are we friends? Are we boyfriends? I don't know. We've never really talked about it."

I sighed. "So let's talk about it. What is it you want from me, exactly?"

He took a step back and then sat on the edge of his bed. "I'm just happy to have you back in my life again, frankly. Anything above and beyond that is gravy."

"So you don't want to have sex with me."

"No, I do, I just…. That's not all that's going on here, is it? Are we just having sex? Is that what you came out here for?"

That was about when I lost the thread. Because we'd been talking a lot during the weeks since Adam had walked back into my life, yeah, but we'd been having phone sex too, and I had just assumed this weekend would involve a lot of naked time, but perhaps I'd misread the situation. And sex was not all I wanted from Adam. "No, that's not all I came here for. But I did expect a little more than a brush-off and drinks with your friends."

He nodded. "We're both still figuring this out, I guess. Can we just…?" He looked at his clock. "Let's just go to sleep. I have something I want to do with you in the morning. We can talk more about this then. Okay?"

I was completely confused. A man who was attracted to me had invited me over to his apartment, and we were just going to sleep? "Uh, sure, Adam."

I WOKE up alone in Adam's bed the next morning. Sleeping next to him had not been an altogether unpleasant experience. He was warm and his skin was soft, and at some point in the middle of the night he'd pulled me into his arms and we'd fallen asleep together that way. No sex, but I felt like the ice had melted.

When I walked into the living room, I found him standing at his window, gazing outside while cradling a cup of coffee in his hands. He didn't notice me right away, so I got a good long moment to just look at him. His face was softly lit by the late-morning sunlight, and he looked calm, his features relaxed, and also a little sad. It was hard to pinpoint what about him made me think that, just something about his carriage and the way his hands curled around that coffee cup.

I cleared my throat.

He turned and smiled at me, the watery quality of his sadness not quite leaving his eyes. "Oh good, you're up. I've got coffee and cereal. Eat, then hurry up and get dressed. We're going to take a drive today. I want to show you something."

"You have not quite got the knack for urban living, my friend. What's all this driving? I thought that was what the train was for."

He rolled his eyes at me and for one fleeting moment looked so much like the fifteen-year-old Adam who haunted my memories that my heart ached.

After breakfast and a shower, I went outside with him. He made me wait on the sidewalk while he retrieved his car from the garage down the block. He pulled up to the curb a few minutes later behind the wheel of a black BMW. When I opened the door, I was assaulted by the sounds of the awful angry punk rock nonsense he'd always liked. He was drumming the beat on his steering wheel while he waited for me to get settled.

I grimaced at him and said, "How are your ears not bleeding?"

He put the car into gear, and we rolled slowly down 84th Street.

"Fine," he said. He pointed to the satellite radio display on the console. "Pick something."

I scrolled through the stations until I found a song I liked. Acoustic guitar strumming flooded the car. I felt calmer already.

Adam groaned. "Sweet merciful crap. What the hell is this?"

"Patty Griffin."

He shot me a sidelong glance as he pulled onto 11th Avenue. "So… talk radio? There's gotta be a ball game on somewhere."

He pressed a couple of buttons on the steering wheel, and soon the car was flooded with the staticky din of a crowd cheering. It became clear soon enough that the announcers were calling that afternoon's Cubs-Phillies games.

"That'll do," said Adam with a grimace.

"That'll do? Oh, please don't tell me you've defected to the dark side now that you've joined the coastal elite. If you've become a Yankees fan, we can't be friends anymore."

He laughed. "No. But let's just say I had a religious experience and have seen the light. Cardinals all the way. This is their year, man."

"Religious experience? What, did one of the players suck your cock?"

Everything went still. Adam stiffened, though not enough to lose control of the car. I froze too. Had I really just said that? Did I want to know the answer?

Eventually he sighed. "You're not… that far off the mark."

Oh God. "I don't think I want to know."

"I was in St. Louis on business last year. I hooked up with a guy who got us tickets to a Cardinals game, seats in one of their private boxes. Most of the people there bailed in the seventh because the Cards were whomping the other team so hard. Like, the score was eleven to two or something. So the two of us were left in this tinted glass box, and one thing led to another, and let's just say Busch Stadium now holds a special place in my heart." He shook his head. "Seriously, though, you're not still rooting for the Cubbies, are you? A team with their record is a bad bet. Putting all your faith in a team that continually lets you down is just a bad business decision."

I wondered if he heard himself. "Bad business decision, eh?"

"Not that I'm immune to bad decisions, but in this case, my eyes are open."

For some reason it didn't occur to me to ask where we were going until I saw the George Washington Bridge whiz by.

"Are we leaving the city?" I asked.

"Why do you think I got the car?"

"Where are you taking me?"

He gave me the sidelong glance again. "I don't want to tell you. You're not going to like it, and then you'll try to talk me out of it, but it's really important that I show you this." His face sobered suddenly, his mouth loosening into something that was not quite a frown, and all the humor seemed to fade away.

So I took his word for it.

We kept to safe subjects—gadgets, baseball—as we drove on a highway in what I assumed was a northward direction. Signs went by for points in Westchester County, all of the towns sounding like the names of country clubs. Eventually he pulled into a cemetery, which was about the last place I'd expected to end up with Adam.

He drove around the narrow streets within the cemetery, then pulled over to the side. He had the purpose and determination of someone who knew where he was going, so it was clear to me that we were there to see someone in particular.

Adam got out of the car without a word. I followed. We snaked our way through a winding path and a number of graves until he found the one he was looking for and stopped. He gestured to the headstone. It was a simple stone, white granite with only the name and the lifespan of the grave's inhabitant: "Steven Boughton, 1954–1992."

"That's my Uncle Steven," he said.

"I don't remember you having an Uncle Steven." I thought I should have remembered Adam going to a funeral in 1992; we would have been in middle school, and we spent almost all of our time together then.

"I didn't know I did, either. Until a little more than two years ago."

He turned slightly and looked at me. His eyes were wide, and his mouth was pressed into a thin line. I believed he was trying to tell me this was significant. Something important had happened to him a little more than two years ago. He'd probably mentioned it in one of our phone conversations, but I couldn't recall what it was.

He sighed. "That was when I came out to my parents officially."

"Ah." That felt like only a small part of the puzzle; it seemed important, but I didn't think it explained anything.

Adam turned and looked at the headstone. "I was home between Christmas and New Year's, spent the whole week at the house. I had just made the decision to move to New York to get Boughton Technologies off the ground. I hadn't broken the other news to my parents yet and wasn't sure how to do it. But I'd dated a couple of guys in California, and things were starting to, well, come to a head, so to speak, so I sat them down and said, 'I'm moving to New York. Oh, and also, I'm gay.'"

He took a deep breath. I had no idea what to do. He seemed upset, but I wasn't sure if I should try to comfort him or say something placating. He might not want me to touch him. As far as I could tell, we were the only people in the cemetery, but even a hand on the shoulder might violate his anti-PDA policy.

He saved me from trying to figure it out by continuing to speak. "The gay thing, I don't know. That was the topic of so many long discussions and arguments that week. It's not worth reliving. Suffice it to say my parents asked me if I was sure a lot. It's over and beside the point. The day after I told them, we were having dinner, and Dad goes, 'Steven lived in New York.' Like, really casual, as if Steven were someone we saw every week. So I asked, 'Who's Steven?' And Dad told me."

Adam brought his hand to his face and chewed on his thumbnail for a moment. The gesture was heartbreakingly familiar. He used to do it during tests when he was trying to work out a difficult problem or while we were getting strategy lectures from Coach Lombard at baseball practice.

"The family doesn't talk about him. Steven, I mean. My grandparents got rid of all the photos of him. His name is never mentioned. Dad turned red while he was telling this story, like he was deeply embarrassed." He put his hand down. "Steven was my dad's youngest brother. I know hardly anything about him beyond a few important facts. My grandparents kicked him out of the house for good when he was in his twenties. That would have been sometime in the seventies, before I was born. He landed in New York City. After that my family lost track of him. Until he died."

"Why did he get kicked out of the house?" I asked, though I already knew.

"He was gay," Adam whispered. "He ended up in the hospital, and when it was clear he was dying, a social worker got in touch with my family. I don't know the whole story, but my dad says that my grandfather flew out here after he…." Adam shook his head. "So Steven is here instead of in the family plot in Glenview."

The only thing I could think was, *Shit*. I considered the timing of his death. "AIDS?"

"Yep. What a tragic fucking stereotype."

He dropped onto the ground, sitting with his knees pulled to his chest. I didn't like standing over him, so I sat beside him.

He said, "I tracked him down when I got to New York. As soon as I found out where he was buried, I drove up here to look, to find out if the story was really true." He draped his arms around his folded legs.

"The first time, I just sat here for, like, an hour. And I thought, 'What a shame.' I mean, all of it. Getting disowned. Catching a terrible disease. I don't know if he died alone, but I imagine he did. There are never any flowers here when I visit unless I leave some."

We sat there together looking at the headstone for a long time. Eventually he said, "I drive up here sometimes. Maybe once every few months. Don't laugh, but sometimes I talk to him. I feel like he and I would have been kindred spirits. We would have understood each other. But no one gave us a chance to know each other. Dad says my grandparents were horrified when they found out Steven was gay." His voice hitched on the word "gay," and he took a deep breath. "I think it's weird to mourn someone you never knew, but I do. Or I mourn the relationship we never had. I don't know."

It was strange to watch him. He was so much a man, big and brawny and strong, but in that moment, he looked so young, like the lanky teenager I'd known and first fallen in love with. I could see him sitting in the corner of my bedroom, his knees pulled up to his chest, his long body folded in thirds while we talked about whatever the tragedies of teenage boys were. His parents ignored him, he had a girlfriend problem, he was sick of Coach ragging on him for running too slow.

That was what he looked like, sitting next to the grave.

"That's terrible. I'm sorry," I said. "But why show it to me?"

The question seemed to surprise him. He jerked his head back and looked at me for the first time since he'd started talking about Uncle Steven. "I need for you to understand, first of all. This is not just a tragedy. This is a tragedy done by my family."

"Your family has changed. They accept you. Don't they?"

"My parents do. I think sometimes that Steven had to die to make that possible, though. That my parents, or my dad anyway, saw what hate and homophobia do, so they were more accepting when I came along. But my grandparents.... Dad made me promise not to tell them."

"Adam." My heart went out to him.

"I started to come here to talk to Steven, and I did a lot of thinking too. And I thought to myself that I didn't want my life to end the way Steven's did. I couldn't die alone. Except that's where I was headed. I'd cut myself off from everyone who cared about me, except my immediate family. I didn't really have relationships, just sex. I was stuck in this pattern I couldn't break out of. And I was sitting here the moment it occurred to me that I wanted to go back home, to find you again. All of you, Ox and Longo too, to find out if we could be four corners again. I just needed an opportunity. Then the Chicago trip coincided with Coach's funeral, and it seemed like a sign. And here you are."

"Here I am."

He smiled faintly. "It was always us, Jake. I mean, Brendan and Kyle too, but you and me always had something special, I thought. Which sounds corny and stupid, but—"

"No, I know what you mean," I said.

"Maybe we just understood each other before we knew there was anything to understand."

I liked that. Once I'd worked out for myself that Adam was gay, I had suspected the same thing.

He lowered his voice as he spoke. "All I really know is that I like being with you. That I missed the hell out of you when I was away. I think I've probably been in love with you since tenth grade, but I was too much of a chicken to face that. And I know I still have a lot to make up to you, to make you trust me, but I need you to know that I've changed, that sitting here with Uncle Steven changed me, changed what I wanted out of life. I brought you here to show you this so you'd believe that."

I did believe him. I wanted to tell him I loved him too, but I wasn't really sure that was the case. I had once loved Adam, but *this* Adam—the quiet, contemplative, contrite Adam, the out-of-the-closet Adam—was someone I was still getting used to.

So instead I reached for his hand. I laced our fingers together. He tilted his head toward me and smiled. We stayed like that for a few minutes, and I let my mind wander. His skin was warm where our palms touched, and he was so *present*, next to me and smelling like sweat and cedar and Adam. I wanted to hug him, to pull him into my arms and tell him that I was there for him now, that I was supportive and loving and open, but I wasn't sure that was the truth.

After a while, he said, "I guess we should head back. Maybe get dinner in the city. There's a French bistro on Amsterdam that's pretty good."

"Sure, Adam. Whatever you want."

He nodded, let go of my hand, and stood up, so I stood also and moved to follow him. He held a hand back for me, so I took it. We walked, hand-in-hand, back to the car.

WE STOOD at the foot of Adam's bed, kissing as if we had all the time in the world, slowly exploring each other's mouths. His fingers wove paths through my hair as I rested my hands on his waist. I took the time to savor and taste and find all the hidden depths of him. I thought to myself that I could have spent hours just kissing Adam, but there was a slow burn of arousal and impatience working its way through my body as I felt Adam's muscles ripple a little under my fingers every time he took a breath. His lips moved against mine just as the stubble of his chin rubbed against my face, reminding me that he was present and male and so much not just a figment of my imagination.

Adam broke the kiss and started to move his lips all over my face. He lowered his hands and started pushing up my T-shirt. "I want to make love to you," he said.

My heart rate kicked up a notch. I wanted that too, so much. I began to unbutton his shirt, and my insides went a little melty as I imagined and anticipated our coming together, hot and sweaty and naked on the bed.

But then I thought about the night before.

Without moving, I said, "What changed?"

He nipped at my neck and slid his hands under my shirt. "Huh?"

"What's changed since last night? You could barely touch me last night, and now you want to make love?"

He looked up and took a step back. "I wanted to make love last night too." His lips were red and a little swollen, and his shirt was unbuttoned but for the two on the bottom, giving me a tantalizing view of the hair on his chest.

"You had a funny way of showing it."

He reached over and took my hand. "Jake."

I raised my eyebrows.

"I was nervous," he said. "I don't want to fuck this up. I've never been in a serious relationship before, not really. I'm not entirely sure how to act."

I flashed back to the night I'd gone out with Kyle and he'd hypothesized that a gay relationship was a lot like friendship but with sex. Maybe there wasn't any more to it. "You were doing just fine. Act like you're my friend and not terrified of me. Be supportive and caring. Treat me like I'm sexy and you want me."

"You are sexy. I want you all the time."

I reached over and undid the last two buttons on his shirt. "Right back at you. But more than anything, just be. Be with me and stay honest, and we'll be just fine. There's no need to play games or any of that bullshit. We never had to wonder how to act around each other before, did we? We just acted."

"I know, but—"

"No buts. Being together isn't that different than it used to be, really."

"Yeah," he said, lowering his eyelids. "But it's deeper, I guess. And sexier." He smirked.

I laughed. "Yeah, and that too."

He kissed me. I wasn't wholly convinced that I'd made my point, but I went wherever Adam led me. He pulled off my shirt, then shrugged out of his own before pushing me onto the bed. There we resumed kissing, and we moved until our bodies pressed together and our limbs tangled.

We wriggled out of our clothes and were soon naked and pressed together, hard cocks grinding against each other, each of us searching for purchase as if we were climbing a mountain. Adam moaned, and his chest vibrated against mine. He put his arms around me and pulled me close and whispered that he loved me. And that was strange. I'd wanted for so long, all through my late teens and early twenties, ten years almost, for Adam to say these words, and it had taken five years of distance and an oddly timed reunion to make it happen, and I still didn't quite believe it. But what I did believe in was the pleasure he brought to me, the simple joy I got just from being near him, from his hands coursing over my body, from his texture and scent. I did care for Adam deeply, and I wanted things to work out for him and for us, but I still wasn't quite—

He bit me, sank his teeth into the skin just above my left nipple, bringing my mind back to the immediacy of us in bed together, panting against each other. He dug his nails into my back as he sucked marks up on my skin, as if he were trying to eat me, but more likely he was trying to get my attention. *Stay with me, Jake,* the hands on my back seemed to say.

I ran my fingers through the hair on his chest, and I sighed and sank into him. He maneuvered us so that he was on top. He settled in between my legs and hooked a hand under each of my knees. He ground his cock against mine, and it was gorgeous, delicious, the amount of friction causing me to both float outside of myself and be reminded that he was right there, that we were together. I kissed him and bit his lip, which made him grunt and sigh and thrust against me.

"Please," he said, my lower lip between his teeth. He licked my chin and then started nibbling at my jaw. "God, please, Jake, for all that is holy, let me inside you. I have to be inside you."

"Yes." I couldn't find the words to say how badly I wanted that too.

He reached for his drawer and returned with the essentials. He shifted to my right side but kept a hand between my legs. He took my balls in his hand and gently massaged them, coaxing all manner of metaphors up through my body: fireworks, lightning bolts, streams of fire. I arched my back off the bed when he ran his fingers over my hole, smearing it with lube and seeking entrance. I put a hand on the back of my thigh and pulled my legs apart as much as I could to give him space. He hummed to himself and kissed whatever bit of skin he could get near: my shoulder, my bicep, my wrist.

"You're so beautiful," he murmured before slipping a finger inside me.

He went slowly. He moved a finger in and out of me until I was begging him for more, and then he added a finger and gently stretched me, all the while mumbling love words and kissing my face. His cock was hard and poking at the spot where my thigh met my butt, and instinct and desire had my body bending toward him, wanting him near me, with me, inside me.

Finally, when he was satisfied and I was half-crazy with lust and desire, he rolled a condom on and repositioned himself between my legs. "You ready?" he asked.

"Oh, dear God, yes."

He chuckled, a low sound in the back of his throat, and then he very slowly pressed inside me. It was heaven, the way I could feel the head of his cock scraping against all those nerve endings, until finally he hit me exactly where I wanted him to. Everything went achingly slowly as the gentle rock of his hips led to the deep massage of the sweet spot inside me. I dropped my head back on a pillow and groaned, feeling an odd sense of relief that we were finally moving together. He pulled me into his arms and kept moving, pushing and pulling in and out of me with increasing speed and force until everything was hot and sweaty and tangled and I thought I'd go blind from the pleasure of it all.

I moved my fingers through his hair, over his shoulders, his back, anywhere I could reach. Then I put one hand on his back in an effort to hold on, and I grabbed my cock and started pulling. I imagined we might fly right off the bed together. It was like we kept climbing up that mountain, but the ultimate goal was to jump off the other side into sweet oblivion. This was dangerous ground we were approaching, but God, the adrenaline rush would be worth it. The end result, the orgasm, the release, the insanity, all of it would be worth it, and I wanted to get there so badly, wanted to get there with Adam.

He was groaning and grunting, and his face was twisted up in pleasure above me. I leaned up to kiss him, and then he mumbled, "Jesus, Jake, I'm gonna come," against my lips.

Everything exploded. I felt myself racing to the top of the mountain and then my body jerked and went stiff for a brief moment, and then I was coming, spurting all over my chest and stomach and over Adam too, and it all felt insane, like flying through the air. He moaned and said my name and then "God, Jake, I love you so much," and then he seemed to curl in on himself and shudder, and then he was coming, roaring with the impact of his orgasm. I held him as he rode it out. He collapsed on top of me.

As we came back down to Earth, I thought, well, maybe that was like diving off a cliff, but at least we were each there at the end to catch each other.

Adam got up a few minutes later to take care of the condom. I followed him into the bathroom, where we helped each other clean up. He took my hand and led me back to the bed, where we climbed under the covers and fell into each other's arms as if we belonged there and it was naturally the most comfortable place for us.

"You blow my mind," he said.

I propped myself up to look at his face. He smiled and closed his eyes.

"I'm tired," he said.

I just looked at his face for a long moment, examining the details of it, trying to conjure up how he'd looked when we were kids so I could properly compare his current freckled visage with the thinner, less chiseled version of our youth, but I couldn't, because that old Adam was no longer and this was the Adam I was left with.

And then I felt it, down in the hidden depths of my heart, the truth that had been trying to make itself known to me all day, the truth I hadn't been willing to admit to myself quite yet.

"I love you too," I whispered.

But Adam was already asleep.

I WOKE up alone again the next morning, but the bedroom door was open and I could hear Adam moving around in the other part of the apartment. From the smell of things, he was cooking breakfast and brewing coffee.

I pulled on a clean pair of underwear and borrowed a T-shirt of Adam's. His shirt was baggy in a way that emphasized how much bigger he was than me, which was interesting considering the fact that we'd been able to wear each other's clothes in high school. I chastised myself for dwelling in the past so much. *You love* this *Adam now; he is your present and your future.* Thinking about that made me smile, so I walked out into the living room prepared to greet Adam and the day.

He was indeed in the kitchen, presiding over a couple of frying pans, making eggs and turkey bacon and humming to himself. He smiled when he saw me and motioned to a cabinet near the sink. "There are plates up there," he said.

"This looks great. I'm starving."

He patted my butt as I walked by. "Of course you are. A night of sweaty lovemaking will do that."

So I set the table and he finished cooking and we flirted as we sat down to eat. It was fun and easy, and I felt content as I dug into my eggs. It was a simple meal, but it was well prepared, the eggs done how I like them, the bacon chewy. After we ate, we showered together, and when I fussed over what to wear, Adam made fun of me, and everything seemed like it should have been, my first night in New York now forgotten.

He had to take a work phone call a little while later, so I sat on his couch and flipped through the magazines he had lying on the coffee table. I was a little surprised to find a copy of a local gay alt-weekly. I flipped through it and found it didn't have much substance, but it did have event listings and a calendar of which gay bars had good happy-hour deals on which nights.

Adam got off the phone and plopped next to me.

"Can I ask you something?" I asked.

"Fire away." He leaned back and then reached over and played with the hair at the back of my neck. "I really do kind of miss your long hair. How long have you had it short like this?"

"Uh, I dunno. I cut it a few years ago. I'm too old for long hair now, don't you think?"

"Eh, maybe. I think you could still rock the look. Was that your question?"

"No." I held open the alt-weekly. "So Mara mentioned you don't go to gay bars."

He shrugged. “I told you that a while ago too. I’ve never really been into all that. I never lacked for companionship. What’s the point?”

I put the paper back on the coffee table. “To have fun? To be around other gay men? To make friends?”

“Says the guy who lives in Boystown.”

“So?”

He glanced at the coffee table. “I’m not like you, Jakey.”

“We already had this argument back in Chicago.” I looked at the paper. I wondered what had compelled him to pick it up. Maybe he’d just felt obligated because he was gay and it was there.

He looked away from me. “I just can’t, okay? I can’t do it, I can’t be a part of all that. I wish you could understand.”

“What? What is it you want me to understand? That you’re still in the closet after all? That you think I’m a clown for participating in all of it?”

“I never said that. Come on, knock it off, you’re putting words in my mouth.” He turned his head and looked at me. “I’m not *ashamed*, if that’s what you’re implying. But I told you, the gay thing, it’s something I do, it’s not who I am. Who I am first and foremost is a businessman, and most of my life is my work. It’s fine if that’s not true for you. If you want to be all ‘gay pride, wee-oo, sis-boom-bah’, whatever, then I can accept that.”

“You can *accept* that?” I became increasingly agitated the longer this conversation went on. “Like it’s some kind of personality flaw? Because let me tell you something, buddy, there’s nothing wrong with me, at least there’s nothing wrong with my sexuality, and it *is* who I am. Don’t *you* understand? There are plenty of people in the world who hate us just for loving each other, who hate this innate thing we were born with, who hate us *for who we are*. Taking pride in who I am, in celebrating my own homosexuality, that’s how I get my life back from those people who hate me. That’s how I stay sane.”

“Look, I’m not saying not to have gay pride or whatever, I’m just not into outwardly showing that part of myself to the world. It’s not like I’m lying to anyone. Plenty of people know I’m gay. That’s not a secret. I’m just not gonna go out there and wave flags or whatever.”

"And not only that!" I was on a roll now. I stood up and started pacing around the living room. "The whole bottoming thing. You could have just said, 'I don't like it,' but instead you gave me that speech implying that bottoming made one less of a man, and that's just total bullshit, Adam, and you should know that."

"Jake, stop."

"Why am I even here, huh? We were great friends once, but that all seems to be gone now."

"That's not true. I love you." He looked up at me and pressed a hand to his chest.

"Yeah? Well, it's not enough for you to love me. You have to respect me too. If you don't, this can never go anywhere."

He stood then. His brow was furrowed in anger. It was a classic Mad Adam face, tinged red, his eyebrows knitted together, his chin out. "Yeah? Well, then you have to stop getting offended every time I try to explain myself. There's more than one way to be gay, you know. Just because I don't do things your way doesn't make my life any less legit. Last I checked, the only thing we all have in common is the desire to fuck other men."

"I'm not offended, really, I just think that—"

"This goes both ways, you know. I'm really trying here, but you keep stubbornly refusing to be open to the possibility that I might just love you and want to be with you without having some kind of hidden agenda. I don't want to change you or force you to do anything you don't want, and all I ask in return is that you act the same toward me."

His reply was so *reasonable* and *logical*. I felt like a heel for implying I wanted to change him, even though I could have acknowledged to myself that I kind of did. But I was still angry. "Maybe we're at an impasse. Maybe you should have stayed gone."

"Maybe," he said, crossing his arms over his chest.

I had to get out of the apartment. I felt like the walls were closing in on me, and the only way I'd ever calm down was to get away from Adam for a while. I could have gone to a coffee shop or something, just cooled my heels for an hour and come back, but I was so full of anger and frustration that I wasn't thinking straight anymore. Suddenly, more than anything, I just wanted to go home. I wanted to be in my apartment, around my own things, where everything was comfortable and safe. I couldn't stand to be in Adam's immaculate apartment any longer.

I stormed into his bedroom and tracked down any loose items of mine lying around his room. I shoved everything into my suitcase and wheeled it back into the living room.

Adam's eyes went wide. "What are you doing?"

"Going to the airport."

"But your flight isn't for another six hours."

"Maybe I'll try to get on a different one."

"Jake, come on, stop it. Let's talk about this."

I took a deep breath. "I hear what you're saying, I do, but I'm really pissed off right now, and I'm still getting used to the idea that you're back in my life, that you've changed in all these ways I bet I don't even know about yet, that you're this different person than you were when you left."

"I'm not that different."

"Well, yeah, I see that too. But all this is fucking with my head a lot, and I'm just so mad at you right now, and I don't know what to do with that, so I think I should just leave."

"No, you don't have to do that. I'll make another pot of coffee, we can sit down and talk, it'll be fine." It sounded like he was talking to himself more than to me.

I walked over to his closet and pulled out my jacket. "I do care about you, a lot, and I miss our friendship, but there's still something not quite right here, and I don't know how to fix it."

"We can work on it."

"Maybe. I want to. But I need to just leave for a while. Is that okay? Can I go home?"

"You want to leave me as I left you, is that it?"

I shrugged into my jacket. "I'm not as vindictive as that. You should know that by now. Can I get a cab just by hailing one here?"

"Yeah, look for the lights on top to be lit up." He closed his eyes. "I really don't want you to leave. So our relationship isn't perfect. We're still working out the kinks. That's no reason to bail."

"I'm not bailing, I just need some space. Being with you nonstop for forty-eight hours is a hard thing when we're still getting used to being around each other again, let alone being *with* each other."

He walked over to the door. "Okay. I'll let you leave, as long as you promise this isn't good-bye forever."

"It's not." I walked to him and kissed his cheek as a gesture of good faith. "I don't think it'll ever be good-bye forever with us. I just need to think about some things. Okay?"

"Yeah. Me too, I guess."

"Good. I'll call you in a couple of days. Okay?"

"Yeah. Please do."

And with that, I left. I went down to the street and hailed a cab and spent the cab ride on my phone with the airline trying to negotiate an earlier flight. As I listened to the falsely cheery hold music, something in the back of my mind tugged at me. I couldn't figure it out, at first; it was just a pin prick of memory and a vague sense of uneasiness.

His words rang in my head. *You want to leave me as I left you*, he'd said. It wasn't that, not at all. I wanted him in my life. And that was the thing; all that anger was really just a manifestation of my fear that he was everything I'd been waiting for, everything I ever wanted, but I wasn't enough for him.

Adam had the posh apartment and the pretentious friends and his own fucking company, and what was I but a quaint reminder of all he'd left behind? How could he possibly want me? How could I keep my heart from breaking when he inevitably left me again?

I would never leave Adam the way he left me. I loved him too much to put him through that. As the cab rumbled over the Triborough Bridge, I glanced back at the island of Manhattan as it slid away. This wasn't the end, I thought, but maybe it would have been easier if it was.

THE Saturday after I returned from New York, I took the train up to Glenview for my father's sixtieth birthday party. I walked out of the train station and saw Brendan's blue sedan idling at the curb. I'd asked him to come get me because my parents were preoccupied with setting up for the party. When I climbed into the car, I said, "Hey, man, thanks for picking me up."

"No problem." He put the car in gear and pulled away from the station. "How are things?"

"Fine."

"Longo said you went to New York last weekend?"

"Yeah, I…." I wasn't sure how much to say. My first instinct was to keep everything that was happening with Adam a secret, but I wasn't sure why. The funny thing was that, of my friends, Brendan, the straight guy, had always been the one most willing to listen to me prattle on about boys. "I went to see Adam. He lives in New York now."

Brendan shot me a sidelong glance as he pulled up to a red light. "Rosie Adam?"

"Do you know another Adam?"

Brendan drummed his fingers on the steering wheel while he waited for the light to change. When we were moving again, he said, "Did you go to see Adam, or did you go to *see* Adam?"

"As in, did I go to see Adam naked?"

He grimaced. "Well, yeah."

"I… we've been seeing each other in that sense, yes."

"Oh, Jakey." It was funny how paternal Brendan could sound. His tone indicated he was disappointed in me. It hurt more than I would have expected it to. I knew Brendan would not shower me with approval, but I had hoped he wouldn't be judgmental.

But I knew my friend well, and his reaction didn't surprise me. "And that is why I didn't want to say anything."

Brendan swallowed and nodded. "I'm sorry." When we pulled up to another red light, he said, "So, you went to New York to see Adam, and you've been seeing Adam for a while now."

"Since Coach's funeral, pretty much."

Brendan kept tilting his head back and forth, as if he were having a hard time making heads or tails of this news. "He's definitely gay, then."

"Yeah." I almost made a lewd joke, but nothing about this situation struck me as funny. "Although everything is up in the air now, because we had this big fight right before I left New York."

Brendan turned the car suddenly, which I recognized as him taking the long way to my parents' house, a trip that would take an extra twenty minutes through back roads and suburban neighborhoods, instead of the more direct route down the highway. So I gave him the *CliffsNotes* version. I told him about going to see Adam in the hotel, about him showing up on my doorstep with the Ducati, about flying to New York, and even about the substance of our fight. Brendan listened, not saying anything but nodding his head occasionally.

When I stopped talking, I looked at Brendan, who was grimacing.

"I'm sorry if this grosses you out," I said, "because it's Rosie and no one ever wants to think of their friends in that context, but…."

"No, it's not that." He tightened his grip on the steering wheel. "I mean, yeah, thinking about Rosie in that way is fucking bizarre, but it's more that, well…." He bit his lip.

"Spit it out."

He sighed. "You don't see a problem with the fact that you've been out for more than a decade but he's still kind of closeted?"

"He's not closeted, not really, he's—"

"Then what was your argument about? You don't think he respects you because he has some kind of thing about gay culture. And keep in mind, too, I had no idea for sure that he was gay until just now, and we were friends for most of our lives. He's got some hang-ups, right? And on top of all that, he's already broken your heart once. Just so we're clear, *that's* the guy you're *seeing*."

I thought of the little epiphany I'd had in the cab to the airport. I understood what Brendan was saying, but suddenly I felt defensive. "Things are different now. I mean, I know you're still mad at him, and I haven't quite forgiven him yet, either, but—"

"Damn right I'm still mad at him!" We pulled up to an intersection, and Brendan hit the brakes a little hard, causing the car to jerk. "I don't get how you can be so quick to forgive him. Because you have. Don't lie to yourself and say otherwise. He left us, remember?" Brendan and Kyle had been just as mystified by Adam's disappearance as I was. They had both gotten angry when Adam didn't return their phone calls or emails, either. I think they had both been able to let go of a lot of that anger, and we hadn't talked about it in a long time, but then here was Brendan, looking like he wanted to punch something. "He left you in the worst way. Don't you remember what that felt like?"

I'd been trying for weeks to make myself forget. "Of course I do. But we've spent a lot of time together since he came back, and… you know what? Forget it. Forget I said anything. None of this even matters because we had a big stupid fight and he lives in fucking New York City and I'm sure as hell not moving and he seems determined to live as far from home as possible, so whatever. It's probably not even going to work out, but I sure as hell wonder why my friends can't be even a tiny bit supportive about this, because Longo's on my case too, like I'm some idiot who didn't think this through. But I have thought it through, a lot, for years. So let's just drop the goddamn subject, all right?" I crossed my arms over my chest.

We both stewed for a long moment. My mind wandered over to wondering what Adam was up to right then, if he was having these same kinds of conversations with his friends about what a bad bet I was. As I'd promised, I'd called him a few days before, but conversation between us was strained and polite, and I felt like nothing was resolved. That was frustrating, because I wanted to fix everything. I always wanted everything to be perfect and happy, but instead things were spiraling out of control, and I didn't know what to do.

Brendan pulled over suddenly. We weren't at my parents' house yet, but I recognized the block as one in my neighborhood. He turned toward me. "I'm sorry."

"I know. Sorry for shouting."

"No, I deserve it. You're right, I shouldn't have bagged on you. I just don't want bad things to happen to you."

"I know. Apology accepted."

"I'm taking out my own shit on you, and you don't deserve it."

"Stop apologizing. I already forgave you."

We sat in the car for a moment longer. Brendan put his hands back on the wheel, and I thought we were going to pull away, but instead he said, "There's something wrong with me."

"Ox, there's nothing wrong with you, I already told you—"

He ran his hands over the steering wheel. "No, I mean, so, we've been trying to get pregnant. Me and Maggie. I mean, obviously. We want kids. And we've been trying for more than a year now and nothing. Maggie went to the doctor to get everything checked out, and there's nothing wrong with her, so clearly I'm the problem."

"I'm so sorry," I said, not knowing what else to say. I had sometimes wondered why Brendan and Maggie hadn't gotten around to having kids yet, because they had both always made it known that it was part of their plan. "Have you been to the doctor yet?"

"No. I know I should, but I can't face it." He shook his head. "You know what really gets to me? Fucking Longo. He goes around sticking his dick in anything that will have him and winds up with a kid he doesn't even want. Maggie and I have been together ten years and want a kid badly, but nothing."

"That's not really fair to Longo."

"I know! I know that. I realize how irrational and stupid that is. I know, even, that Longo loves his little girl and is, against all odds, a pretty good dad. But whenever I see him lately, I just get so angry."

I wasn't sure how to help him, or if I could. "I'm really sorry," I said. "I wish there was something I could say or do."

Brendan shrugged and pulled away from the curb. "Such is adult life, eh? Everything was much easier when the biggest thing we had to worry about was whether we needed to replace our baseball gloves." He took a deep breath. "Just be careful, all right? With Rosie, I mean. I hope things work out. I'm here if they don't."

"Thanks, Ox. And I hope things work out for you and Maggie."

When we got to my parents' house, I talked Brendan into coming inside to say hi to my mom. I unlocked the front door and called out to announce my arrival.

"Kitchen!" shouted my mother.

I dropped my luggage near the stairs. We walked back to the kitchen and she gave us both hugs. "Brendan, it's so nice to see you. You look handsome. How's your pretty wife?"

"She's great, Mrs. Isaacson."

Mom smiled. "Jacob, *bubele*, no problems with the train?"

"Nope."

"Your father went to the liquor store, but he should be back shortly."

"You need a hand with anything?"

"Have you had lunch? You should really eat a sandwich. You're too thin these days."

I rolled my eyes, but I let my mother make turkey sandwiches for me and Brendan. We ate standing at the kitchen island.

My mother said, "Oh, Jake, I saw this great article in the *Trib* about a gay couple that adopted a baby girl with cerebral palsy. How cute is that?"

I had seen the same article. "It's pretty cute."

"That could be you!"

"What?"

"I mean, you don't have to adopt a kid with cerebral palsy, but one of these days, you'll be able to get married anywhere in this country and raise a family the same as anybody else."

"I gotta find a husband first."

"Sure, sure," she said, as if this were a minor detail.

I glanced at Brendan, who was quietly eating his sandwich. I wondered if he knew that we were in similar boats. It was highly unlikely I'd ever have biological children, although I wasn't even sure I wanted them.

To Mom I said, "Don't you have a daughter who lives just a few blocks away and two perfectly respectable grandchildren already?"

"Of course. But I want good things to happen to you too, dear."

"Aren't you kind of seeing someone, Jake?" asked Brendan, picking a piece of turkey off his sandwich.

"Don't think I won't come after you in your sleep," I said.

"Jacob, is this true? Do you have a boyfriend you've been keeping from me? You must invite him to the party!"

"Mom, he's not even my boyfriend. He's just…." I trailed off, and Brendan raised an eyebrow. I didn't want to lie to my mother. "He lives out of town. He can't be here for the party."

"Soon, though. Next time he's in town. Assuming you've met him in person and this isn't one of those Internet things." She pursed her lips to make her disapproval known.

"I've met him in person."

"I'll say," said Brendan.

"Seriously, dude," I said.

My mother laughed. "Oh, you boys." She gathered up our plates. "Brendan, you'll come to the party tonight, of course."

"Oh. Well, actually, Mrs. I., Maggie and I had plans, so…."

"Bring her too! I'd love to see her."

Knowing when to throw in the towel, Brendan nodded. "I'll see if she's up for it, okay?"

"Great. Now go." She pushed Brendan toward the front of the house. "I'm going to put my ungrateful son to work. I'll see you tonight, okay?"

Brendan nodded and beat a hasty retreat.

KYLE showed up for the party too, with Alexa in tow. I worried that would be a problem for Brendan, but he seemed to take it in stride, and anytime Kyle said something that pushed one of Brendan's buttons, Maggie was at least there to soothe him.

Although, if Brendan had wanted to avoid Kyle, it was pretty easy to get lost in that party. There were fifty people crammed into my parents' house, which was about twenty more than could fit comfortably.

I held court over the couch for most of the night, getting slowly drunk on the beer various people kept passing me. This was fine with everyone involved, I thought; Dad mostly circulated, telling jokes and making sure everyone was having a good time while Mom fussed about whether there was enough food on each of the many serving plates she'd set out.

Brendan sat with me for a great deal of the time. We didn't talk much, but it was comfortable. Kyle ran around after Alexa, who seemed determined to shove her hands into every food bowl and steal canapés off guests' plates. She was three and seemed like a real handful. When my sister, Rachel, finally showed up, Alexa was at least distracted by my niece and nephew, who weren't much older. The joy on Kyle's face when Rachel relieved him of his need to watch the kid was pretty funny. He kissed her full on the mouth, which left her standing there stunned for a moment. Then he dropped onto the couch next to me.

"I love your sister," he said.

"She's married, dude."

Kyle laughed. "I don't want to fuck her. She looks too much like you, for one thing. She's just my favorite person right now."

I reached for another beer. "Thanks for that."

Kyle patted me on the back.

Maggie wandered over. Since the three of us sitting in a row effectively took up all the cushion space on the couch, she sat on Brendan's lap. He smiled and put his arms around her.

"Hello, boys," she said.

"Hi, Maggie," Kyle and I murmured simultaneously.

"Hope I'm not intruding on your Guy Time."

"Not at all, my dear," Kyle said. "You know we adore you."

One thing I'll give Brendan: he loved his wife, and it was obvious whenever she was near. He grinned and flirted with her while they exchanged bits of information relating to things they'd seen at the party. The scowl he'd been wearing for a lot of the day disappeared. He hugged her and rested his hand on her shoulder, and I tried to ignore—or at least not react to—the blatant PDA, but I thought they were sweet together too. It was such an Adult Thing to have a relationship like that.

I tried to picture past boyfriends at a party like this. David had only met my parents on a handful of occasions, and never for any length of time longer than dinner. I hadn't wanted David to be a part of my life in the way my friends were. I wanted to keep everyone in their separate boxes. But my mother had insisted on meeting David after we'd been together about six months and kept making noise about making him part of the family. I'd mostly ignored her.

Of course I'd known through everything that David was not The One; he was a placeholder to tide me over until I met the man who could make me forget about Adam.

And Adam, of course, belonged right here. Hell, his parents were standing on the other side of the room, chatting with my mother, and I was pretty sure I'd seen one of his brothers roaming around the house too. These were his people, and we'd once all been his friends, and I could so easily picture the two of us, huddled in a corner and talking conspiratorially. We'd probably done just that at my dad's fiftieth birthday party, at his fortieth. Only now Adam might hold my hand. He might curl his fingers around my arm. He might steal a kiss. Instead of conspiring to liberate a few beers from the cooler, we'd work out where we could go to make out.

Thinking about that made me feel worse. I slid my butt forward a little so my head could sink into the couch cushions.

"So Jakey," said Maggie. "Your mother sent me to find out about this new guy you're dating."

All three of us boys groaned, Brendan the loudest. Maggie elbowed him right at his breastbone. He coughed.

Kyle raised an eyebrow at me. "Rosie?" he asked.

I shrugged. "Kind of. I guess. Maybe."

Maggie reached over and punched my shoulder. "Get out of town!"

"It's not… I mean, we had a fight and… I mean, I guess we were seeing each other, but I don't think it's going to work out and…."

"Don't bother with the lecture," Brendan told Maggie. "I already did."

"Me too," said Kyle, "and we see how well he listens."

"I don't know, guys," said Maggie. "This could be a good thing. I know I wasn't around when you guys were little, but when I first met Brendan, he always talked about the two of you like you were a collective unit. 'I'm gonna go get a drink with Jakey-and-Rosie.' 'I'm gonna throw a ball around with Jakey-and-Rosie.' Like you were one person. So you could each be the love of each other's lives. An epic love story for the ages!"

Brendan took her glass of wine away. "No more of this for you."

"This is kind of a big deal," said Maggie. "I mean, isn't it? You and Rosie?"

"Eh," I said, wanting to underplay it so we'd change the subject.

She groaned. "You boys are awful. Not a romantic bone in any of your bodies."

"I'm plenty romantic," said Kyle, puffing out his chest. "I have of late been getting to know a young woman named Jennifer, in the biblical sense, of course, and she inspires me to bring flowers and pay for dinner."

"Wow, sounds special," said Maggie.

"Wait for it. He's about to ruin it," Brendan said.

"Yeah, next he'll tell us about her huge knockers," I said.

Kyle rolled his eyes. "While she does have an ample bosom, I do actually like her as a person. Mostly."

"What's the catch?" I asked.

"She hates kids." He laid his head on the back of the couch and put a hand on his forehead. "I mean, I'm not too keen on kids, either, but I like *my* kid. So her blanket-hating all kids is a little problematic."

"Does she know about Alexa?" I asked.

"I did tell her, yes, and she said something about that being okay because Alexa will be with Michelle most of the time, and I didn't have the heart to correct the poor girl. Although at the time, I was trying to get into her pants. I succeeded, by the way."

"You're a pig," said Maggie.

"Well, yes, but that's neither here nor there. The larger problem is that I have a perfectly nice girl who I like a great deal, but I will have to dump her because she hates my daughter."

"Maybe she'll come around," Brendan tried. "Same way you decided kids were all right when Alexa was born. Maybe she'll like this kid."

"I don't think I can undersell the depths of her hatred. I'm afraid to introduce her to Alexa for fear she'll get out the mace." Kyle sat up and shook his head. "I don't like this business of being in my thirties. Life was so much simpler ten years ago."

As if our conversation had summoned them, the kids chose that moment to come tearing through the living room. Alexa beelined for her dad with my sister's kids in tow. She jumped in Kyle's lap, and he grunted as he absorbed the impact.

"Hey, kiddo," he said. "We were just talking about you. Saying terrible things."

"No you weren't," she said with a giggle.

Kyle sighed and gave her a hug. "You're right, I could never say terrible things about you. You're Daddy's perfect girl, aren't you? Even if I never find another woman to love me, I'll still have you, right?"

I hadn't seen Alexa in a while. She'd grown so much it was hard to believe she was the same kid. The poor thing was basically a blonde Kyle in tinier form. As she tried to process what he was saying to her, she put a hand on her head and scrunched up her nose.

Kyle smiled and kissed the top of her head.

"Uncle Jake?" asked my nephew, Joey. "Grandma said you had some trucks in your room."

"Oh, yeah. There's a big purple box full of cars and things. It's right next to the closet. Have at it."

Joey gave a little cheer, and he and his sister ran off. Alexa slid off Kyle's lap and went after them.

Kyle elbowed me. "Leave it to the gay kid to have boy toys but keep them in a purple box."

"Hey, the purple box was my mom's. And that 'gay boys play with Barbies' thing is a stereotype. You know perfectly well I was into plenty of boy things."

Kyle laughed. "Sure, *boy things*. That's why you got into sports. You were checking out the other boys' *things* in the locker room, weren't you?"

I shrugged.

Kyle brought his beer to his lips. "Oh, me too."

Brendan rolled his eyes. "Of the four of us, how am I the only straight one? How did that happen? How did I manage to pick the three of you for best friends?"

"It's because you're so sensitive, sweetie," said Maggie. "You blend right in with these boys."

Kyle and I both cracked up at that. Brendan's face went scarlet.

Maggie stood up and adjusted her skirt. "Well, I'll go see if Mrs. Isaacson needs help with anything and leave you boys to talk about boy stuff some more." She gave Brendan a kiss on the cheek and then disappeared into the crowd.

"So," Kyle said when she was gone. "Rosie, huh? That's still a thing?"

"I guess. I don't know."

Kyle narrowed his eyes at me. "Part of me wants to know if he's good in bed, but part of me really doesn't want to know."

"That's gross, Longo," said Brendan.

"I'll talk about Jennifer's tits if that makes you more comfortable."

Brendan frowned. "It's not the gay thing. It's that it's *Rosie*. It's… incestuous."

"Not as much as you'd think," I said.

Kyle laughed. "Yeah, *how* long did you have a crush on him?"

I coughed, the beer I was sipping getting stuck in my throat. "How long have you known about that?"

"There was a period of time pre-David in which your eyes did this silly puppy-dog thing whenever Adam walked into a room."

"Yeah, we all kind of knew about that," Brendan added. "But that's why what he did was so awful, right? I mean, let's review. He started being really pissy around you when you started dating David, and rather than call him on his bullshit, you just kind of absorbed it. Right? So then he *kisses* you before taking off for parts unknown. So he strung you along, and then he ditched you."

"It's not exactly like that."

"We're on Team Jake," Kyle said. "I'm always going to pick slow and steady over the wild hare. But you seem to be on Team Adam. Which is kind of fucked up if you think about it."

I sipped my beer and shook my head. "I appreciate that you guys have my back, but just… I gotta work this one out for myself. And in the event that Adam really is the guy for me, if we *do* work things out, I want you guys on board for that too."

"We are," said Kyle.

"We support you, Jakey, but we also reserve the right to stop you from making stupid decisions. Jury's still out on Rosie."

"Thanks, guys." I let that hang there for a moment while all three of us sipped our drinks and gazed out at the party. Then I said, "But just for the record? He's great in bed. And he's got a really big—"

"Stop!" shouted Kyle, laughing.

"Dude, gross," said Brendan.

"Just saying."

ADAM called me a couple of days after the party. His call seemed to have two purposes: to ask repeatedly if we were "cool" and also to tell me he'd be in Chicago on business in a couple of weeks and he wanted to see me.

"All right," I said.

"Really? Because I'll understand if you don't want to—"

"Adam. We had a fight. We're working through it. I'm still willing to give this a shot if you are."

"I am. Thank you."

"Fair warning, though. Brendan blabbed, so now my mom knows I'm seeing someone. I might have to tell her one of these days."

Adam chuckled. "My parents are still blissfully ignorant. I'm working out the best way to tell them. My mother can conveniently forget I'm gay if I don't have a boyfriend. Now I'll have to tell her I'm dating little Jakey Isaacson from across the street, and that all her worst nightmares have come true. That might be fun, actually."

"Can we agree I'm not 'Little Jakey' anymore, please?"

He laughed. "Sure, Jake." He lowered his voice. "There's nothing little about you anyway."

I felt like we were back on solid footing, for the most part. That is, until he showed up on my doorstep a day early. When I opened the door, I saw he had his suitcase with him, which struck me as a little presumptuous. He'd told me he'd be staying in a hotel, which seemed ideal because I didn't want a repeat of what had happened in New York. I was working out how to tell him that I didn't think his staying with me while he was in town was the greatest of ideas when he said, "I want you to fuck me."

I must have stood there for a good minute with my mouth hanging open as the words slowly penetrated. "You want… what?"

He pushed me inside, pulling his suitcase into the vestibule and letting the front door of the house slam shut. I glanced at my landlords' door, not remembering if I'd heard them come home or not. Although on reflection, I doubted this was the first time a guy had stood at the base of the stairs up to my apartment and uttered those words to me. I was pretty sure, however, that this was the first time Adam had ever spoken them.

He pushed me against the wall and kissed me hard. My head collided with the vestibule's ugly wainscoting, but I did not care, because Adam tasted like fire and risk and *Adam*, and I hadn't realized how much I'd missed him, missed having him in my arms, until that moment when I got him back again.

My brain registered a sound coming from the ground floor apartment, what sounded like a chair being pulled across a hardwood floor, so I pushed Adam away and said, "My neighbors. Let's go upstairs."

I hauled his suitcase up, and he followed behind me, occasionally reaching up to fondle my ass. Once we were in my apartment, I dropped his suitcase near my bedroom door and then pointed at my couch. "Sit," I said as I went into the kitchen. I found a bottle of red wine and took a couple of glasses out of the cabinet.

When I walked back into the living room, he was sitting on the couch with his hands on his knees, rocking a little. I wasn't sure if it was nerves or if he was just biding his time. I put the wine and the glasses on the coffee table and then sat next to him.

"Wow, classy," he said.

"Full disclosure: I'm trying to lower your defenses so that I can take advantage of you later."

He laughed. "Good to know."

We chatted and drank the wine, and I started to worry that I'd misheard him when I'd opened the door. When we got to the last dregs of the bottle, I leaned over and kissed him, wanting some sign of what he wanted. He put his hands on my lower back and slowly slid them up. His palms were hot where they touched me. It was an easy, affectionate gesture, but I still felt nervous about everything.

"Jake," he whispered. "Tonight I… I want you inside me."

I couldn't pull away from him, but I slid back slightly, so that I could see his face even while our hands were still on each other. "You're serious."

"Very."

"Why?" was all I could think of to say.

He shot me an awkward half smile. "I've given this some thought. It's something I've always been afraid of, but I want to see what it feels like. I want to feel what you do whenever I'm inside you, because you make this face, and it's so gorgeous, you always look like you're about to die from the pleasure of it. And I want to do this for you, Jake. I love you and I trust you in a way I've never trusted anybody else, and I want to do this to prove that."

"Adam, you don't have to prove anything. I—"

He put his fingers on my lips. "You like to top sometimes, don't you?"

"Well, yeah, but—"

"I want to be an accommodating lover too. With you, Jake, I want these things with you."

I couldn't come up with anything to say that sounded less stupid than "Thank you" so instead of speaking, I stood up and offered my hand. When he took it, I pulled him up and led him to my bedroom.

This felt like a big moment, and I struggled with how to handle it. Did he want it romantic or rough? Should we strip off our own clothes or undress each other? Should I pull the condoms and lube out of the drawer now or wait until the right moment?

I paused a moment too long, maybe, but he filled in the space by wrapping himself around me and pulling me into a beautiful kiss, soft but passionate, and I thought, *There's no going back now.* Adam was never going to be just my friend again, and I didn't think I could live without him here with me like this, and for all of our problems and incompatibilities, here he was, offering himself to me, loving me. What else did I need from him?

Without speaking, we started to undress each other. We stood to the side of my bed and kissed as we peeled off each other's clothes, caressing each other's skin when it was exposed. Adam closed his eyes and leaned into me, moaning as I planted kisses along his shoulder and ran my hand over his cock.

"Are you sure about this?" I asked when we were both naked.

"Yes," he said, though his voice wavered.

I pushed him onto the bed so that he lay on his back. I grabbed lube and a couple of condoms from the nightstand drawer and placed them next to his head. Then I crawled on top of him and kissed him with everything I had, my unspoken way of conveying that I understood the significance of this gesture, that I loved him all the more for it. I appreciated that he trusted me, and I wanted to make this really good for him so I didn't betray that trust.

He put his arms around me, and I positioned myself so I could rub my cock against his. I could have come just like that, just from the gentle pressure of my balls rubbing against his, of our shafts pressing against each other, the friction sending tingles and sparks through my body. He whispered my name, and I started to come unglued, feeling my body arch and jerk as I got closer to hurtling over the cliff. But not yet; this couldn't end yet.

I kissed my way down his chest, rubbing my face in the hair there, loving the texture and smell of his body, loving *him*. "Adam," I whispered. "Adam, Adam." Over and over, feeling like I'd won the prize, like this body beneath my hands was one I'd been craving forever. He answered me by saying, "Jake," back to me like a misdirected echo. I licked and bit and sucked as I moved down his body, and he lightly ran his fingers through my hair. He gently bucked his hips as I got closer to his cock, as if he were seeking something only I could give him.

I took him into my mouth, and he groaned. I ran my tongue up the underside of his shaft and took a moment to savor the taste of him, salty and sweet, and to inhale the scent of Adam's sweat and whatever essence made up Adam. He wriggled under me as I touched him, which I liked. I liked knowing I could undo him the way he was undoing me. I ran my fingers over his balls, gently squeezing, pulling all kinds of sounds out of him. I was loving every minute of this, loving the size and shape of his beautiful cock, how it fit in my mouth, how I'd discovered just how to drive him wild. I glanced up and saw he was pulling at his own hair as he shifted his lower body, as if he were trying to get relief. I backed away a little.

"Goddamn, but you are a dirty tease," he said.

I grabbed the bottle of lube. "Such flattery."

He laughed, and it sounded half crazy.

Lube now in hand, I went down on him again, this time loosening my throat. He gasped as I took him in until I could press my lips to the base of his cock. I felt him stop breathing for a moment as I started to move up and down his shaft, and then he let out a strangled moan. I was glad he was nearly delirious with pleasure, because things were about to get interesting.

I kept my mouth on his cock, licking the head and tasting a salty bead of precome, and I poured some lube on my fingers. As gently as I could, I ran a finger over his entrance. As I expected, he stiffened, but he didn't lose his hard-on. That seemed like progress. I kept up sucking on him, pressing my tongue into his skin, doing all the things I knew he loved while I pushed his legs further apart and explored the undiscovered country of his body. He stopped breathing again as I started to rub lube around the ring of muscle.

I took my mouth off his cock for long enough to whisper, "Relax. I've got you."

Then I slid in a finger.

He jerked as he adjusted to the sensation, but, again, didn't lose his hard-on. I kept sucking his cock as I explored, and I managed to get him to relax enough for me to slide in a second finger. Then I curled my fingers and found his sweet spot.

He jerked so hard I thought we would both topple off the bed.

But then he let out one of those strangled moans again. He put a hand firmly on the back of my head and tugged on my hair gently before pushing me back onto his cock. I took this as a sign to keep going, so I stretched him, being sure to pay homage to his body, repeating the things he seemed to like.

My own anticipation mounted through all of this, and I kept thinking, *I'm going to be inside Adam*, something I'd been wanting for a very long time. My cock was hard just with the anticipation of that, and my heart raced as we got closer to the point where I'd be able to slide inside his big body.

"You ready?" I asked him, lifting my head.

"I think so. Yeah."

As I moved away to put on a condom, he started stroking his cock. The sight fueled my lust for him, and I couldn't wait to be a part of something so hot and exciting. I watched him for a moment and thought about how best to do this, overwhelmed briefly by the mission at hand.

"Hands and knees," I said.

"Huh?"

"Your first time, it's better if you're on your hands and knees."

"But I like it when we face each other."

I did too. I loved being able to kiss him while he was inside me, but I knew better. "That's varsity-level sex there. Because of angles and positions and stuff, it's really better if you're on your hands and knees. It will hurt less at first. Trust me on this."

He nodded and rolled over. He propped himself up on his elbows and presented his ass to me. It was a beautiful sight. I groaned just contemplating it, and he turned around and looked at me with an eyebrow raised.

I knelt behind him and ran a hand up his back. His skin was clammy and smooth. He had a birthmark on his right shoulder blade that I'd never noticed before. I bent over him and kissed the space where his shoulders met, kissed him all along his spine. I licked his skin and tasted his salty sweat. I trailed kisses down to his lower back and moved between his ass cheeks. Feeling daring, I licked him there. This was, I thought, maybe one of the most intimate acts, getting down into the places that one doesn't usually present to the world. I loved having access to that. I loved that Adam still seemed mostly relaxed. I licked his entrance, and he shivered, so I did it again. And again. I cupped his balls with one of my hands and kneaded them while I continued to eat him out. He shivered and groaned and shook, spiraling out of control, and every sound he made traveled right through my nervous system, straight to my dick, making my body yearn and hum for him.

I moved back a little and then trailed kisses back up his spine, getting a little more aggressive this time, biting and sucking as I moved. I sucked up a mark on his shoulder, and he shook beneath me the whole time. I got as close to his ear as I could, which trapped my cock between his ass cheeks. I thrust a little, letting my cock slide against his skin. It felt marvelous, being pressed against him, and I liked the pressure of him rubbing against me, sending little pulses of pleasure through my body. But I wanted to be inside him, and my wanting was starting to become like an ache.

"If I do anything you don't like," I said softly, "if it hurts too much or you want me to stop, you tell me to stop, and I will. I won't do anything you don't want me to do. You got that?"

"Yeah," he said, and it sounded like a whimper. "Please, Jake."

I lubed up my cock and then poured more lube on my fingers. I inserted two and stretched him a little more. He groaned as my finger scraped over his prostate. I decided that he was as ready as he'd ever be, so I positioned myself behind him, holding my cock in my hand, and pressed forward slowly, until the head of my cock met its first resistance.

I put a hand on his lower back. "Relax," I said. "Deep breaths."

He nodded and let out a huff, and then started breathing slowly and deeply. I pressed forward slowly, gauging his reaction as I went but wanting so badly to shove myself inside him. I hadn't topped in a while, and he was tight. His body squeezed me in all the right places, and I wanted that tightness over my whole cock, pulling that orgasm right out of me. I wanted to thrust my hips forward and pump in and out of him fast and hard, but I didn't think he was ready for that just yet. I was also pretty sure he was going to tell me to stop at any moment, though he didn't. Instead he started to push back against me.

"Ugh, more, Jake. Please more."

So I pushed forward a little more, sliding into him slowly, and dear Lord, but it felt good.

"Stroke yourself," I told him.

He managed to get a hand between his legs and started tugging on his cock while I continued to push forward until I was in to the hilt. I massaged his back and asked, "You okay?"

"Yes. Good. Move."

So I moved. I pulled out slowly and pushed back in slowly a few times. The pleasure was so acute it was almost agonizing. His body was hot and tight and squeezed me nicely, until I thought I might come before we really got started. I paused for a moment to adjust, and then gradually picked up speed.

Adam curled his hand into the sheets and pushed back against me. "Oh, Jesus God. More. Faster. More."

That was all I needed. I didn't quite unleash everything I had on him, but I moved faster, sliding easily in and out until we were both crying out with the pleasure of it. I grabbed his hips and moved in and out quickly, caught up in the sensation of his body squeezing me and pulling pleasure and fire and ice out of me all at the same time. I gazed at his back, at the way the muscles in his shoulders tensed and loosened, and I admired how big and broad he was. And I thought, *I love this man*, and I did, I loved him with my whole heart, and I wanted to keep this connection between us, this thing we were sharing, for as long as it would last.

"Christ, I'm gonna come," he said, sounding surprised. He repeated, "Gonna come, gonna come," a few more times as he furiously stroked his cock. Then his back dipped and his shoulders tensed, and he let out a shuddery moan. His body clamped down on me, sending shivers through me, but I powered through it, slid through his orgasm. Then it all became too hot and tight, and I was clobbered by my orgasm as everything overwhelmed me and I came deep inside him, filling the condom, crying out and digging my fingers into his skin as I rode it out.

We collapsed on each other, neither of us able to speak or move for quite some time. Eventually it became too itchy and sticky to ignore the mess we'd made, so we got up and showered together. We each lovingly ran soap over each other's bodies, and while we did so, our eyes kept meeting, and I felt like we were telling secrets in the dark. I wanted to ask him how he was feeling, but I was still nervous, too afraid that his answer would be negative. So I didn't speak, and we cleaned each other off and then rubbed towels over each other. While he dicked around in the bathroom, I changed the sheets. Then we settled into bed together.

"This feels like a cliché," I said as he pulled me into his arms, "but, uh, was it good for you, baby?"

He chuckled, the rumble through his chest vibrating against me. "The things you do to me, Jake. I never imagined that it would feel so good."

"Really? So you're okay?"

"I mean, I don't know that I'm a total convert, because I like fucking you a hell of a lot. And this is totally weird, but I can still kind of feel it? Like you're still inside me. Which means I'll probably be sore tomorrow. But that, Jesus. It was like riding the edge of an orgasm the whole time you were inside me, and when I came, it was so intense I thought I would lose my fucking mind."

I got turned on again listening to him talk about it. "So now you understand my perspective. It's never a hardship to bottom for you." I almost added *especially not with that big dick of yours*, but then I felt a tiny bit inferior, so I stopped talking.

He kissed my forehead. “Thank you for…. Well, thank you. For everything. You’re amazing.”

“I know. I am pretty amazing.” I grinned at him in an effort to show I was mostly joking and not a complete narcissist. “I do love you, you know.”

He squeezed me. “I had a hunch.”

“Yeah?”

“I mean, you’ve never said, but I hoped anyway. I love you too. So much. I’m glad my first time at this was with you. I don’t think it could have been with anybody else.”

“I hope your last time is with me too.” That had sounded romantic in my head, but it came out sounding like a threat. “I mean, I hope you stay with me for a long time and don’t do it with other guys but that we do this again lots in the future? Ugh, never mind.”

He laughed, heartily this time, a roaring belly laugh. “No, I get it.”

I laughed too. “Oh, I adore you, you big oaf.”

IT WAS Kyle's idea. He thought a reunion of sorts between the four of us would somehow restore the peace, so he had us all come to Dickie's.

I'd taken the train in, and Adam said he'd meet me at the station, that he'd be spending the afternoon in Glenview. I should have been less surprised when I walked out of the train station and saw him straddling the Ducati. I didn't even say anything. He offered his cheek for kissing, so I indulged him with a quick peck, and then I took the extra helmet, strapped it on, and hopped on the back of the bike. We rode through the streets we'd ridden through a thousand times when we were in our early twenties, and everything seemed oddly familiar viewed from the back of the bike.

The Ducati rumbled below us as Adam pulled into the parking lot of Dickie's and killed the engine.

"I haven't been here in forever," he said as he took off his helmet. "I see it's still a dump." His tone was not so much nostalgic as neutral, more "Oh, this is still here?" than "So many memories!"

I took his hand and led him inside, where Kyle and Brendan were already sitting at the bar. They both turned to greet us as we came in. A long, awkward moment commenced in which they sized up Adam and vice versa. I moved to order us each a beer, walking away from Adam, but he snagged my forearm and pulled me back to him, as if I were a security blanket. I squeaked when he squeezed my arm.

Luckily Kyle broke the stalemate. "Hello, Rosiekins. I see you're no longer the twelve-pound weakling you once were."

Adam eased his grip on my arm but didn't let go. He said, "Hi. Can we just kill the elephant in the room now?"

Kyle mimed cocking a shotgun.

Adam sighed and finally let go. "Look, I'm sorry for everything, all right? About leaving, about not being in touch, all of that. I was going through some shit. I'd like to try to make it up to you, and I hope you can forgive me. Jake has."

Kyle narrowed his eyes. "I don't have to sleep with you to forgive you, do I?"

"Please don't," I said.

Kyle ran a hand over Adam's pecs. "Because that's a sacrifice I'd be willing to make."

"Longo! Stop flirting with my boyfriend!"

That made everyone freeze again. I sighed and moved to the bar to get drinks for me and Adam, chastising myself for referring to Adam as my boyfriend, realizing that it just highlighted how different the dynamic between us all was now. Kyle had wanted this reunion to bring everything back to normal, but there was no going back. We had to create a new normal.

I glanced at Brendan, who hadn't spoken since we'd walked in the door. He looked down at the bar and pushed his half-empty glass around with the tip of his finger. The bartender served up two of whatever the happy-hour special beer was. I handed one to Adam.

Finally Brendan spoke. "Why *are* you flirting with Rosie? Don't you have a Jennifer to flirt with?"

"This is true," said Kyle. "I haven't broken it off with her yet."

Adam sipped his beer and leaned against the bar. "What's her fatal flaw? They all have one, don't they?" I appreciated that he was trying to be genial in a way this group needed, like we really were all still friends.

Kyle shrugged. "It's true. This one doesn't like children."

"Oh, because you're a big fan of the short set."

Everyone froze again. I wondered how often we'd keep walking over these land mines. To Kyle I said, "It, uh, hasn't come up yet."

Adam frowned and looked around. "What did I miss?"

Kyle sighed and reached into his pocket. He flipped through his wallet until he arrived at a professional portrait of Alexa with a huge grin that was all cheeks and teeth. He showed it to Adam. "That's Alexa. She's three."

"She's yours?" Adam asked, taking the wallet to get a closer look at the photo.

"Yeah. Her mom and I broke up about a year after she was born, and we share custody now. We weren't married or anything. Alexa was just a happy accident."

Adam handed Kyle's wallet back. "I'm sorry, man. I had no idea." He looked around at all of us again. "What other vital bits of information have I missed in the last five years? I'm guessing from the ring that Brendan got married. To Maggie?"

Brendan nodded.

"Kids?"

"Not yet."

Conversation got going with everyone filling in each other on what they'd been up to while Adam was gone. Things seemed to be going well. Brendan even talked some.

At one point, Kyle's phone rang. "Ack, it's Michelle, I better take this." He went outside to take the call. Then Brendan excused himself to go to the men's room.

That left me and Adam at the bar. I put a hand on his waist and said, "This is going okay, right?"

He reached over and pushed my hair out of my face. "Yeah, I'd say so. Awkward sometimes, but I guess I shouldn't have expected everyone to just welcome me back as if nothing had happened. Although honestly? I expected Longo to be the bigger asshole. I never would have anticipated the silent treatment from Ox."

"He's got his own shit to deal with."

Adam nodded. "Man, the last time I was in this bar, I think I was focused more on not admitting I had a crush on you than I was on drinking. Longo kept quizzing you about David. Remember?"

"I remember."

He leaned closer to me. "I listened to you talk about David, and I kept thinking, *That should be me*. It should have been me who was with you, who you talked about with your friends."

"Now it is."

He smiled. "Now it is. I almost kissed you in the men's room that one time. I wanted to scream at you that you should have chosen me instead of David."

I put my hands on his shoulders. "You should have kissed me."

"I'll kiss you right now. Do you think it's okay? Will we scandalize the townies?"

"Who gives a shit?"

We both moved to close the space between us, and our lips met gently, a sweet little kiss just to say *I love you and I'm glad you finally chose me*, and that was about when both Kyle and Brendan arrived back. Kyle whistled. Brendan grunted.

"So this is a real thing," Kyle said.

"Did you think I was lying?" I asked.

"No. But there's a big difference between hearing you talk about it and actually seeing it with my own eyes. And it's a little weird, too. I'm still wrapping my head around the Rosie-being-gay thing."

"Incest," Brendan said.

"Yeah, that too. It's like watching my brothers kiss. If I had real brothers instead of you guys, I mean. Man."

I pulled away from Adam slightly, but he threw an arm around me.

Brendan stiffened a little and then said, "I have to go." He shook hands with Adam and then bolted out of Dickie's. Adam watched him go, then excused himself to go to the men's room. Kyle glanced out toward the parking lot. "What got up his butt?" he asked.

"It's weird. I knew it would be."

"What? You and Adam? Yeah, it's weird. Change is always weird. We'll adjust."

I turned toward the bar and signaled for the bartender to pour me another. "Ox seems pretty pissed still."

"He is. He'll get over it." Kyle scratched his chin. "I guess here's where I give you the speech about the changing nature of friendships. How we can't stay frozen in time forever."

"I wouldn't have asked you to. I didn't come here tonight because I thought everything would be like it was five years ago."

"No, I suppose you wouldn't have. Well. Does he make you happy, at least?"

"Yeah. Most of the time."

Kyle clinked his glass against mine. "That's what's important, then."

"Everything okay with Michelle?"

"What? Oh, yeah. Alexa has a case of the sniffles, and Michelle thinks it's tuberculosis or some such. I talked her off the ledge with the promise to take Alexa to the doctor tomorrow." He shrugged. "Such is my glamorous life these days."

Adam came back then. He gave me a kiss on the cheek before sitting on a stool. Kyle laughed.

"Yeah, this is going to take some getting used to," Kyle said.

When Adam looked the other way, I waved my hand to get Kyle's attention and mouthed the word, *Thanks.*

De nada, he said.

I SPENT that night at my parents' house, and Adam spent the night at his, and that was kind of surreal, but I was too drunk and tired to take the train home.

The next day was a Saturday. Brendan called in the morning with a peace offering and told me to collect Adam and meet him at the batting cages.

"He's going to make us play baseball, isn't he?" Adam said as we boarded the Ducati. It hadn't escaped my notice that he'd pushed it across the street and only stopped when he was at an angle that he wouldn't be seen from his house. My own parents had gone to some family friend's bar mitzvah services.

I pulled on my helmet's strap. "That's my guess, yeah."

"I haven't actually played in years. That job I had in California, that company had a softball team, so I played on that, and dominated of course." He cracked his knuckles. "But I've been too busy to play much since there."

"You obviously find time for the gym." I squeezed his bicep.

"Well."

We rode through the back streets of Glenview and arrived at the batting cages. Kyle was in the parking lot, pulling equipment out of the back of his car. Adam parked the bike and then trotted over to help. He eyed the car seat in the back of Kyle's SUV.

"This is such a grown-up car," he said.

"I know, it's terrible," said Kyle. "She'd better grow up to be a baseball player, to at least justify my owning all this crap. I found two pairs of cleats in my storage locker. Two!"

"How is her case of the sniffles?" I asked.

Kyle handed Adam a duffel bag. "Oh, she's just fine. Michelle—that's my ex—is in nursing school, so she gets a little excitable when it comes to diagnosing things these days. She had a class this morning, so I took Alexa to the doctor at her orders. Alexa is the picture of a perfectly healthy toddler. The pediatrician thinks that whatever she had has already worked its way through her system. So I dropped her back with Michelle, who will watch her like a hawk for the rest of the day. Because of course, neither I, her father, nor the doctor with all the degrees and experience actually know the real truth."

Adam chuckled. When Kyle gave him the stink-eye, Adam grinned and said, “I’m still getting used to the idea of you as a father. It’s kind of strange.”

“I’m still working on the idea of you as a homo. Things change, Rosie. Get used to it.”

“I’m not complaining.”

Brendan’s big blue sedan pulled into the parking lot then. He parked on the other side of Kyle and got out of the car. He regarded us all warily but then turned to Adam. “I’m sorry for storming out last night.”

“It’s okay,” said Adam.

And with that, we moved on.

Adam opened the duffel he was holding to see what was inside. It held a couple of bats, an assortment of batting gloves, and a half-dozen balls, all of which looked like they’d been through a few games. “How old is this equipment?” Adam asked.

“Not as old as you think. When was it? Three or four years ago, Ox and I got it into our heads that we should coach a Little League team. It, uh, didn’t go so well.”

“Their team finished dead last in the division,” I told Adam.

“Not all of us are coaching material,” said Kyle.

“Speak for yourself,” said Brendan.

Adam hiked the duffel over his shoulder. Brendan and Kyle bickered good-naturedly about strategy on the way into the main building. Brendan offered to pay everyone’s fee, which Adam took issue with. Eventually we all stood at one of the cages, and Kyle made Adam go first.

“Can you even hit a baseball anymore?” Kyle asked. Brendan trotted out to turn on the pitching machine. I decided to stand behind the backstop fence. It seemed safer there.

“I can hit a baseball,” said Adam.

The machine whirred to life. Brendan ran around the batter's box and stood next to me behind the fence.

Kyle said, "Could you even hit a ball in high school?"

Adam dropped his bat and looked at Kyle. "I had the best batting average on the team!"

As soon as the words were out of his mouth, a ball whooshed by his face.

"Fuck you, Longo," he said.

He picked up his bat and assumed a stance. I supposed old habits die hard, because I found myself analyzing it. It was his Ken Griffey, Jr., stance, with his elbow too high. He swung and missed the next ball.

"Put your damn elbow down," I said.

Kyle and Brendan both turned to stare at me, but Adam did as he was told, and he hit the next ball hard; it arced through the air before landing in the net.

"Yeah, boy," Adam said.

He made quick work of the next two balls before handing the bat over to Kyle. Kyle took the bat but held it away from his body. "You've clearly cast a spell on it or something. It's cursed. I'm going to get beaned in the head."

"Oh, shut up," said Adam, laughing.

Adam came around the fence. He stood next to me and smiled. I reached over and patted his shoulder. Yeah, maybe it was weird, but we were all finding our common ground again. If the four of us had ever had anything in common, it was baseball.

Kyle hit the first ball, but it didn't go very far. He missed the second and third.

"You guys are distracting me," he said.

"We are doing no such thing," I said.

Then, as if by some unspoken agreement, all three of us started razzing him. "Hey batter, swing batter," I called out.

Kyle hit the fourth ball. It would have fallen short of a home run, but it was a solid hit. He focused on the fifth, but it whooshed by him.

"Jake-Jake," he said, motioning me to his side of the cage. "Although maybe if you rub Adam's ass, you'll have better luck than I did."

I considered doing just that, but Brendan was glaring, so I settled for turning my cheek toward Adam. He gave me a quick peck, and then I went up to bat.

It had been a while since I'd had to hit a baseball. Assuming the stance was pretty easy; I had enough muscle memory from playing as a kid. But the physics of actually hitting a ball suddenly baffled me. I felt Adam behind me, staring at me, and I was reminded of all the times we'd come to the batting cages when we were in high school, all the times I'd overthought this very situation because I wanted Adam to think I was a good ballplayer. I had him now; I was sure that my relative ability to hit a ball had no bearing on his feelings for me. Thinking about that took the heat off. I didn't care as much about hitting the ball as I did about spending an afternoon with my closest friends, as I did about being with Adam.

So when the ball came at me, I swung the bat without really thinking about it. I was surprised when I actually hit the ball, when I heard the sound and felt the bat vibrate in my hands from the force of the hit. Adam hooted behind me, but I blocked him out, wondering if I could do it again.

I did. I hit the second and third balls. I whiffed on the fourth, hitting it foul so it went behind me and hit the backstop. But I caught hold of the fifth one too. I was still feeling pretty astonished when I handed the bat off to Brendan.

"Why couldn't you have done that when we were in high school?" Brendan asked.

"Jake somehow acquired the ability to hit a baseball from a mere peck on the cheek from Adam," said Kyle. "If I give Adam a tongue kiss, will I be able to hit home runs?"

"Don't," I said, resuming my spot at the backstop fence to watch Brendan.

"I know why you couldn't hit a damn ball in high school," Kyle said.

"I could hit a ball. I had a decent average."

"You were too distracted by Rosie."

I rolled my eyes, but Adam seemed to perk up at this. He turned to face me, and he had a wide grin on his face. "Really?"

"Shut up, all of you," said Brendan.

Brendan walked up to the plate and did a whole routine involving twirling the bat around, digging his sneakers into the sand, and getting comfortable in his stance, as if he were a major league player. He did it for our benefit, I was sure, probably to show off, since he was the only one of us who still came to the cages regularly. He'd told me once that hitting baseballs relieved stress.

Brendan hit all five of his balls with enough force to break a window, and while not all of them would have qualified as home runs, I couldn't deny his hitting prowess.

"Wow, Ox," said Kyle as Brendan passed the bat back to Adam. "You picturing your enemies' heads on those balls?"

Brendan just grunted and resumed his place behind the cage.

The four of us took turns chatting and hitting balls and laughing and joking, and I was happy to see both that Adam was blending back in pretty well and that he had a good sense of humor about Kyle teasing him relentlessly.

When our time at the cages was up, Brendan invited us over to his house for dinner. "We'll grill some burgers or something."

Adam glanced at me like he wanted me to say something, but I wasn't sure what he was getting at, so I just shrugged. He nodded and said, "That sounds really great."

Kyle's phone rang then. "Dammit!" he said. He answered it, "Michelle, she's fine, the doctor said—oh. Yeah, all right. I can be there in fifteen."

"What's up?" asked Brendan.

"Michelle is dating this asshole named Timothy." He affected a hoity-toity accent when he said "Timothy." "It's not Tim or Timmy, always Timothy, and apparently he scored reservations at some exclusive restaurant in Chicago, so now Alexa's sniffles were a mere trifle, and oh, can she stay with me for the rest of the weekend?" He sighed. "So, Ox, you mind if I bring a date to your barbecue?"

"Is he an asshole because he's an asshole, or is he an asshole because he's dating Michelle?" I asked.

Kyle held up his hands as if he were weighing something in each. "A little of column A, a little of column B. He's not a harmful asshole, and he's pretty good with Alexa, which is why I'm letting it be, but this is the third time this month she's called me in to take Alexa so she could go on a date with him. That's pretty presumptuous. What if I have a date?"

"And how is Jennifer?" Brendan asked.

"Ugh," said Kyle. He walked over to his car and climbed in. "I'm gonna detour to Michelle's. I'll see you in a half hour, give or take."

Adam asked Brendan for his address, and once we'd conferred, Brendan got in his car. He took off while Adam was still futzing with the bike.

"It's such a grown-up thing to have a cookout," Adam said as he slid his helmet on.

"I don't know if you noticed, but we are grown-ups." I put my hands on his waist. "Baseball antics notwithstanding."

"I'm just adjusting, is all."

"I'm really glad you can be a part of this. Part of my life again."

He turned his head slightly. The helmet blocked most of his face, but the little crinkles near his eyes indicated he was smiling. "Yeah, me too," he said.

We flew over the suburban roads to Brendan's house. I felt weirdly content, hanging on to Adam with the wind whooshing past us. There'd been some tension that morning, but there had been a lot of good too. Brendan was making a real effort, Adam seemed appropriately contrite, and everyone had had a good time.

We rolled into Brendan's driveway and hopped off the bike. As Adam took my helmet, he gave me a quick kiss. I felt a little confused about our roles in this whole tableau; was Adam rekindling friendships, or were we presenting ourselves as a couple to my friends?

Confusing the matter was Maggie, who greeted us at the door with a lot of enthusiasm. She immediately hugged Adam.

"Oh, it's so good to see you!" she said. She took a step back and swiped some invisible dust off his shoulders. "You look great!"

"Thanks, so do you."

"Hi, Maggie," I said, feeling invisible.

"Hey, Jakey. Brendan is already out back fiddling with the grill."

As she led us through the house, Adam looked around, taking it all in. Brendan lived in a large but modestly appointed house that was nice but kind of cookie-cutter, classic suburbia. We found Brendan on the back deck, dumping charcoal into his grill.

"This is a great house," Adam said.

"Thanks," said Brendan.

Things got a little awkward then. No one knew what to say. Maggie quizzed Adam on what he'd been up to in his absence, and Brendan kind of ignored us. I sidled up to Brendan and asked, "What changed?"

"What?"

"I thought things were going pretty well when we were all at the batting cages, and you invited Adam back to your house, but now you're being kind of rude."

"No, I'm not."

I opted not to argue the point, and Kyle showed up then anyway, so everything became a frenzy of *oohing* and *aahing* over Alexa. Adam was surprisingly good with her, kneeling down so he could see her face and talking to her like a person instead of devolving into baby speak. He indulged her when she started rambling on about the doll she was holding. She pointed one of her little fingers at Adam's face and asked what the spots were. He tried explaining freckles, but she lost interest and went to go talk to Maggie.

"She's very cute," Adam said to Kyle. "You'll have to beat the boys off with sticks when she gets older."

"I don't intend to let it get that far," Kyle said. "Just as soon as I can afford to buy a house, I'll buy a shotgun so I can sit on the porch and cock it whenever boys get near. Either that, or I'll just have to put her in a plastic bubble when she turns thirteen and not let her out until she's finished college. Or turns forty-five."

"That seems kind of extreme," Adam said.

"Nope. Men like me exist in this world, and I do not intend to let them anywhere near my daughter."

Alexa wandered back over. "Daddy?"

"What, baby doll?"

"I'm hungry."

"Want me to get her a snack?" Maggie asked.

Kyle squinted at Alexa. "Okay. But we're going to have dinner soon, so nothing too big. And no sugar."

"I've got celery and peanut butter."

Alexa nodded and toddled after Maggie. Brendan successfully got a fire going and announced that he needed to leave the grill for a little while to let it heat up. While we waited, we wound up tossing a ball around Brendan's backyard. Without even thinking about it, we'd positioned ourselves at our old bases, and we threw the ball around the horn like we'd done a thousand times in practice. We talked about professional sports for a while, quoting stats at each other and indulging in cross-town rivalries. Alexa came outside again, and we let her throw the ball to us.

We ate dinner on the picnic table set up on the deck. Adam set next to me and kept touching me in a way that I bet he thought was covert, but Brendan kept shooting us looks, so Adam's affections did not go unnoticed. I figured Adam would refrain from most PDA, the kiss at the bar the night before a notable exception. He'd been generally more affectionate with me this whole trip, and I wondered if he was doing it because that was what he thought I wanted or if he wanted it too.

"So, Ox, Longo, what are you guys up to these days?" he asked. "Where do you work?"

"Sadly, I am still at the same company I was when you left. Moving my way up the ranks in the ad department at the same pharmaceutical company." Kyle rattled off the names of a couple of drugs he'd had a hand in advertising. "I do print campaigns, mostly. Sometimes I write the fine print. 'This drug has the side effects of dry mouth, indigestion, skin lesions, and death.'"

"That's charming," said Brendan.

"You, Ox?" Adam asked.

"I work for my dad." Brendan's dad owned a hardware store downtown.

"Don't be modest," Maggie said. "Brendan's father is setting him up to take over the business."

This probably wasn't really news to Adam. We'd all known Brendan would stumble into the family business eventually. Brendan was also, it turned out, a whiz with numbers, and he'd passed his CPA exam before he'd made the decision to work at the store. He kept the books and worked as a cashier a couple of days a week.

"We all know what Rosie's been up to," Brendan said. "I saw that profile of you in *Computer World*."

That surprised me. I'd had no idea Brendan was keeping tabs on Adam too.

"I'm thinking about expanding," Adam said. He glanced at me. "Maybe set up an office in the Midwest. My business partner won't leave New York, but I suppose that doesn't mean I have to stay there."

"Really?" I asked. Adam in the Midwest was definitely good news.

"It's a possibility. Still working out the details."

Dinner went okay, I thought. Alexa kept distracting us by being a three-year-old and doing cute things. Kyle would tell her to behave or he'd ruffle her hair, and at one point he said, "Now I'm glad I brought a date. I'd feel like a fifth wheel otherwise."

Brendan wrinkled his brow. "Why? It's not like you're the only single—oh, right." He frowned. "I forgot."

Adam bristled at that, but I could see him put some effort into relaxing his shoulders. He didn't want to get offended. I ran a hand down his back.

And things got awkward again.

After dinner, I helped Maggie clean up. I was alone in the kitchen when Adam came in. He walked up to me and put a hand on my waist. "I don't know if I can do this."

"Do what?" I asked.

"Pretend like everything is hunky dory. Spending time with Ox and Longo is reminding me how wide the distance is, I guess. Ox is pretty pissed at me."

"He's not."

"You don't have to lie to protect me."

I sighed. "They're trying to protect me. Or they're still reeling from you just vanishing and then suddenly wanting to be best friends again."

"I know it doesn't work that way, but… protect you? Why am I threat to you?"

It bothered me that he was playing innocent. "Come on, Adam. You hurt me pretty bad when you left. There's no reason for anyone to think you won't again." And that included me. I was enjoying this time we were spending together, and I wanted it to last, God, I wanted that more than anything, but I still thought it was only a matter of time before something happened that would make Adam freak out again and leave. Plus there was the whole matter of us living in different states, and potential Midwest office or not, that still didn't put us in close proximity. Would it really be worth it for me to travel between Chicago and wherever he wound up? Because Midwest headquarters could mean Milwaukee or St. Louis just as well as it could mean Chicago.

"I wouldn't, Jake. I love you."

The smart retort about how he'd loved me five years ago and still left was there, but I said instead, "I know, but look at it from their perspective. You've spent, what, two days with them? I've at least had these past few months to get to know you again. It's going to take time."

"I know. And I expected it would, just… you know. It seemed so easy earlier. When we were at the batting cages or just tossing the ball around. Like when we were kids."

"You're the one who keeps pointing out we're not kids anymore."

"I know."

He leaned over and rested his forehead against mine, so I put my hands on his shoulders, and we stood like that for a moment, perhaps psychically communicating what we needed to tell each other.

I heard shoes squeaking across the linoleum. Adam practically jumped away, but I grabbed his arm before he could go too far. Maggie was our intruder, and she just smirked at us.

"It's fine. You guys make a cute couple."

"Thank you," I told her.

"Brendan's feeling a little weird about it, but he'll come around."

"You sound sure," said Adam.

"Kyle's already on your side, he's just giving you a hard time because that's how he is. I mean, don't do anything to hurt Jakey, or you'll have all of us to answer to, but yeah. If things work out for you two, Brendan will come around."

"Thanks, Maggie," said Adam. "I…. Thanks."

WE WERE snuggled up in bed, Adam curled up behind me, and I was perfectly content to lie there and wallow. My sheets smelled like Adam and us and sex, and I was starting to think that maybe I wouldn't wash them right away after he left when he kissed my shoulder.

He trailed kisses along the ridge of my back, up my neck, and then he sucked on my earlobe.

"Feeling amorous, are we?" I said.

"Mmm. Seems I can't get enough of you."

It was too soon after our most recent bout of lovemaking to even contemplate going at it again, and I could feel his flaccid cock pressing against my butt besides. Still, it was nice to lie there and be lavished with attention.

He said, "I have to say, being with you is far better than I ever imagined it could be."

My heart rate sped up to a happy beat, and I pressed back into him. "You spend a lot of time imagining?"

"Oh, sure I did."

"I'm surprised we never fooled around as kids."

"Well, we were so tied up in our own teen angst about it that—"

"No, I mean when we were younger, when it would have seemed more innocent. Like, I have gay friends who have told me that they kissed or fooled around with other boys when they were really young. Or, I mean, when they were old enough to know what they were doing but still too young for anyone to have drilled into their heads that kissing other boys was wrong."

Adam was silent for a long moment, his breath feathering across the base of my neck, but then he pulled away. I rolled over to see what he was doing. He lay on his back. Not wanting to break our connection, I curled against him, linking my leg with his and draping myself over his chest.

"You don't remember, do you?" he said.

"Remember what?"

"When we were, I don't know, maybe eight? Nine at the outside? There was one night we went 'camping' in your backyard." He curled one arm around my waist and used his free hand to make finger quotes. "It was late, and your parents had gone to bed, and we had that package of contraband snack cakes that we were stuffing our faces with. Then you lay down, and I noticed for the first time that you were wearing these pajama bottoms, I think they had the Superman logo on them, and it was clear from the way they were laying that you weren't wearing any underwear. And this thought just popped into my head. I suddenly really needed to know what your penis looked like."

I laughed. "Really?"

"Yes, really. I'd seen other penises before, obviously. I have four brothers, but besides that, Mom used to drag me and Danny to the Y for swim classes because she thought we were lazy, so I saw boys I wasn't related to in the locker room. But somehow I thought that, because you were my friend and I had all these different feelings for you, yours would be different somehow."

"That's some amazing boy logic right there."

There was a slight smile on his face when I lifted my head to look at him. "Well, so, without even thinking, I asked you if I could see it. And you being you, you said, 'Sure, if I can see yours.'"

The memory started to come back to me. "I think I do remember this now. Man, if that wasn't a sign of what was to come—"

"The funny thing," Adam interrupted, "was that although your dick looked pretty much like every other one I'd ever seen, I found the act of watching you pull your pants down really exciting. Then—do you remember now?"

I did remember. I remembered lying on my back and pushing my pajama pants down my hips and letting Adam look as long as he wanted. I remembered my blood rushing as I let him look. I remembered the giddy thrill I felt when I pulled up my pants and coaxed Adam out of his, and I had a vivid memory of what his penis had looked like then.

"So after that," Adam said, "you rolled over and fell asleep, and I spent the rest of the night lying awake, listening to you snore and thinking that I really would like to know what it felt like to touch your penis."

"I don't snore."

"Shush. You do too. I don't mind it, for what it's worth. Anyway, I started to feel ashamed after that. Maybe it's because she raised five boys, but my mom had very strict policies about nudity in the house, and when I had enough time to think about it, I started to feel like I'd done something wrong with you."

"You didn't. Natural curiosity."

"I get that *now*. But my parents are Catholic. *Jerking off* is a sin. I think Mom would have been horrified if she'd known what we did."

"She'd be more horrified by what we're doing now, I suspect." He jerked a little, so I went for a subject change. "By the way, now you have free and open access to touch my penis whenever you like." I grabbed his hand and put it on my half-hard cock.

He got into the spirit of it and started stroking. He kissed my jaw. "I love you, Jake."

"I love you too."

We kissed. There were a few halfhearted attempts to get another session going, but ultimately, by some unspoken mutual agreement, we settled back onto the bed and into each other's arms.

He sighed. "I guess it didn't seem weird at the time. I suppose one of the reasons our friendship always worked is because we're both gay."

"I know, baby. We've already had this conversation. Let's just go to sleep."

"No, I…. That's not what I meant. It was, like, kind of an innate thing, I guess. I understood it at the time, but I didn't. When you came out, I was really surprised. Remember that night at Dickie's?"

"Of course. But what I remember is you getting mad at me. You barely spoke to me for weeks after that."

He shifted on the bed. "I wasn't mad at you. I was… frustrated with myself, more than anything."

I sat up. "No. I distinctly remember you being angry with *me*. You still spoke to Ox and Longo, but you barely spoke to me, and when you did, you were short with me. Don't lie to me, Adam."

"I'm not lying. I was a total mess on the inside. I mean, I'd known since… well, probably since that night in your backyard, if I'm honest with myself, but I did a lot of lying to myself too. And you coming out… God. Maybe I did resent you a little, but mostly because you had this thing I couldn't have. You told us you were gay, and you seemed… proud. I felt so awful and terrified and so deeply ashamed." All of this was delivered haltingly, with long pauses in which he didn't breathe. Once it was out, he shifted. He put his hands behind his head and looked at the ceiling. "You just said, 'Hey, I'm gay,' and it seemed so easy for you, but everything inside me felt like it was being torn to pieces." He took a deep breath. "Not to mention that I wanted you, I'd wanted you for so long, but I couldn't have you."

"You could have had me." I pulled my knees to my chest and angled my body so that I could look at him, but he looked stubbornly at the ceiling.

"No," he said. He bit his lip. "You wouldn't have wanted me then. You used to get mad because I couldn't say 'I'm gay,' and you were right. I still had to come to terms with the fact that my life wouldn't be what I'd always thought it should be."

"What did you think it should be?"

He stared at the ceiling and blinked a few times before he answered. "When I was a kid, I thought my brothers were the coolest. You know what happened that same summer we camped in your backyard? Doug got married. You know what Matt, Greg, and Danny have done since? They got married and had kids."

"You could still get married. Not legally in most states, granted, but—"

"They were always talking about girls. I even dated a few even though I knew better, mostly so I could come home and say, 'Yeah, that Maureen, she's great, yeah?'" He moved one of his arms and draped it over his eyes.

I racked my brain. Did I remember Maureen? If I recalled correctly, she was the girl he'd dated when we were in our early twenties, around the time I came out to him.

"I dated Maureen for almost three months and never slept with her, you know that? She wanted to do it. One night, we were at her apartment, and she moved to give me a blowjob, and I just couldn't get it up. I was too freaked out. How lame is that? I was a goddamn virgin until I was twenty-five years old."

I didn't know what to say to him, if I should try to comfort him even though he clearly wasn't done talking yet. I put a tentative hand on his chest. I felt a little bad for thinking it, but even with as much turmoil as was etched on his face, he looked so incredibly handsome. His naked chest was on display, with my gray sheet draped over his middle. He lifted his arm a little and looked up at me.

He said, "When I was in California, I used to wonder, what would have happened if I'd stayed? If I'd kissed you and then told you everything, all about how I felt. But I… I mean, you were with David then."

"I broke up with David when you kissed me."

But of course the truth was more complicated than that. I'd loved Adam for so long. If he'd shown up at my doorstep that day and said he wanted me, I would have been his in a heartbeat. Then again, I wasn't sure if I would have been able to deal with him when he was still closeted. Hell, he was out, and I was still struggling with his reticence in public. I shifted so that I was lying next to him again. He turned his head to look at me.

“I don’t know if knowing that would have changed anything,” Adam said. “I know I never met David until recently, but I thought that you and David were a pretty solid couple.”

“We were, sometimes, but it was complicated.” Of course Adam thought what I’d wanted him to think, which changed all the time. Sometimes I wanted him to think my relationship with David was a flimsy thing and that I was still available. Sometimes I wanted to make Adam jealous, so I wanted him to think David and I were great together.

But this conversation was not about David.

Adam took a deep breath. “I know running away was the cowardly thing, the easy thing in a lot of ways, but it didn’t make me any happier. And then I got to California, and I thought, ‘Fuck it, I’ve kissed a guy, it’s all out there now,’ and I went out with the first reasonably attractive guy who showed interest. He turned out to be an asshole. He was really into some kinky Dom/sub stuff that I didn’t understand at the time, and he wanted me to give up more control than I was willing to. At first, I thought he wasn’t a bad guy, we just weren’t that compatible, but then it kind of went bad and….” He trailed off and looked away from me.

“Did something happen?”

Adam let out a breath. “He wanted to fuck me. Used to call me a useless cunt when I said no. But I wasn’t ready yet. I was so new to everything, and, I don’t know, I think I bought some of the homophobic bullshit I heard from my brothers growing up, that gays were pussies or pansies, that taking it up the ass was a symptom of that. I don’t believe that, I honestly don’t, but I think I internalized some of it, and I just couldn’t do it. The guy left me eventually.” He turned his head and looked at me, finally. “I really thought my life was over. I was in California and I felt so completely alone, and I missed you so much, Ox and Longo too, but you most of all, and I missed my family, and everything was a mess. I kept trying to talk to my parents about it, to get them to see… but my mother kept shutting me down and refused to talk to me for a good long while after I moved away. And I… I had one really bad night that I….”

It surprised me when he started to cry. It wasn't even that I doubted he was able to cry, although if anyone would have bought into the lie that crying wasn't masculine, it would have been Adam. It was more that I didn't understand the depth of his suffering until that point. Then he just fell apart right in front of me. A big tear streaked down his cheek.

"What happened?" I asked. I gave up trying to resist comforting him and reached over. I put a hand on his stomach and moved closer, until the length of my body pressed against the side of his.

Very quietly, he said, "I felt like I'd lost everything. That I was completely alone. I hated myself so much. I was completely miserable, and I didn't know how to fix it. I had a prescription for painkillers. I'd had my wisdom teeth out a few weeks before, but they didn't bother me much, so I hadn't been taking the pills. Then one night, I took them all."

"Shit." It felt like my stomach dropped right out of my body. "Oh, Adam." I pulled him into my arms. Just the knowledge that there was a chance he might have left me permanently like that broke my heart.

"My roommate found me," he said, close to my ear. "He took me to the hospital. And, well, things got better after that. I made friends in California, I was doing well at work. I decided to focus on my career, and I started planning Boughton Technologies. Life got less lonely, and I started to figure out what being gay meant for me."

"Thank God." I pulled him close and realized I was crying a little too. "Thank God it didn't work. Thank God you're okay. I don't know what I would have done if you…."

He moved his hand and wiped at his tears. "But you were here. You had David. Or that's what I thought."

I pressed my face into his shoulder. And I told him the truth. "Even if we hadn't broken up, it wouldn't have mattered. I didn't have you. You were my best friend." I started to lose it, my throat sore with swallowed tears. "You're my whole fucking world, Adam. It was always the two of us together, our whole lives. There is no me without you. And you were gone five years. I spent every one of those years, every hour, every minute, every second waiting for you to come back."

"Jake," he said as he put his arms around me. His voice was watery.

"You came back," I said, my own voice quivering. "You came back for me, and it's better than I dreamed of, and I love you so much. You can't ever…. Don't ever doubt who you are. Nothing that you are is inferior or bad or less. You are a good man."

He clutched at me, holding me tightly. "I think… I think I had to go away. I had to figure out how to be gay. How to be *me*. I had to go out with a few guys who were all wrong for me, and see what was out there, and learn about Uncle Steven and all of that. I wanted to be a better man when I came back to you, and I think I am. I'm still scared sometimes, but I'm not ashamed anymore."

To say I was moved would be an understatement. I didn't know what to say, so I kissed him. It started sweet but soon ramped up into something more passionate as we opened our mouths and opened to each other. Adam's suicide attempt swirled through my mind as we kissed, and I couldn't help but think that he felt remarkably alive under my hands, his body warm, the smell of his sweat in the air. I thought it remarkable, too, that we'd come together in this way, that all the years we'd known each other had culminated in this one moment, that in some ways this was wholly different from anything we'd ever experienced together before—that we were naked in my bed and pressed together, reveling in the kind of romantic love that knocks you off your feet and leaves you breathless—and yet nothing had changed. It was me and Adam, and we had each other, and nothing else mattered.

I felt drained, happy to be kissing him but too tired to initiate sex again. When we pulled apart at last, I said, "We should sleep."

"Yeah." He lifted a hand and rubbed his eyes. "My parents don't know about the pills. I asked the hospital not to call them and I didn't want them to know. I haven't told them about us yet, either. I will, I'm just not sure how. I've seen or talked to them a half-dozen times while I've been in Chicago this trip, and I keep mentioning I'm seeing someone, but Mom just clams up and refuses to talk about it. I suppose one of these days, I'll just have to blurt out, 'I'm in love with Jake from across the street.'"

"I haven't actually told my parents yet, either. I plan to, though." Although I wasn't really sure about that. Part of me was still waiting for this to fizzle, kept waiting for him to come to his senses and leave. Still, it felt like there was something substantial between us this night, and I wanted to revel in it.

He laughed softly and put his arms around me again. He took a deep breath. "I want for us to be partners in all things. I move to Chicago, we get a place together, we share our lives. That's how it should be."

That sounded perfect to me. I snuggled against him.

"God," he said. "I didn't know it was possible to love anyone as much as I love you. Is that crazy?"

"It's not crazy. It's like that for me too."

He kissed the top of my head. "Well, here's to our mutual insanity."

BRENDAN met me for dinner in Chicago a few nights later, after Adam had flown back to New York. I was still feeling a little shell-shocked from Adam's visit, and I'd been missing him something fierce since I'd left him at the airport. I'd been consoling myself primarily by daydreaming about our future; he'd said more than once that moving back to Chicago was a real possibility.

I wondered, though, what would happen after that. Adam had talked about getting a place together, and that was too fast for me. Why couldn't we just have a normal relationship for a while? Live in separate apartments, go out together sometimes, get to know each other again. I'd introduce him to my friends slowly, I'd get Kyle and Brendan back on board completely, and everything would be lovely until we were ready to take the next step. Assuming he wasn't just saying he'd move to Chicago to appease me or, worse, as a way to keep me sleeping with him. The latter seemed unlikely, but I still wasn't sure I could throw all my trust behind him. I still didn't feel confident that he was actually coming back, that he wouldn't just vanish again. Maybe that was my hang-up. Probably it was. I wanted to believe him. I didn't quite yet.

I'd invited Brendan to dinner because I felt like things were unresolved. Well, that, and I was lonely without Adam, so I'd been filling up my social calendar to distract myself. But I wanted to avoid discussion of Adam with Brendan at first to verify that our friendship was okay, so we kept to safe topics. Until I asked how Maggie was.

"Good. I, uh, have a doctor's appointment next week."

"Oh. That's good, right? Then you'll know for sure. And who knows, maybe it's nothing."

"Maybe."

We ate silently for a few minutes, which gave me a chance to stare at the overdone Japanese decor in the sushi restaurant in which we were eating. Brendan was a little inept with chopsticks and kept dropping his rolls into the little bowl of soy sauce.

"How's Adam?" he asked.

I felt a little relieved that Brendan had brought him up. "He's fine. Back in New York for the time being."

"Okay. Good."

I don't know why, but that angered me. Something about Brendan's tone—he'd said "good" like he meant "good riddance"—rubbed me the wrong way. "You think it's good that Adam went back to New York?"

Brendan grimaced. "I didn't mean that how it sounded. Just, you know. It's probably good he went home, so that you can get some distance."

"Distance?"

He squirmed. I guessed he'd told me more than he'd intended. "Make sure you're making the right decision."

I stared at him for a moment, hoping his real meaning would appear in big letters over his head. Eventually I said, "I don't get it. Do you still have a problem with Adam? Even after you invited him to your house? You said you didn't."

"He's been back for, what, a few months? I'm willing to give him a shot, but you can't expect for everything to go back to the way it was before he left just because you've lost your mind where he's concerned."

Lost my…? I was offended. It took me a while to formulate a response. "I understand why you're mad, but after everything, I've managed to find a way to mostly forgive him. I wish you would too. He's been through a lot the last couple of years, and he's changed, I can tell he has. I've spent a lot of time with him. You've barely even given him a chance."

"Why should I?" Brendan shook his head. "You want all of us to be best friends again, and I can't do that. You and Longo are my best friends. My parents, Maggie, you guys. That's my family. Adam chose to leave. He chose to break up the family."

"I know that. I was there when he left, remember? I think—"

"He did break up the family when he left, you know that? Sure, the rest of us stayed friends, but we all know it wasn't the same. And he hurt you badly. I know he did."

"I don't know how to explain it, but we've been working things out. He's really sorry about what he did. I really think—"

"Because you can't see what's going on right in front of you." The words came out exasperated. He took a deep breath and sat back. When he spoke again, he was much calmer. "I know you had a crush on him back then. I used to watch you moon over him, but I never said anything, because I figured Adam knew too. You weren't that subtle. And I thought he would put a stop to it. Just like he did with Lindsay Howell in tenth grade."

I hadn't thought about Lindsay Howell in years. She'd been our class's vice president, a pretty, outspoken girl. At some point when we were sophomores, she decided Adam should be her boyfriend. She lay siege to Adam and ultimately launched an all-out assault, but Adam wasn't interested. He gave her some variation on the "I'm flattered but you're not my type" speech, or so he told us later. I never asked what he actually told her, although I understood in retrospect why he'd turned her down. Either way, whatever he said got her to focus her energies on someone else.

I was surprised Brendan thought these situations were in any way similar. "Maybe I did have a crush, but it was more than—"

"So what happened exactly?" Brendan tapped the stems of his chopsticks on the table. "I don't know if you ever told us. He made some kind of move on you, and then he skipped town."

"He kissed me. I did tell you that."

“Right. He kissed you. And somehow none of us knew he was gay until that moment.” Brendan paused for a moment, going very still. Then he put his chopsticks down and looked up at me. “You knew.”

“I knew. He never said anything, but I knew.”

Brendan shook his head. “I still don’t get it. How could all of this stuff be going on that I never knew about? Why didn’t you tell us? Why didn’t *he* tell us? He lied. All those years he was dating girls, he lied. To us, Jake, he was lying to his closest friends.”

I didn’t want to make excuses for Adam, but I found myself coming to his defense anyway. Brendan was right, but he wasn’t. “He wasn’t ready.”

“Well, bully for him. You were. We never judged you. We wouldn’t have judged him.”

“I know that. He must have too. But his parents are much more conservative than mine, and I think everything was tied up in his feelings for me, and—”

Brendan waved his hand. “Well, it doesn’t matter now.”

But it did matter. Suddenly everything clicked into place. The four of us had been friends since boyhood, and it had always been a balancing act. I hadn’t thought we were that delicate; we’d gotten through my coming out and Brendan’s relationship with Maggie and Kyle having a kid without much damage. Or had we? Sitting across the table from Brendan was starting to feel a little like sitting across from a stranger. He’d never said any of this to me before. I’d never seen him so mad.

“How can you forgive him?” he asked. “Because you have, haven’t you? Not just ‘mostly’ like you keep saying, but you’ve totally absolved him of all past wrongdoings.”

Brendan was right. I was loathe to admit it, but I had forgiven Adam. I shrugged. “Maybe I just understand him in a way you don’t.”

“Because you’re both gay.”

“Yeah. Under everything else, I get what he went through, I understand why he did what he did. He didn’t handle himself well, what he did was really awful, but I know why he left.” I sighed and leaned on the table. "Did you know his mother saw us kissing? He came to my house and kissed me in the front yard, but he didn't know his mother was watching from their kitchen window. She let him have it afterward. She didn't throw him out of the house exactly, but she did scare the hell out of him. He was going through some really awful shit at the time, and I don't blame him for running away. Not anymore."

Brendan looked at his plate.

I said, "Look, I don't expect you to forgive him. I wish you would, but I understand why you can't. And I know that we can't just pretend that nothing has happened. Things are different now anyway. I understand now that we can't go back to how things were before he left. He wants a relationship with me. A romantic one. The dynamic is different."

"Is that what you want?"

"I'm still deciding." I wasn't sure what I wanted anymore. It was easy enough to look back on the time before Adam's departure with fondness and a longing for things to go back to the way they had been, but it was also easy to overlook how miserable I'd felt as I pined away for him. That definitely wasn't what I wanted. I couldn't help but think of our last few nights together too, how my heart ached when I thought about what he went through, how sad I was without him near.

"I'm in love with him," I said. "Other than that, I don't have anything figured out."

"Look, you're my friend and I've got your back no matter what you decide. I just want to make sure you're making the right decision, so you don't get hurt again. And as for Adam, well, maybe with time I'll be able to forgive him, but I'm not there yet."

"That's all I can ask."

Brendan picked up his chopsticks again and used them to push the remaining sushi rolls around his plate. "I love you like a brother, Jakey, you know that. Longo too, and even Rosie, deep down. But Rosie's become like my estranged brother. He's the guy I used to be close with but never call anymore. You know what I'm saying?"

"I understand."

"All right." He sighed. "I'm sorry. You're really in love with him?"

"I really am."

He made another attempt at picking up a roll with his chopsticks. "I don't understand that. I just can't wrap my head around it. But if he's what you want, well, go for it, I guess."

Ah, Ox. For all his speeches about how he didn't have a problem with "the gay thing," I wasn't sure he totally embraced it, either. He was a straight guy married to a woman; I was sure there was some part of him that struggled with the idea of ever loving a man, the same way I struggled with contemplating loving a woman. So I got where he was coming from.

I'd hardly touched my dinner at all. I picked up my chopsticks and tried. I didn't have much of an appetite, but I kept shoving rolls in my mouth because it was easier than talking at that point.

WHEN we were twelve, Adam inherited this shed behind his house from his brother Doug. Our neighborhood didn't have enough trees to build tree houses, but there was this old shack behind Adam's house that his family mostly used for storage until Doug claimed it and made it into his clubhouse of sorts. It wasn't a large structure; before Doug took it over, it had been used to house the Boughtons' ancient riding lawn mower and miscellaneous yard tools like rakes and hoses. Doug told me once that his usurping of the space had been Papa Boughton's incentive to finally get rid of the lawn mower, which hadn't worked in years anyway. I'm sure the Boughton parents were just as happy to get some of the boys out of the house, given what a chaotic place it was most of the time. Before Matt, the oldest, left for college, the house was a zoo.

When Doug was a couple of years into high school, he offered the shack/clubhouse to his younger brother Danny, who in turn offered it to Adam by saying, "You can have the faggy clubhouse."

Adam and I cleaned it out and painted the inside walls red because it was Adam's favorite color. We put up a couple of posters advertising rock bands and our favorite baseball players. We got some carpet squares that a local store was getting rid of and used them to make a mismatched checkerboard floor so we wouldn't have to sit on the hard concrete. When Adam's mother replaced the sofa in their house, we took the old cushions and used them as seats. Adam declared that the clubhouse was to be a girl-free zone, which his parents viewed as a cute way of keeping out his little sister, but we were among the few of our classmates who were still stuck in our "girls are gross" phase well into middle school.

The No Girls rule was fine by me, anyway. At twelve, I was starting to figure out that I felt the same way about boys as most of my male classmates felt about girls. I'd heard the word "gay," but mostly as a playground taunt; I didn't really understand what it meant yet.

Sometimes we invited Brendan and Kyle to the clubhouse—we were all friends by then, though we didn't get really close until high school—but more often than not it was just me and Adam, sitting on cushions across from each other, talking and eating junk food. We talked about baseball a lot, and our classmates at school, and teachers, and everything.

One afternoon, the two of us were seated, splitting a plate of pizza bagels that his mother had made for us. Adam wiped some tomato sauce off his lip and said, "You know what would be cool? If this were our house. If we just lived here."

I looked at the narrow walls of the clubhouse. "Here? In this tiny room?"

"Sure, why not? No parents. No brothers or sisters."

"No kitchen, no bathroom."

He frowned. "Okay, maybe not *here*. But when we finish high school, we should get a place together. Just the two of us."

"Okay," I said. That seemed pretty reasonable. Adam was probably my favorite person in the world then, and I never got tired of spending time with him. Us living together sounded like a pretty cool idea. I considered that for a minute. We'd go to college, of course; that had always been part of The Plan. I pictured us sharing a dorm room and playing college ball and taking classes together, just like we did in school then. Then I thought about what would really happen when we grew up. "But what happens when we have to, like, get married?" That struck me as a wholly unpleasant possibility.

"I guess our wives could live with us. Like, all of us in the same house," he said. He put his hands behind him and leaned back on his palms. "Too bad we can't just, like, marry each other, you know? I don't want to get married to some stupid girl."

"No, me neither."

I thought about what he'd said for a moment. It made a certain kind of sense, the two of us as companions for the rest of our lives, sharing a big house the same way we shared the clubhouse. But the possibility of us marrying each other seemed so completely absurd that I laughed.

"What's so funny?"

"We can't marry each other. That's totally stupid."

"Duh, I said we couldn't. I just thought it might be nice."

I was still giggling. "If we could get married, would you wear a dress to the wedding?" That struck me as funnier. I pictured Adam in a big frilly wedding dress. I laughed so hard I doubled over and rolled on the floor.

"I would not wear a dress. Knock it off, dumbass."

I just kept laughing.

"If anything, you should wear the dress. You're prettier."

I highly doubted that. I lay on my back and kept giggling.

"You're an idiot," Adam concluded, laughing a little himself. "Fine, forget it. It was a stupid idea."

ADAM called that night after I got home from dinner with Brendan. I had been home maybe twenty minutes when the phone rang. I was feeling a little frustrated and defeated. But Adam's voice perked me up some.

"I was hoping to be able to tell you this in person, but I only just found out it's a real thing today, and I couldn't wait," he said.

His tone was excited, so I guessed it was good news. "What is it?" I asked.

"Boughton Technologies will be opening its new Midwest headquarters in Chicago. I got a really good deal on rental office space that I looked at the last time I was in town."

"Holy shit! You're moving to Chicago!"

"Yeah, as soon as we finish construction on the new space. It's really great, perfect for what I want to do. I can't believe how good a deal I got. I wanted to tell you the day that I saw it, but there was another potential tenant and I wasn't sure that it would really work out. I didn't want to say anything until I knew for sure. But basically, over the next couple of months, I'll be flying back and forth between New York and Chicago to try to set up the new office. I'm appointing my business partner as head of the New York office, and then I'll relocate to the Chicago office permanently."

"That is unbelievably awesome!" My glee could hardly be contained. Now things really felt like they were rolling into where they should be. Adam and me living in the same city wasn't just a dream; it was becoming a reality, and it felt right, like that was the way fate should have played out.

"It's really a step forward for the company, and, I think, a natural progression. I want to start doing more work with the telecomm companies that are headquartered in the region, so this really does make sense for us."

It didn't escape my notice that he was talking about this as if it were a business transaction. I didn't really care. In the moment, I was too excited. This was a real thing we were moving forward with. We would be in the same city and have a wild romance. I sat on my couch and took a deep breath, trying to get my emotions back under control. Because all of a sudden, I was also hit with a wave of panic. I was thrilled that Adam would be moving back to Chicago. I was also terrified.

It all seemed too fast, suddenly. Adam in New York meant I'd have time to adjust, I'd have time to figure out what our relationship was and what it meant and how to proceed. Adam in Chicago meant I'd have to make some decisions.

"So," he said, oblivious to my sudden bout of turmoil, "I found out this afternoon that this space I want is a go. The new office won't be open for another six months, probably, but I will definitely be in Chicago plenty." He sighed happily. "I'll be there in a couple of weeks. I've got a bunch of meetings with potential clients, and I want to hire some people."

"That's really great. I'm looking forward to it." And I really was. I wanted to see him. But I wasn't ready to make any major life changes regarding our relationship just yet.

The same didn't seem true for Adam, who just kept plowing ahead. He said, "So, not to get too far ahead of ourselves, but we should start making plans for when I'm back in town. I mean permanently, not in a few weeks. Where we're going to live and all that. It probably doesn't make sense to start apartment hunting too soon, but I was thinking, maybe in the Loop? Close to work for both of us?"

"What's wrong with where I live now?"

He clucked his tongue. "C'mon, Jakey. Just because we're a gay couple doesn't mean Boystown is our only option. Chicago's a pretty liberal place, we could live anywhere. I mean, I hope you weren't assuming I would just move into your place. It's too small for both of us."

I hadn't even assumed we would be living together. "Uh, no, that's not really what I meant. I don't know what I meant. This all just happened really fast. I mean, you just told me you're moving here. Give a guy a few minutes to think about that."

Adam laughed. "Yeah, okay, sorry. I've been thinking about this all afternoon. So now you think about it, and we'll talk later."

"Sure."

"I gotta run. I'm meeting Mara for a drink so I can break the news to her that I'm leaving New York. I'll be sad to leave my friends here. This was really the right decision, though. New York has never really felt like home."

"Okay. Tell Mara hi for me. I'll talk to you soon."

"I love you, Jake."

"Love you too."

I KEPT a picture of the four of us. I don't know who framed it—probably my mother—but it sat in a simple wooden frame on my desk in college, on my dresser at home, on the bookcase in the Boystown apartment. We were about sixteen in the photo, and it was clearly taken after a game, the four of us in a row on a bench in our uniforms with a field in the background. Brendan sat on the far left, his cap pushed back on his head to show a tuft of blond hair and his face lit up by a big open-mouthed smile as he waved to whoever was taking the photo. Kyle sat to his right, his arms crossed over his chest, his attempt to look surly belied by the fact that his mouth was crinkled as he tried to hide a smile. Adam sat next to Kyle, the front of his uniform smeared with dirt from sliding into a base. He was wearing that inscrutable grin he so often wore, one that made me think he had a juicy secret he wanted to tell me. I was sitting on his right, my hand on my head to keep my cap from blowing away in the wind, and I'd always liked this photo of myself for two reasons: I actually looked kind of cute, in a skinny teenage boy kind of way, and Adam had his arm thrown around my shoulders.

Sometimes that photo felt like a fossil, especially in the days when Adam was planning his move back to Chicago, when it felt like everything was about to change irrevocably.

I didn't want things to change. For all I knew that we'd never be four corners again, that things had changed when Adam had kissed me the first time, if I was honest, part of me still hoped everything could go back to the way it had been, with the four of us as best friends. Even the romantic relationship between me and Adam didn't seem that different in the scheme of things. Adam and I had always been closer to each other than we had been to Kyle and Brendan, at least until Adam left. As a kid, I'd thought this was just because of our proximity, and later I thought it was because we were both gay, but that didn't explain why I was closer to Adam than to Kyle. Because it could have just as easily been Kyle. I made fun of Kyle because he invited it, but I knew he struggled with being queer sometimes too, that we'd had that in common. And I loved Kyle like a brother, but I didn't love him the way I loved Adam.

In my head, we'd been in a holding pattern since Adam had left, just waiting for him to return so we could become a perfect unit again. Brendan and Kyle and I hung out or went to bars or had dinner together or what have you, and I thought we were biding our time. Everything was the same as it always had been, except we were waiting for Adam to come back. It was stagnant. It was like someone had pushed the pause button and life wouldn't resume until Adam came back.

Except it wasn't like that at all. Because while I sat around waiting, Brendan and Kyle were living their lives. Brendan fell in love and started spending a great deal of his time with someone who wasn't us. Kyle's relationship with Michelle didn't pan out, but he started canceling plans on us to spend more time with his daughter. I started to realize that Brendan wasn't mad about Adam leaving *per se,* but he was angry about Adam coming back and disrupting everything again. That he'd adjusted to life without Adam while I had been waiting for Adam to come back. I had boyfriends, yes, but nothing really changed. I didn't change my life to be with David or any of them. And whenever I broke up with someone I was seeing, I went back to waiting for Adam.

Maybe I was the one who was stagnant.

GOING to the movies was one of the most date-like things we did. Adam had been working out of a hotel in the Loop, and he called me one afternoon, saying, "I need to get out of here. Come see a movie with me." So off we went to see an action flick that starred a Hollywood leading man Adam adored—with good reason, because the man was hot—and the movie was terrible, but Adam let me hold his hand and then fall asleep leaning on his shoulder.

He had to wake me up when the movie ended, and as we walked out of the theater, he said, “So the movie was that good?”

“Sorry.”

“Uh, you want some coffee or something?”

I yawned. “It’s your fault for keeping me up all night.”

It had been a tricky balancing act, his bouncing back and forth between New York and Chicago. When he was in town, he usually stayed at a hotel, or at least got a room at one. Since the new offices were still under construction, Adam and his employees mostly worked out of his hotel room, meaning he actually had to be there, at least during the day. He spent most of his nights at my place, though. Which meant I didn’t sleep a lot when he was in town.

I couldn’t decide if it was a problem. Things were intense between us when he was around. He’d be in town for a week or two, and we’d spend as much of our free time together as possible, which meant I was forced to neglect sleep and my other friends for the duration of his visit. Then he’d be gone for two or three weeks and I’d feel utterly bereft and lonely, lying awake at night and missing him like crazy.

I was counting on things calming down when he moved to Chicago for good, because this was starting to wear on me.

He made lewd jokes about the movie and its star as we walked down the block to a coffee shop. He installed me at a table and went to fetch us a couple of lattes. So I sat back in my chair and watched him from across the shop. Sometimes I loved to just look at him, and he looked particularly good that day, in a fitted blue-and-white check shirt tucked into a pair of worn jeans that showcased his butt nicely. I sat there and thought, *That’s my boyfriend*, with a whole lot of pride and also, *That’s Adam Boughton*, with a whole lot of awe.

He returned and handed me a cup. He smiled at me when I took a sip. It took me a moment to realize there was nothing amiss, which meant that Adam had known my coffee order without my having to tell him. It’s cliché, but there was something romantic about that.

“Well done,” I said.

He grinned. “I know.”

He took the top off his cup and added a packet of sugar. It was funny how some things never changed. Adam had taken up coffee drinking when we were fifteen because he thought it made him seem more adult, but he hated the taste of it and always added a ton of sugar. I loved that he still did this. I loved that I even knew that.

He reached over and poked my arm. "You look like the cat that got the canary. Anything special going on?"

"Nope. Just that I love you. I'm basking in it."

"Aw." He put the top back on his cup. "Oh, so, I forgot to mention, but it looks like the official moving day will be October nineteenth." That was about a month away. "So I thought I'd make an appointment with a realtor so we can start looking at places."

"What's wrong with my place?"

He raised his eyebrows. "Nothing. But we already talked about this. If we're living together, we can get something with more space, and if we join forces, we can afford to live a little closer to both of our jobs."

"Out of Boystown, you mean."

He sat back and took a sip of coffee. He shook his head. "We can live in Boystown if you really want to, I guess. I don't care about the neighborhood. But you sit on a train for close to forty minutes every day to get to your job, so I thought you'd be happy to cut your commute time."

I saw the logic in what he was saying, but something about his presumption irked me. "I like my apartment. I don't know if I want to give it up yet."

He frowned. "I already told you, I don't think your place is big enough for both of us."

"So maybe you should get your own place."

The words just tumbled out of my mouth before I thought about them. I didn't mean them. I wanted to live with Adam. Or I thought I did.

It was sort of like being back on the baseball team, though. Adam had always had strong opinions about how the game should play out, and he often manipulated his teammates (except for Kyle, who had his own ideas) into doing his bidding. He did his best to control the outcome of every game. If he knew an opposing batter tended to steal bases, he yelled at us all to stick close to our posts. If he knew we were facing a power hitter, he made us back up. He could wave his hand and get the whole infield to follow his lead.

And now he was dictating how his life with me would go. Or that was what it felt like.

"What gives?" he said. "I thought this was already decided."

"You decided."

"Uh, no I didn't. We've been talking about this."

"You've been talking about this. You never asked me if I wanted to move in together, you just assumed we would when you moved here."

Adam's eyes widened. "We've been talking about this for months. You've never once said you don't want to live together."

I crossed my arms over my chest, feeling irritated with both of us. "I just don't know," I said.

Adam stared at me for a long moment. He took a sip of his latte before he said, "You still don't trust me." It was an accusation.

I couldn't come up with an answer.

While it was true that I was still waiting for the other shoe to drop, the truth now was that I wasn't ready. I did trust Adam, I believed that he loved me, but this was too intense. It was too much. I'd loved Adam for so long, and I was still getting used to the idea of us actually being together, and he was still trying to change everything. I needed to keep something of my old life to stay grounded. I needed to know there would still be a net to catch me if he woke up one morning and realized he'd made a mistake. And I couldn't think of how to express that to Adam without pissing him off. So instead I sat there and tried to come up with something to say that would placate him and end this stupid argument. But I couldn't come up with anything.

"Jesus Christ," he said after a minute ticked by without either of us speaking. "What is it that you want me to do? I know that I hurt you, but I've done everything I can to prove to you that you can trust me again. I've told you things I've never told anyone, I've done things way out of my comfort zone. Hell, I'm moving to Chicago, all so I can be with you. But I can't stay in a relationship where I'm the one who does all the work. You have to give me something back, Jake. You have to do some of the work, too. Because I can't sit here sacrificing everything to be with you while constantly worrying that you're about to say no to it all. I can't give you everything I have if you don't give me anything in return. I can't do that."

"It's not really about that," I said. "I mean, I love you, but—"

He held up his hand. "Didn't you give me a whole speech about how it wasn't enough for me to love you? How I had to respect you too? Well, I do. The same goes for you. Maybe under everything, *you're* the one who doesn't respect *me*. You've never been comfortable with the way I live my life, right? I'm not marching around all out and proud and whatever, so I'm not good enough, is that it?"

"Adam." I worried he was right. "Don't put words in my mouth. I never said that. I—"

"I can't believe that after everything, you still think you're better than me."

"That's not what this is about."

"Then what is it about?"

I still could come up with nothing to say. I was having my own doubts as it was. How can you convince a man you love him when part of you is seriously freaking out about the happily ever after? It wasn't Adam I doubted in that moment in the coffee shop. It was myself.

"Forget it," he said. A quiet growl escaped his lips. He stood and walked out of the coffee shop, leaving me alone with his latte.

I MADE it home without falling to pieces. It was just a fight, I told myself. We'd argued plenty in the last six months. We'd have a chat about it and be right as rain, just as always. Except he'd never walked out on me like that before. And suddenly the reason we'd never gotten together all those years ago became clearer. Here I'd been thinking the stakes were low because Adam hadn't been a part of my life for five years; if things went south, he'd just disappear again and I'd go back to living the way I had while he was gone. But I was wrong. The stakes were so much higher now; the hurt went so much deeper.

If he left, it was because I really had driven him away this time.

And below it all, I knew he was right. We'd been seeing each other for half a year and I still didn't really think of us as a couple, still hadn't told my parents. The prospect of moving in together made me nervous, but I didn't understand exactly why until I realized the risk involved.

At first, it seemed the only reason I'd balked could have been my own cold feet. I enjoyed the time we spent together. He'd taken over a couple of drawers in my dresser, had clothes hanging in my closet, had his own toothbrush and razor sitting at the edge of my sink. There was no rational reason that I should be so freaked out about us living together, since we'd been basically doing that for months, albeit sporadically. Except that if it all blew up in my face, I didn't think I could survive the fallout. I needed Adam. Even when he'd been gone those five years, I'd been living for him. I'd never been able to really live without him.

I changed into pajamas and curled up on the couch and very resolutely decided not to think about him. I was flipping through TV channels when I thought I heard "Boughton" mentioned. I stopped flipping and realized I'd found a news show on a tech-related channel. A picture of Adam giving a speech at some convention flashed on the screen, and the commentator said, "Boughton Technologies is reportedly establishing a Midwest headquarters. Adam Boughton himself has always been said to have some really great ideas about how to make new technology more accessible. The Chicago office means the company is expanding and may have a wider distribution. What do you think?" He turned to his co-host.

"Oh, definitely," said the other host, a woman. "I hope this means good things for him. I'd love to see him doing Steve Jobs-style keynote speeches at major events. He's not hard on the eyes."

I couldn't help but laugh at that.

But the first host then said, "I don't think you're his type, Jane. Didn't you hear? This month he's on the cover of *Out City* as one of the country's ten most successful gay businessmen."

They flashed the magazine cover on the screen. I almost couldn't believe my eyes. For one thing, Adam looked *good* in that photo. He was clean-shaven and his hair was sexily disheveled, and he wore a nicely fitted gray suit with a purple tie. He was grinning in the photo in a way that made him look so happy and carefree.

So he'd done the story after all, the one he hadn't wanted to do. And I knew he'd done it for me.

And I realized, too, that what I perceived as his reticence was mostly in my own head. For all of his speeches about how gay wasn't part of his identity, he'd stopped being shy about it in front of other people. We'd held hands and kissed and spoken openly about our relationship in public a number of times, and he'd never batted an eyelash. He *had* changed. He'd done everything I asked and then some. He'd come back for me, he was here to stay if I let him. I was the one being stubborn.

The commentators were cracking jokes about Adam no longer being an eligible gay bachelor—apparently the story had mentioned a boyfriend—and they made a few campy jokes that I felt a little offended by, ending with the female commentator saying, "The hot ones are always gay, am I right?" I stood up and flipped off the TV. I went into my room and fished through my drawers for clean jeans and a T-shirt. Once dressed, I left my apartment.

THERE was a newsstand in my neighborhood that I knew carried *Out City*. It was a glossy monthly that seemed to have a fairly limited circulation, and I rarely read it, which was how I rationalized things as I tried to forgive myself for not noticing that my boyfriend was on the cover.

I found the magazine with little trouble. The guy working the newsstand whistled and said, "Well, he's a delicious hunk of man," pointing to the cover.

"I know," I told him, considering playing the "I'm sleeping with him" trump card but instead forking over the money and tucking the magazine under my arm. As I walked to the El, I called my mother quickly, and then I hopped on a train.

I didn't get around to reading the article until I was speeding northward on the Metra. The first few paragraphs were a straightforward profile of Adam the Tech Genius, although whoever had written the profile had made sure to explain often how hot Adam was. The article was all "the handsome tech guru" this and "No doubt his youth and good looks add to his appeal" that, and then had this gem: "Boughton defies all the nerd stereotypes and is basically six feet of muscle, with a boyish grin and a dusting of freckles on his nose. He looks like he belongs on a movie set, not in a cubicle or a boardroom. I joked with him about living up to stereotypes about gay men and vanity, though he claims he only works out to relieve stress."

It was toward the end of the article that the writer mentioned Adam's love life. "Sadly, he's off the market. One thing Boughton is not shy about is his boyfriend. 'I've got a guy in Chicago,' he tells me, practically gushing. 'He's really wonderful, the best man I know. I'm completely crazy about him.'"

Well, gee. No pressure.

I got a cab from the train station to my parents' house. When I'd called, my mother had said to come on over to the house, which made the presence of Linda Boughton all the more strange. The only person I wanted to see less than Adam's mother in that moment was probably Adam himself.

I walked into the kitchen, where they were seated, and greeted my mother and Linda politely. Mom stood. She gave me a hug and kissed my cheek and asked what was wrong. I rolled my eyes toward Linda. My mother nodded like she understood I wanted to speak to her alone. She gestured to the magazine. "What have you got there?"

I could have shrugged it off, just said it was some in-transit reading material and tossed it in the trash. Instead I dropped it on the kitchen table. Linda gasped.

"That's Adam," she said.

"Yep," I said.

"He never said anything about doing an article like this, let alone being on the cover."

"I kind of think he didn't want you to know. He didn't tell me, either, actually."

Linda looked at me askance. "Well, why would he?" There was accusation and anger in her voice. "He doesn't talk to you anymore."

Had Adam really not told his mother we were back in touch? I felt my anger building until I realized I hadn't actually told my mother, either. Well, I figured, it was time to burst some bubbles.

"That's not true," I said. "Adam and I have been back in touch since Coach Lombard's funeral. More than back in touch."

Mom glanced at me and then sat back down across from Linda. She picked up the magazine and studied the cover. "He looks good. It's a flattering photo."

Linda shook her head. "I can't believe Adam would do something like this. 'The Ten Most Successful Gay Businessmen'? Why would he put himself out there like that?" She grabbed the magazine from Mom.

"Because somebody asked him to? Because he's proud of who he is?" I suggested.

Linda huffed and started flipping through the pages.

"Page fifty-eight," I told her.

I busied myself with getting a glass of soda from the fridge while Mom and Linda read the article. I knew when they'd gotten to the end when Linda gasped again. "He's seeing someone in Chicago? He never said. What guy?"

I sat at the table and pointed to myself. Both women's jaws loosened.

"Jacob." My mother's tone was admonishing, though I wasn't sure if she was admonishing me for keeping the secret or for springing this on Linda the way I had. She reached over and combed my hair out of my face with her fingers. "You mentioned something about seeing someone at your father's party, but I wasn't sure if you were serious. How long has this been going on?"

"Almost six months. Since the funeral, I guess."

"Why didn't you say anything?"

And why hadn't I? "I wasn't sure if it was real, I guess. We had a lot to work out. And I was still upset about what happened when he moved to California." I'd given my mom a short version of that story when it had happened. I hadn't admitted to my crush, just said that Adam and I had had an altercation. I think my mom assumed it was a fight.

Linda stood up. "He was right to leave Chicago. I thought he never wanted to come back."

I'd spent five years convinced that something I'd done had sent Adam away. The fact that his mother had played such a big role in his departure was still relatively new information, and I was still processing it. But I saw some of that now. Linda had told Adam to stay away from me. She'd told him to leave. She knew what was going on all along, and she thought the best solution was to separate us. She'd almost gotten her wish.

I got angry. I said, "He's moving back to Chicago for me. He did that article for me, because he wanted to prove that he wasn't afraid of being gay. He still sort of is, though. I think a big part of the reason is that his parents keep saying they support him even though they actually don't."

Linda closed her eyes. "He doesn't know what he really wants."

"He knows exactly what he wants," I said. He knew better than I did.

"It's a phase."

I looked at Mom, hoping for help. I saw that we'd both had the same reaction. Mom stared at Linda for a long moment.

"It's not a phase, Linda," said my mother. Then she gestured at me to speak.

"A phase is something you go through in college when you're curious and your world is all possibilities. For me, it's not a phase. I've been gay my whole life. I'm turning thirty-one next month, and I've been dating men since I was eighteen. I had crushes on them before that. That's hardly a phase."

"But Adam—" Linda started to protest.

"Adam's the same. Adam is exactly the same. And he spent most of his life terrified that everyone he loved most would abandon him if he told them what was going on in his head. He's finally now getting to a place where he can love himself for who he is, where he can love another man and be loved himself, where things finally make sense for him. And I'm guessing he didn't tell you that he and I have been seeing each other because he knew you'd react the way you're reacting right now."

I stopped talking. A lightbulb went off. That was what had really happened five years ago, and that was what had happened again that afternoon. He didn't want to be abandoned, so he pushed everyone away before they could do it to him. That would end then and there, I decided. If he'd have me, I planned to hold on to him and never let go. I took a deep breath.

"I'm telling you now, so that you have time to adjust to the idea, so that when he comes to you to tell you he's moving in with me, that he's in a relationship with me, that, heaven forbid, he wants to marry me, you are a lot more loving and supportive of him than you are right now, than you have been to this point. Because Adam spent so many years hating himself that he needs people to love him for who he is, not for who they want him to be."

Linda's face scrunched up, and she stumbled backward as if I'd hit her.

"He told me you saw us kissing. That day right before he left, he kissed me. And you told him to stay away from me. You talked him into taking that job halfway across the country. *You* sent him away. I never wanted to do him any harm. I care about Adam so much, and he cares about me, and that's what that kiss was about. And you tried to stop that. Because you… I don't know. You think it's a phase. You don't want him to be who he is. But you don't get to make that choice. Adam is a good man. He needs your love and support, not your denial."

Linda grasped the back of a kitchen chair, and she looked down. She mumbled something that my mother seemed to understand and then, more loudly, said, "I need to be getting back now."

"I'll walk you out," Mom said.

I sat at the kitchen table and waited for Mom to return. I could hear her and Linda talking as they made their way to the front of the house, but I couldn't make out the words.

My own words echoed back at me. I knew what I'd said was true and that I had to take it to heart as much as Adam's mother did.

The front door closed, and I sat back in my chair while I waited for Mom to come back. The panic came on like a snowball rolling down a hill, starting small but escalating as I realized I really *had* just said all that to Adam's mother. I was horrified that I'd been so forward. I regretted that I'd been so mean, although I still thought most of it needed to be said. Of course none of it really mattered if I'd been the one to push Adam away this time, if there was a very real possibility I had lost him.

Or did it? David had told me once that he just wanted me to be happy. Maybe that was what love was. It would destroy me to lose Adam, but if telling off Adam's mom did some good, maybe it would be worth it. Life would be better for Adam from now on, with me or without.

My mother walked into the room with an expression on her face that I'd seen a zillion times as a kid. Her eyebrows were lifted and her lips were pursed, and the look was all about love and sympathy. It was the same expression she'd worn every time I'd skinned a knee, every time I got picked on at school, every time I struggled with my homework. The same love in her eyes had been evident the night I'd told her and my father that I was gay.

I burst into tears.

She was by my side in a second, pulling a chair up to me and then pulling me into her arms, the same way she had countless times when I was a kid, with her arms wrapped around me, pulling me close so I could cry on her shoulder.

"I'm so sorry," I whimpered.

Her chest moved against me as she took a deep breath. "Oh, Jacob, *bubele*. How long has all that been pent up?"

"I don't know," I said through my tears. Now that the floodgate had opened, I couldn't stop. "I just realized all at once that I was sitting right next to the reason Adam struggled so much with being gay." I sniffled. "I just realized it's not about me."

Mom stroked my hair. "What isn't?"

"I thought that he hated being gay, and that meant part of him would always hate me. Because I'm out and proud, I would always represent that thing that he hates. But he… he did that article because he figured out how not to be afraid. That's what he was trying to tell me this afternoon, but I… I was so tied up in my own nonsense." I managed to get ahold of the tears and stop enough to speak without it coming out too garbled. "I thought that because he wasn't proud of being gay it meant he wasn't proud of *me*, that he was ashamed of me, ashamed to love me. But I see now that's not the case. He really…. He wants people to love him. He's terrified of letting people down."

That was how I knew he was back for good, too. He'd fixed the thing that had driven him away. He was ready now in a way he hadn't been five years before.

"Did something happen?" Mom's voice was gentle and vibrated through her chest as she spoke. She was soft in the way I always thought she should be, so loving and comforting. Being one of six kids meant Adam had to fight with his siblings for his parents' attention, I realized. No one had ever handed him anything, least of all love.

I'd been doing the same. I was no better than the thing I'd accused Adam of being. I was holding out on him, waiting for things to be a way they never could be. Adam was moving forward with his life, making plans, adjusting to the way things had changed. I was still stuck in the same place.

"We went out today and had an argument. He thinks I still don't trust and respect him. But I do, I so completely do. I kind of worried it was true at first, though, or I didn't argue with him when he accused me of it, and he got mad. He stormed away. But that wasn't the problem. I love him, Mom. I love him so much. I think about what he's had to go through, and it breaks my heart. And now I've pissed him off and he might leave me, and I don't know what I'll do if—"

"Shh," she said. "The way you stood up to Linda just now, that was… well, not how I would have handled the situation, but it was clear that you care about him very much."

I eased away and wiped at my eyes. "You'd like him now, Mom. He's so smart and clever, and he's been completely open with me. And I pissed it away because I didn't think I was ready. Because he made me feel a little self-conscious."

She gave me The Look again. She reached over and wiped at my tears with her thumb. "Oh, sweetie. Straight relationships are hard enough. I can't imagine how it must be for you and Adam with all the extra stuff you have to deal with."

"Now that he's moving to Chicago, we've been talking about moving in together. What do you think about that?"

"Are you ready for a step like that?"

"I don't know." Was I? It terrified me, but how was I ever going to get on with my life without taking a step forward? "Yes, I think so. I want to be with him."

She smoothed down my hair. "You know I love you. I want what's best for you. I want you to stay safe, and that includes with your heart. As your mother, I feel obligated to tell you all the things moms are supposed to say. Normally I'd demand to meet your boyfriend, but I guess I don't need to. Instead I'll tell you the same thing I told Rachel when she moved in with Ken."

I thought back on the day my sister had made the announcement that she was moving into an apartment with her now-husband. I couldn't remember what my family had told her. "What did you say?"

"If this is what you want and you feel ready to take this step, then you have my blessing. But, um, what do moms tell their sons when they know for certain their sons are having sex? Be careful. Use a condom. You know."

"Ew, Mom."

She laughed. "When you and Adam work things out, bring him to dinner with me and your father, okay?" She smiled. "You know what else I asked Rachel when she moved in with Ken?"

"What?"

"I said, 'Are you going to marry that boy?' But now I wonder if that's appropriate here. I mean, if the answer to that question is yes, you're not going to do something silly like move to Toronto, are you? Because maybe Linda was willing to let her son go to California, but I selfishly want to keep you close by."

"I'm not moving to Canada. But if he forgives me, yes, I want to spend the rest of my life with him."

She smiled. "I think that's the best answer I could hope for." She leaned over and kissed my forehead. "I love you, Jake. Don't ever forget that, okay?"

"I won't. Thanks, Mom."

She stood. "Good. So what are you doing still sitting here squawking at me? Go get that boy."

IT WAS getting pretty late by the time I got back to Chicago. I was up and running off the train almost as soon as it pulled into Union Station. Then I hailed a cab and went to Adam's hotel. I walked through it as if I belonged there, and then I waltzed down the corridor to his room.

It wasn't until I was standing about to knock that I had reservations about what I was about to do. I pressed my ear to his door to ascertain if he was alone, remembering suddenly that a large percentage of his senior staff was staying in the same hotel. I heard the din of a sporting event on a TV but otherwise no speaking. I knocked.

I heard him come to the door, but there was a pause in which he must have looked through the peephole and wondered if he should open the door. But he did eventually.

"Hi," I said. "Can I come in? I want to talk to you."

He sighed. "Yeah, all right." He moved out of the way and held the door open for me.

I walked into what was a fairly large hotel room with a king-size bed and a couple of sofas. He flipped off the TV and gestured toward one of the sofas. I hesitated. I still had the magazine in my hands, though now it had been rolled up into a tube. I uncurled it and showed it to him.

"Ah," he said.

"Why didn't you say anything?"

He shrugged. "Honestly, I thought the magazine was coming out next week, and I wanted to surprise you."

"Okay. Well, you should probably know, I went to see my mother tonight, and your mother was in my house, and I showed this to both of them and then confessed that I was your awesome guy in Chicago."

He frowned. "Well, that explains why my mother has called four times in the last hour. I kind of didn't want to talk to anybody, so I didn't answer." He reached over for the magazine, so I handed it to him. "So she did include the stuff about you, huh? The reporter wanted to sell me as this hot eligible bachelor, but I told her I had a boyfriend."

"I thought you didn't want to do the article."

"I didn't. Not at first, anyway, but then I thought about it, and I figured maybe something like this could go a long way toward proving that I'm not ashamed anymore. I was proving it to myself, to you. I thought the article might be some good press for my company as well. Show we're a company with progressive values or whatever. One of the other tech companies just got a lot of good press for extending spousal benefits to same-sex couples, and their stock went up. I mean, not that it was purely a business decision, but I thought about that too."

"Wow."

"Yeah. So when the reporter called me again, I said, yeah, sure, I'll do the article. I wasn't expecting the cover, though, for what it's worth. She only told me about that a couple of weeks ago."

"You *are* better-looking than all of the other guys they photographed."

He laughed. "I don't know if I'd go that far."

Tension somewhat defused, I let him steer me toward one of the sofas, and we sat down next to each other.

"Look," I said, "I want to apologize for this afternoon, for my hesitating about this whole moving-in-together thing. I, uh, went to see my mother, and I might have sort of told off your mother, and I realized some things."

He raised an eyebrow. "Okay, you're going to have to back up there. You told off my mother?"

So I told him about what had happened when I'd gone up to Glenview, about showing both moms the article, about defending

Adam to his mother. When I said that she kept insisting his homosexuality was "just a phase," he closed his eyes and looked so profoundly sad for a moment that I wanted to reach over and hug him, but I didn't. I didn't think it was time quite yet. I recounted almost exactly what I'd said, and I reiterated that I thought he was a great man and I understood now how I'd misread the situation.

"Oh," he said when I finished. "You really said all that?"

"I really did, and then your mother kind of ran out of the house. I felt bad about being a little bit mean." Unable to keep my hands away any longer, I reached over and trailed my fingers over the side of his face. "And I told her that you deserve to be loved for who you are, not for who she wants you to be. I realized the same applies to me. You were right when you left the coffee shop earlier. If I want you to love me for me, then I need to love you for you. If we're to move forward, then I have to move forward with you. I'm… I'm really sorry, Adam. And I came over here tonight because I can't lose you again."

He closed his eyes again and leaned into my hand a little. I cupped his cheek.

"I know you're reluctant to move in together because you think I'll leave you again," he said, "but I promise I won't."

"I know that. I understand that now. That's not even what this was about. You're changing a lot about your life to be with me, and I haven't been willing to leave my safe little bubble. And that's not fair."

"Okay. I mean, if you want to slow down—"

"I don't, not really. The main reason I was panicking about moving in together was that I was worried about everything changing. We're moving into some uncharted territory here. I was worried you would leave again, that you'd wake up one day and realize you had very good reasons for leaving. I thought moving back to Chicago would be regressing for you. But it's not, it's a step forward. And I see now that the only way you would leave is if I push you away. Which I did this afternoon."

"We had a fight, Jake. I wasn't planning to leave. What was it you said to me a couple of months ago? You said there is no you without me. Well, same goes. We've come too far together to throw it away because we had an argument. I had to leave the coffee shop because I was so upset I thought I might start yelling and throwing things, but I intended to call you tomorrow."

"Really?"

"Yeah, really. Dumbass."

I laughed despite myself. "I shouldn't have said what I said. It's not even about whether you're out or not. It's about me now and my own issues. I don't even want to change you. I just want us to be together. But it's scary out there, and my apartment is such a safe place for me. Everything happened so fast that I think I just got caught up in my own insecurities. Plus, you know, my default way of operating for a long time was, 'I can't get involved because what if Adam comes back?' but then you *did* come back, and you're with me now, and I guess I freaked out. None of it even seems real sometimes."

Adam reached over and pulled me into his arms. I let myself be hugged tightly. He smelled really good, like toothpaste and Adam, and the T-shirt he was wearing was really soft.

"I'm so sorry," I said. "I do love you. I trust and respect you and all those things. Completely. I'm totally yours. And I believe it when you say you love me. And I want a life with you. But I was worried about our future. And Brendan is still pissed at you, which wasn't really helping matters, because I thought…. I don't know what I thought."

"You thought that when I came back, everything would go back to the way it was. We'd be the four corners of the baseball diamond again, just like in high school."

I pulled away from him and tried to surreptitiously wipe at my eyes. "Yeah. That's basically what I thought. But I'm realizing now that things between us were changing even before you left town. We grew up and became adults and learned how to get on in the world without each other. And I was stuck, waiting for times to be simpler, but instead they got more complicated. And frankly, I don't want to go back. This relationship with you, our future together, that's what I want."

He smiled. "That's what I want too."

"So fuck what I said before. Let's do this thing. Let's have this crazy relationship and move in together and make love as often as possible."

He kissed me. It was fast and hard and aggressive and everything you could have asked for in a hot kiss. I put my hands on his face and held him there while I opened my mouth to let him in, and I felt more connected to him than I ever had before. Here was my Adam, the man I'd been waiting my whole life for.

"Think our new place will be anything like the clubhouse?" he asked once we'd finished trying to climb into each other's mouths.

"Yeah, pretty much, except you're not allowed to put up any Nine Inch Nails posters."

When I put my hands on his chest, I felt him vibrating with laughter. He kissed me again. "Also somehow I don't think we can talk my mom into delivering homemade snacks."

"Probably just as well."

"Mmm." He put his arms around me. "We're good now, right?"

"Yes. We're very, very good."

EPILOGUE

SO I married him.

We had a quiet wedding in my parents' backyard with us, our close friends, and our immediate family present.

It came about in maybe a less than traditional way. One afternoon, Adam and I sat at the table we'd set up in the living room of our apartment on the North Side. We were both doing office work, although my attention wasn't really on mine. Adam was working to unravel some unwieldy piece of code, and all of his attention was focused on that as he made notes on a piece of graph paper and counted out numbers on his fingers. I loved watching his mind work sometimes. He would have been the first to tell you that the media surrounding him was full of hyperbole about his relative genius—he thought himself a man of above-average intelligence but hardly a genius, as he'd told me on a number of occasions—but I wondered if he was just being modest.

He seemed to figure something out, gasping as he made some connection and then furiously typing on his laptop. When it seemed safe to interrupt him, I said, "Hey, Adam?"

"Uh-huh."

"Look at me, baby. Give me your hand."

He lifted his head and shot me a skeptically raised eyebrow, but he held out his hand to me. I wrapped my hand around his.

"I just had a crazy thought."

"About the report you're working on?"

"No." I clutched his hand. "About us. What if we got married?"

A smile spread across his lips slowly. "Well, I think that would be pretty great."

What followed was a crash course in everything straight couples take for granted. We talked about having the ceremony in New England so that at least the marriage would be legal *somewhere*, but that seemed silly once we established that neither of us had any desire to live anywhere but Chicago. It took two months of meetings with a lawyer to get all the legal stuff worked out and an awkward day at the courthouse when we tried to register our civil union and we wound up with a clerk who acted like she'd never seen a gay couple before. We made the decision to have the wedding in my parents' backyard in Glenview—close to the scene of the crime, I figured, mere yards from where Adam and I had shared our first kiss. Adam thought it more romantic to have the wedding in the same backyard we'd played in together as boys, where our friendship had been formed, and partly where we'd first fallen in love with each other as teenagers. But we wrestled a lot with the issue of the marriage not being a legally recognized thing. My mother kept arguing that the civil union was better than nothing, but then we had all these arguments about segregation and second-class citizenship, and, well, it wasn't pretty.

"Look, it's not going to be easy," Adam said to me late one night after a meeting with our lawyer. "Maybe it would be better to go to some state where our wedding would be totally legal and not a civil union consolation prize. Or maybe someday soon the state of Illinois will allow us to get married legally here. Maybe it's not a real wedding. But it feels right."

It felt right to me too.

I'd even called David to let him know I was getting married, mostly because I thought he should hear it from me before he got the news from some other source. He congratulated me and didn't seem the least bit surprised. "I wish you well, Jake, I honestly do," was what he said to me.

"Thanks," I said. "I'm sorry for how things went with us. I always valued your friendship."

"Yeah," he said, sadness in his voice. "Well. We stopped being friends a long time ago, didn't we?"

"I suppose we did."

I took some time to mourn that friendship too. It was strange, after David had been a part of my life for so long, not to have him be anymore. I got a card a few years later telling me he'd moved to Ontario with the love of his life and that they'd adopted a baby girl and a couple of cats, and he seemed very happy.

So, almost two years after Adam came back into my life, he and I put on suits and exchanged rings and vows with the rabbi from my parents' synagogue presiding. My parents and my sister and her family were there. All four of Adam's brothers and his younger sister showed up with their families in tow. His parents, his mother especially, had given him a hard time about getting married, but they showed up and sat in the front row of chairs. I'd like to be able to say that Adam and his mother kissed and made up, but things between them remained strained. Adam's relationship with me was something she tolerated but never really accepted.

Brendan and a very pregnant Maggie came too. Brendan had come around eventually. Things were still a little strained between him and Adam, but once he understood that Adam and I were the real deal, he stopped being quite so stubborn. Kyle brought Alexa, whose mother had thrown a fit when Kyle had told her he was taking their daughter to a gay wedding, but Kyle had argued it would be good for her to see that many kinds of love exist, and he'd gotten his way. Adam's friend Mara flew out too, and a smattering of our other friends were there. Overall, it was a small wedding, but it was perfect.

We both felt strange about spending our wedding night in one of our parents' houses, so we got a hotel room in Glenview, where we spent what felt like hours making love.

Eventually we lay together in bed, completely tangled in each other and the bedding. He held me tightly, and I rested my head on his chest. I put a hand on his belly, and he put his hand over mine. It was a strange thing to see the platinum band on his hand. Adam had picked the rings out and had taken great pride in finding something both beautiful and quite masculine.

"That's a nice ring you got there," I said.

"Yeah?"

"Uh-huh. I have one just like it."

"You don't say."

"My husband gave it to me."

His breath caught in his throat. He sighed and then kissed the top of my head. "Husband," he murmured. "Well, I guess we really are partners in everything now, eh? We got our wish."

"Yeah. Wait, what wish?"

He ran a hand over my head. "I mean, I know the apartment is not as glamorous as the clubhouse, but…."

I laughed. "You wanted us to marry each other. Who needs stinky girls, right?"

"Exactly. Dream come true. Who knew it would be possible? I wish I had known twenty years ago that one day I would be this happy. That any of this would even be possible."

"Worth the wait, I say."

His chuckle rumbled through his chest. "Yeah. After everything, I think that going through what we did just makes this all the sweeter. I love you, Jake."

"I love you right back."

KATE MCMURRAY is a nonfiction editor by day. Among other things, Kate is crafty (mostly knitting and sewing, but she also wields power tools), she plays the violin, she has an English degree, and she loves baseball. She lives in Brooklyn, NY.

Visit her website at http://www.katemcmurray.com.

Also from DREAMSPINNER PRESS

http://www.dreamspinnerpress.com

Also from DREAMSPINNER PRESS

http://www.dreamspinnerpress.com

Dreamspinner Press
For more of the
best M/M romance,
visit
Dreamspinner Press
www.dreamspinnerpress.com

CPSIA information can be obtained at www.ICGtesting.com
Printed in the USA
BVOW030147240912

300910BV00007B/41/P

9 781613 726969